UNSETtLEd
StAteS

Advance Praise

"A good old-fashioned mystery novel that goes beyond its elegantly crafted whodunit into the deeper, messier mysteries of mental disorder and religious belief. *Unsettled States* is as thoughtful and thought-provoking as it is fun."

— Kurt Andersen, author of *Heyday*

"Casey weaves together diverse and seemingly discordant storylines, and in the end settles the score in unexpected ways. *Unsettled States* is the work of a great writer working at the top of his game."

— Daniel Frisch, author of *Looking Forward to Monday Morning*

"Diversely average characters given extravagant but believable situations with satisfying but sometimes unexpected resolutions at the end. A remarkable literary achievement."

— Michael Mailer, writer & filmmaker

"The lives of citizens in a small Connecticut town are anything but simple in this enchanting book ... The dysfunction hovering over suburbia is not exclusive to the life of a cop or a voyeur, as the story's drama encapsulates the dissolution of two prominent couples' marriages. The characters are well-developed, and the plot's pacing is consistent, with more than a few surprises thrown in to make for a fulfilling read."

— Philip Zozzaro, *US Review of Books*

"Good character development and fast pacing add to the book's appeal, as do some moments of levity that effectively vary the tone ... An often-thrilling novel that's likely to satisfy mystery buffs."

— *Kirkus Reviews*

Other novels by Tom Casey

Human Error, St. Martin's Press, 1996
Strangers' Gate, Tor/Forge, 2006

Praise for *Strangers' Gate* and *Human Error*

Strangers' Gate

"From the brilliance of the opening chapter, one is aware of a writer with an exceptional point of view. I know of no other American novel where the protagonist is an accomplished pilot who can write the story with his own fair share of winged prose."

— Norman Mailer, winner of the American Book Award, author of *The Naked and the Dead*

"*Strangers' Gate* is the best noir thriller since James M. Cain's *The Postman Always Rings Twice*. Casey is a star of the fist magnitude."

— David Hagberg, author of *Soldier of God*

"Tom Casey is a pilot's pilot and a writer's writer. This fast-paced story rockets you from one bed to another as it builds to a climactic and bloody finish."

— Walter J. Boyne, author of *The Boy in the Striped Pajamas*

Human Error

"Tom Casey evokes the personal and corporate dramas that follow in the wake of a major airline crash with tremendous power. Anyone who has ever wondered about the lives of commercial pilots or the corporate intrigues and strategies of the major carriers and their regulators will find a world opening to him in this novel. As there are great sea stories, this is a great story of the air. A suspenseful and informative read."

— Robert Stone, winner of the National Book Award,
author of *Dog Soldiers*

"A first-rate debut novel."

— *Kirkus Reviews* (starred)

UNSETtLED StAteS

A NOVEL

By
Tom Casey

Cover design by Elizabeth Cline

Library of Congress Control Number: 2024903086

Published by
HERESY PRESS LLC
P.O. Box 425201
Cambridge, MA 02142
heresy-press.com

ISBN 979-8-9887173-5-5

For Silvia Erskine
Partner, Mentor, Artist, Friend

and

In loving memory of Marisa Bisi Erskine
(1923 - 2023)

Ye living ones, ye are fools indeed
Who do not know the ways of the wind
And the unseen forces
That govern the processes of life.

—Edgar Lee Masters

1

"Tell me about penis envy."

"Well, Gerry, contrary to Dr. Freud, I find the affliction more common in men than women. Would you like an appointment to explore your interest, or do you want to tell me about your gun?"

Detective Gerard Mallory's eyes lit up, and he laughed. Caroline always made him laugh: Caroline Singer, MD, psychiatrist. They were having lunch, sitting in a booth at Alfonso's Trattoria across the town square from the courthouse.

"I have an interesting issue in front of me."

"What kind?"

"It's regarding a resident caught peeping into a neighbor's window."

"Oh?"

"He's a local, grew up here and went to school at Granville High."

"How old is he?"

"Thirty-three. He lives alone in a cottage at the lake and works at the McAndrews Library. He's well regarded there."

"Did you arrest him?"

"Yes, but I let him go with an understanding that he sees you."

"Is he open to therapy?"

"He seems willing to try. He feels pretty ashamed about the whole thing."

"What's his name?"

"Bradley Davis. Appears to be highly intelligent. Can peeping be a phase?"

"Possibly." Dr. Singer finished her glass of Pellegrino and folded her hands. Her expression grew serious, professional. "But peeping could be the tip of the iceberg. There could be a lot behind it."

"Such as?"

"He might have suffered sexual abuse. We don't know his psychopathology. He could be acting out unconscious desires."

"By peeping through windows?"

"By living vicariously. By peering at other lives as if through Microsoft windows, to use a modern analogy."

"That's a curious thought."

Dr. Singer continued. "He might have other mental anomalies such as bipolar disorder, anxiety neuroses, eating disorders, substance abuse, or an arrested personality in different degrees. There might be sexual perversions and associated problems such as guilt, depression, or shame. Reactive behavioral impulse. Life can be overwhelming. We'll have to see."

"There is no normal, is there?"

Dr. Singer laughed and shrugged. "In any moment there is a 'normal,' but it stays indefinite, always shifting."

"Will you see him?"

"Of course. If he's willing."

"I think you'll find him to be an interesting patient. He seems shy, but, as I said, he's very bright."

"You understand that I can't share any patient information with law enforcement unless …"

"I understand. But if you learn he's buried his parents under the porch, you'll let me know, won't you?"

"You know I'm required to disclose anything suicidal or inferring criminal intent."

"Many thanks for this, Caroline."

2

A small sign on the door announced the offices of:
CAROLINE SINGER, M.D.
PSYCHIATRIST

A tall, slender man in his early thirties peered at the sign and pressed the doorbell button. In seconds the lock opened. He went through the first door to a small hallway and a second door on the right. That door was unlocked and gave into a small waiting room with yet another door that was closed. Rooms within rooms, he thought, noting the unremarkable furnishings. The walls were a bland institutional green. A painting of a lonely house on a bleak landscape made the couch beneath it seem small; in front of it a tree-trunk wooden table was uniquely ill-suited. He was trying to have an interpretive insight—something about how the room itself was a portrait of dysfunction—but the inner door opened, and Dr. Caroline Singer appeared.

"Bradley Davis?"

"Yes," he said.

"Welcome, Bradley. Please come in."

The young man took her measure. She was tall, in her mid-forties, handsome and bespectacled. She reached out to shake his hand. Her handclasp was strong, sure, and confident, her voice quiet but commanding, with that sexless authority some professional women convey. She stepped away from the doorway to usher him in and invited him to sit in a chair facing hers. The window blinds were drawn. Beside them was a couch along the wall.

When they were both seated, she took out a paper tablet to take notes.

"Don't you record the sessions?" he asked.

"I sometimes take notes, but therapy is like talking to a friend. You don't have to record their words to remember what they say to you, isn't that true?"

"I guess so."

"I'm a good listener. So, how are you feeling?"

"I'm fine," Bradley said.

"Good."

"Except maybe a little embarrassed. Under the circumstances."

"It's not uncommon to feel awkward at first." Dr. Singer smiled. Bradley noticed how even her smile carried an aura of unqualified authority. "Detective Mallory told me about your arrest, but let's put that aside for the moment. I want to learn a little bit about you and answer any questions you might have about therapy. He did mention that you have a mother in town, is that right?"

"Yes."

"Do you live with her?"

"No. I moved out after college, about ten years ago. But I see her fairly often."

"How often is that?"

"At least once a week, sometimes more, depending. She lives alone. She's a semi-invalid."

"An invalid?"

"She drinks."

"I see. And you? Do you drink?"

"Not nearly like she does. It's her life—it's become her life. She rarely leaves home."

"And you work at the library, is that correct?"

"Yes, at the McAndrews County Library."

"And where do you live?"

"I have a cabin. Up on the north side of the lake. It's a small house, really, but I think of it as a cabin. It has a great view. I live alone."

"Have you been in therapy before?"

"Not real therapy. College career counseling is all."

After a brief silence, Dr. Singer said: "Let me explain the goals of therapy. What we do here is simple on the face of it. We establish a relationship, rather like a friendship. It is a clinical relationship, however, unlike any other. The point of analysis is for you to understand the motives behind your actions. You talk and I listen. There is only one rule, but it is a most important requirement: you must always tell me the truth. You might not know the truth, but you must not be inhibited in what you say. Nothing is off limits. There is no need for embarrassment. I will become your confidant in all things personal. You will tell me what you feel and think and do. We will explore your motives to see if they comport with your desires. Together we will endeavor to liberate you from complicating inhibitions. Only by talking freely and honestly can we discover what your true intentions are, and if your actions are in line with your goals."

"It doesn't sound difficult."

Dr. Singer smiled wryly. "Well," she said. "Why don't we get started." She indicated the couch with her hand, inviting him to lie on it. "If you don't mind."

Bradley hesitated. "Do all your patients actually lie down?"

"Those in analysis therapy do, yes."

Bradley got up from the chair and went over to the couch. He rested his head on a pillow, facing away from where Dr. Singer sat out of his sight. "May I close my eyes?"

"Certainly. The idea is to relax."

Bradley closed his eyes and folded his hands, making a steeple with his index fingers. After several moments of silence, he said, "Shall I tell you about my mother?"

"If you wish."

"I'm *supposed* to talk about my mother, right?"

"You can talk about anything, Bradley. But yes, since you brought her up, why not begin with your mother." There was a pause. The pause grew into a silence. Dr. Singer waited for Bradley to speak.

"She was very drunk that morning," he said.

"Tell me about it."

Haltingly at first, and then with greater detail, Bradley began to recount to Dr. Singer a recent visit to see his mother, and his analysis commenced.

"Mother?"

Bradley frowned. Hearing no response from inside, he opened the door, leaned in, craned his neck and called again, louder this time.

"Mother?"

Tentatively, he stepped into the foyer. Visiting his mother always triggered tremors of ambivalence, so even as he arrived, Bradley's mind was formulating strategies of escape. He noted that the house was cool and continuously damp or wet—ill, if that can be said—sweating or suppurating, with that smell of musty corruption, cigarette smoke and her wretched perfume, an odor unequaled by any elsewhere. His mother's voice, interrogative, grimly buoyant, frail, garbled, and thick with phlegm, called: "Bradley?" Then she coughed volubly, cleared her congestion, audibly swallowed, and said again, "Bradley? Is that you?"

"Yes, Mother."

The adjacent parlor door was slightly open. He stared at its invitation to enter with that mix of elation and sadness which even as a boy the sound of her voice excited in him. He never knew what to expect from her. When Bradley pushed against the door, it opened, and he found Eleanor extended full-length with her head on a pillow set against the arm of the brown davenport. Supine, eyes glazed with drunkenness at 10 a.m., cigarettes, medications, and a box of tissues beside her, she was a solitary who even as a young widow in her thirties had demanded to be left alone and now, in her sixties, looked like someone in her eighties on a deathbed.

"Mo-ther," Bradley pronounced with disenchantment. She ignored it. Resisting a powerful urge to flee immediately and never return, he entered the room. Her eyes followed him. He sensed she was not entirely convinced of his presence, that he might be a dream or hallucination. With her tongue protruding slightly from a corner of her mouth, her smile resembled the grin of an exhausted dog. Her wiry hair the color of ash was pulled into incongruous pigtails held in place by small brown bands bejeweled with colored buttons.

The parlor had a bookcase on one side, a dark but tasteful Persian carpet, and colorful pillows from Pakistan. The coffee table was a polished slab of Brazilian mahogany. There was a ceramic cheetah in the corner. A large brass cage hung from a chain above the cheetah where an African gray parrot stood silent, gloomy, and stone-still on a perch. The windows looked out through trees to the Armistice Monument for Fallen Soldiers at the center of the village roundabout.

Bradley sat in a chair beside the coffee table, facing his mother where she lay in her pale green bathrobe, a blue blanket over her hips. By comparison, Bradley was well-dressed. Even on days off he wore jacket and slacks and collared shirts; he didn't own a pair of blue jeans and never wore T-shirts. He had prominent ears and a noticeable nose, with a wide mouth that seemed to smile constantly, inadvertently, often with an air of inappropriate delight that deceived: it made earnestness seem ironic and cynicism gleeful.

Eleanor cuddled her drink with both hands, keeping it close to her breast as she contemplated the parrot. She met her son's eyes in a double-take and then looked away. "Bradley," she said at last, softly, thickly, almost abstractly, his name issuing like a sigh or a summary of some bittersweet memory.

"Hello, Mother."

She reached out her hand, rather like a diva, not looking at him. He took it and squeezed it. Then she began to laugh, and then cough, coughing laughter that a lifetime of cigarettes had combined into one reflexive convulsion.

"Sit with me, Bradley, that's a good boy. We're a family again when you're here. It consoles me."

"Don't begin that," Bradley said, petulant, looking also at the parrot, who was watching him with one eye.

"Don't be fresh, Bradley. I'm your mother." She turned her head leftward to look at her son directly. Though physically weakened, her gimlet eyes could open an oyster from across the room.

"You never let me forget it." He shrugged, smiled, and met her gaze with satirical warmth.

This banter pleased her. Even as her necessities had become trivial, in some corner of her mind she saw herself a matriarch who had endured hardships that only the great in mind and spirit can know. Bradley was her only child. She cleared her throat in a husky clamor of hocking and swallowing and finished with manipulations of the tongue to lick her lips. An audible passing of gas issued from under her blanket.

"Your father was a great disappointment to me," she said, after an interval of labored breathing.

"Mother, please. Why mention him?"

"He was too serious, practical to a fault," she went on. "Deliberate about everything. A horrible bore." She raised her index finger for emphasis, seeming to be addressing no one in the room, talking to herself. "And cheap, Bradley. As I've told you, he had the first dollar he ever made when he died. An unseemly vice. A dreadful man."

Bradley winced. "Oh, Mother, stop browbeating the poor guy, he's been dead for decades."

But time had no influence on his mother's memories. They were her weathers, her sunshine and clouds. It continuously surprised him to realize that she was mostly in conversation with herself and that the ghost of his father hovered and drifted continuously with other ghosts in her imagination. From childhood, Bradley had heard little that was positive about him: his mother's accounts insisted he was feckless, unimaginative, humorless, and irresponsible. His thrift earned her contempt over time. She made fun of him for riding a bicycle, which she felt shamed his masculinity.

Bradley took his father's side. "He was a good-natured, sensible, mild-mannered man who worked hard to support his family."

"A dreary failure, even in death," she countered, taking Bradley's presence as an opportunity to revisit her animosities. She often spoke to her son through defamations of his father. Eleanor cuddled her glass again, more at ease; her lips moved as she thought; she leaned her head forward and took a long sip of her scotch.

"He was that way," she said, her words a weary sigh.

"Who? What way?"

"Your way, Bradley," she said, putting her glass on the table next to the box of tissues, raising her eyebrows in a slow-gathering expression of maternal disappointment. "I'm not a fool."

Bradley, in a sudden pique, shifted in his seat and began to drum his fingers on his knees. "What could you possibly be referring to?"

She rose up slightly and turned to him. "Where are my grandchildren?" Her tremulous voice rose in an involuntary harrumph of disapproval.

"Am I gay? Is that what you're implying?"

Eleanor shrugged. "You work in a library!"

"Good lord, Mother, where do you get your notions?" Bradley's tone was droll and annoyed, and yet there was an understanding between them, an underlying dynamic as much involved with humor as reproach.

"You might have gone to law school. You could have been a doctor."

"Stop it."

"Oh, Bradley, you're everything I never wanted," she said, and began to laugh in spite of herself. Then she turned away from him. Bradley smiled and then laughed grimly; laughter as an exhalation, laughter as a sigh.

Eleanor lay back against the pillow once again and moved her shoulders from side to side reflexively as though re-reaching for that more comfortable mood of a moment before. Bradley began to clean grit from beneath one of his fingernails with a matchbook, reflecting. She liked to refer to his "eccentricities." It was an old song. At a very young age, he had comprehended her ruthless self-absorption: abstract, alcoholic, needy, controlling, and fed on illusions. What a family, he thought— family being himself, the parrot, his mother, her liquor, and her ghosts.

"Darling, will you make me a scotch?" She gestured with one hand to her empty glass.

"What's the magic word, Mother?" he said.

She looked up at him with rheumy eyes and wicked glee. After a pause, she raised her eyebrows and said, "Now?"

Laughing, shaking his head, Bradley stood, took the glass, and then bent over and kissed his mother's forehead.

A wooden wheel-cart bar caddy was parked between the dining room and the kitchen. On top of it was a silver bucket filled with ice. He put three ice cubes into the glass and poured a liberal measure from the scotch bottle. How did she live like this day after day? he wondered as he carried the brimming glass back to her.

"Thank you, dear," she said, receiving the drink into the palms of her hands, fingers clutching at it like a Venus flytrap closing fast on a bug.

"It's a strange life you have, Bradley."

"Is that so? From what province of normalcy do you make that judgment?"

"I suppose I can console myself by saying, Well, he's different."

"Mother, you know next to nothing about my life." Bradley dismissed her with a wave, sighed and looked at his watch. "I have to go soon."

"Isn't this your day off?"

"Yes."

"When will you be back?"

"I'll look in on you in a few days."

"I'll be here." Eleanor shrugged. She had a sip of her drink and then added, "Unless I die." She put her drink down on the table, and her eyes met his again. "Of neglect." She began to cough because she had started to laugh again.

"Stop it, Mother."

He knew her patterns and could anticipate seizures of amusement, self-pity, or invective, sometimes occurring simultaneously. He watched her moving her lips in silence and knew she was formulating a thought completely removed from the conversation. She sat up and leaned on her elbow. "I had talent, Bradley. I could have been great at something."

"Please, not that again." Bradley sat in the large rattan chair so that he could face his mother.

"I gave up my promise to live with you and your haircut of a father in this godforsaken town." She picked a cigarette out of the pack lying next to her glass on the table and lit it with a Dunhill lighter, inhaling deeply and exhaling in a slow, meditative cloud. Her smoking reminded Bradley of earliest days when she mothered him from the unfathomable, unreachable alien world of her adulthood. "This town …" She scowled, repeating the word as though trying to find something redeeming in the idea. "How could this have been my life?"

"What's wrong with this town?"

It was all familiar. He could see her thoughts collecting into a statement: "The man next door is a volunteer fireman!"

"What on earth?"

"A peasant! I'm surrounded by people who wallow in mediocrity."

"Write your memoirs," Bradley said, brushing her comments away with a wave of his hand. "Malign your neighbors. Malign me. It's good therapy."

"I might still. It will be called *Motherhood: A Log of Regrets*."

Bradley guffawed. "I'll buy you a pencil."

"Ha!" she said. "It might cost you a nickel. You're just like your father."

"Stop it." Bradley was growing impatient. These visits achieved nothing. She would hardly remember he had come. He was beginning to feel angry, but his mother's jaw dropped slightly and her face registered an expression of deep sadness and fear. She was old now, and she knew it, old in spirit, weak against decline, in defeat. And so, predictably, she retreated into reveries of a shining past, exalted primogeniture, conjuring the myth of her own precocity and promise.

"Your grandfather stood for something," she said with the earnest insistence of someone who wanted to stand for something herself. He was a champion in her eyes, a demigod far more numinous than any biblical divine. Bradley remembered him, a kind grandfatherly giant who strode out of his mother's fantasies with some semblance of true heroism. He had good looks and a commanding personality; tall, lean, capable, the glint of humor and light of intelligence in eyes that absorbed the follies around him, often with amusement—a genial man but a curiously unconnected soul as he aged, someone who bore little resemblance to his youthful avatar, fading from vigor as the elderly will, retreating from an active life to watching television and listening to recriminations of conservative talk radio until he died in his chair of heart failure. His death was the beginning of Eleanor's decline. "When God forgets you, that's when you begin to fade from the world," she had said as they left the church to bury her father. She was afraid of being forgotten. She lived for her memories, most of them figments which rose up from mythmaking and hovered as daydreams.

Recalling his grandfather gave Bradley a thought. Keepsakes in a trunk at the foot of his mother's bed contained her father's valued artifacts, his pilot helmet from World War Two, his Army Air Corps wings, and other items precious to him that were sacred relics to her.

"Excuse me, Mother; I'll be right back."

Bradley went from the parlor to the kitchen and down a hall on the other side to his mother's bedroom. He stopped at the hall bathroom.

As he stood relieving his bladder and peering out the window, he saw a woman walking a dog and experienced that thrill of the unobserved observer. This detonated stimulating and pleasurable associations. Afterward he went to his mother's bedroom. There he quickly found the leather case he was looking for in the trunk at the foot of her bed: his grandfather's authentic brass marine binoculars from World War Two. He took the case, put it on the steps outside the door to the mudroom, where he'd noticed bags of trash collecting. Then he went back to the parlor entrance and, leaning in, said, "Would you like me to take out the garbage, Mother?"

She gave him a questioning expression, and then said, "There will always be garbage in this world," not quite in response to his question but rather emphatic to some other notion in her mind, as if the noun was not garbage but *worry* instead, or *responsibilities*.

"Could you, Bradley? There's a thoughtful boy." She was in the moment now, but her voice was fading and had the quality of summary again, even regret.

Bradley went back to the kitchen pantry. As he took bags to the bin, backyard memories and bright colors of childhood flooded his mood: the shapes of flowers in spring, the summer he got stung by bees, baby birds in porch nests, small animals gamboling in the grass, clouds overhead, and the mystery of rainfall and lightning and thunder. Rich impressions of life rose out of this place where he first knew the world. After closing the bin beside the garage, he got the leather case and put it into his car. When he returned to the parlor, he didn't sit down this time but stood in front of the couch.

"All done," he said.

"Thank you, dear."

"I have to go now, Mother."

She had a sip of her scotch. Then, squinting at Bradley and amused at something, she began to laugh and cough. "Next time I'll bake a cake." She lit another cigarette with her ancient Dunhill lighter.

"Don't."

"I just might."

"Good-bye, Mother." Bradley, bending over, gave her a kiss.

"Adieu, Chéri," she said.

"Adieu."

As he left the parlor, anticipating imminent freedom, other images scurried through his imagination and began to excite him. When he opened the front door to leave, he heard his mother say again, "Adieu, Chéri." That's sweet, he thought. He smiled and turned to wave, but it was the parrot talking. His mother was already asleep, ice melting in her drink, cigarette still burning in the ash tray. It was almost time for lunch, and later he had an appointment in the city. When he was gone, the parrot, sensing his departure, moved back and forth on its perch, sighed audibly, and with astonishing ventriloquicity, muttered in his mother's voice, "Such a disappointment."

Bradley told Dr. Singer about his first-time peeping. When he returned home from his mother's house with his grandfather's wartime binoculars, he went immediately to a place in the woods (his special place on a ledge hidden by trees) to see what a difference magnification might make on his ability to observe Grace Addison in her garden. It made an astonishing difference. But what a surprise! Good Lord, what is this? he thought, with grim fascination, as he watched Nelson Hawkins kiss Grace Addison. Then they went into her library. How is Nelson Hawkins in the picture? Not only could he see them clearly, he felt he was among them. Witnessing something he did not foresee, he could do nothing but watch. Hawkins was a neighbor on the lake and a writer he admired. He occasionally came to the county library, where Bradley worked. Recently, Hawkins had given an inspired presentation on the evolution of Realism in the nineteenth century. But what he saw now upset his admiration. He felt a stab of jealousy. It was like unexpectedly seeing your girlfriend happy with someone else at a movie theater in another town. They were kissing, for heaven's sake. Kissing! Nelson Hawkins was kissing Grace Addison, and both were married!

While Bradley spoke, Dr. Singer made notes. *Mother lives alone, alcoholic, depressive, possibly bi-polar, unfulfilled and competitive with her son. Patient may be somewhere on the autistic spectrum but admirably forthcoming. Parrot hilarious. Sibling rivalry?*

Near the end of the session there followed a long silence, as though Bradley were struggling to make an admission against the desire to conceal it. Dr. Singer waited.

"I'm supposed to tell you secrets," Bradley said.

"Candor allows us to discuss matters that bother you."

"Sometimes I go to a place in New York City."

"What place is that?"

"It's called Mistress Angela's Dungeon. It's a kind of role-play place."

"I'm aware of it."

Bradley was plainly shocked. "You are?"

"Is it a stretch to believe I might have one or two patients with problems related to what you've seen there?"

"I guess not."

"What sort of role-play do you engage in when you are there?"

"Just doing things."

"*Things* is a broad term. When you are there, do you dress as a woman?"

"Yes."

"But nowhere else?"

"No."

"Do you get sexual gratification dressing as a woman?"

"Yes. Well, sort of. I mean, but everything there goes according to a script. Kind of."

Dr. Singer smiled at his syntax: sentences that struggled. "And your grandfather's binoculars? You use them for peeping?"

"Yes."

"Well." Dr. Singer closed her notepad as a signal that the session was over. "We'll take that up next time."

Bradley sat up.

"Let's meet again on Thursday, and every Thursday at this time if that works for you."

"Thursdays are good."

"I'll see you next Thursday, then."

3

He killed her. But even as he strangled her, he didn't mean it to happen. After he saw what he had done and was sure she was dead, he quickly left the house. He stepped into the yard, shutting the interior door behind him and checking to see it had locked. He let the wooden screen door close gently. Insects were voluble. The night sky was clear. There was a slight wind sibilant in the tops of the trees. He breathed deeply the cool air. Revived by oxygen, consoled by darkness, he retraced his steps to the car. Otherwise all was silent. *Nothing is different.* He tried to believe it but knew it wasn't so. His relationship with himself, with the world, and with God was different. *Everything* was different.

The moon was setting. For the moment he had no fear, nothing that felt like fear. He felt lightheaded and somewhat surprised by his calm. Once in the darkened yard, he turned to look at the house. It was not a large house, but it had that welcoming aspect of warmth and security. The light in the living room was on as he had left it. A gust of consternation passed through his euphoric mood—yes, oddly euphoric, probably manic, a giddy mix of deliverance and dread. He didn't expect it and couldn't explain it. Life was like a tangled rope, he thought without ironic inference; everyone's tangles were different. He lingered in the yard, in faint moon shadows, when all at once, like a strange hush in a stadium crowd, the noise of insects stopped suddenly. For a moment the yard was entirely silent, and the earth seemed to absorb him into its intention. Faint luminescence allowed just enough light to identify a path beside the road. He walked on the path, which was waterlogged from recent rain. The ground was softening. Pushing aside barberries, he reflected that he had come here to achieve redemption, or if not redemption precisely, deliverance: deliverance or reckoning. The road was remote, but he saw the advancing headlights of a car through the trees farther down. The car moved slowly. As it got closer, he concealed himself, and the woods seemed to yawn in the passing lights. As the car went by, something in his soul shuddered. The brightness faded swiftly. He stayed under cover and moved cautiously on the uneven ground. When he could see his car, he grew excited with that thrill a child feels approaching the house where he will soon be safe from real and imagined threats of night. Another vehicle approached from the opposite side. He could see the headlights. He waited in the shadows until it had passed. Then he walked gingerly to his car, got into it quickly, started the motor, and drove off with sudden relief, almost elation.

The road was narrow. An adrenalin tingle became rather like a glow in him. The double yellow line curved left and right and looked like a ribbon moving this way and that as he went. A feeling of relief ebbed slightly as the rational process of driving blunted euphoria. Still, the diminution was slight, and his mood stayed curiously, blasphemously buoyant. This elevated mood continued until, as if in a dream, a police car materialized close upon his rear with blue lights flashing. The squad car bleeped its siren once, signaling intent while choosing not to disturb the peace with a full-throated wail. He slowed, pulled off to the right, stopped. Continuing to check his rearview mirror, he sat for a moment in silence, not moving. A bright spotlight coming from the squad car behind him illuminated the dashboard of his car. Through the mirror on the driver's side, and as if out of a blinding vision, he saw a police officer exit the cruiser. He muttered a curse under his breath.

Police procedure for managing a traffic stop at night involved putting the perpetrator in a sudden unfamiliar context. A disorienting phalanx of bright and flashing lights and the spotlight achieved this. The man saw that the officer was female, of average height but heavyset. He watched her unhitch her revolver at the holster with one hand and turn on a flashlight with the other. When she got to the window on the driver's side, he lowered the window. She shined her flashlight into his eyes.

"Do you know why you were pulled over?" The flashlight beam moved from his eyes to the passenger floor and the empty back seat.

"I don't think I was speeding."

"Your left brake light is out."

"Well, thank you, Officer," he said. "I wasn't aware of it."

"May I see your license, registration, and insurance, please?"

Her badge said GARVIN. As he reached into the glove compartment for his registration, his mind was considering many reasons to be anxious about the stop, not least being that a record would place him in this place on this date at this time. But did it matter? He could be anyone out and about his business. He kept his registration and insurance card together in an envelope. He found the envelope, checked for the documents, withdrew them, and handed them with his license to the police officer. She scanned them with her flashlight beam, noting his name and address, and then she shined the flashlight beam into his eyes again, blinding him.

"Have you been drinking?" she asked.

"No, ma'am."

"Where are you coming from?"

"I'm on my way home."

"No, sir. I asked where you are coming *from*?"

"From Granville. I live in Wilberforce. I'm on my way home."

"Is this your current address?"

"Yes, it is."

The officer was turning the license card over and over, as though to be sure it was authentic. "Wait here, please," she said and went back to her squad car.

Embedded in the *sir* and the *ma'am* of this exchange were certain inflections that held the menacing politesse of law enforcement. Looking up into the rearview mirror, the man could see the officer running a check on him. The spotlight was very bright. He could see shadows of the hairs on his arms. Crickets chirped in concert to crescendo, their sound trailing off and then rising again while minutes passed. He drummed his fingers on the steering wheel. Then the door of the cruiser opened and the officer got out, no longer holding the flashlight, and returned with his documents. She handed them back to him, her manner friendly now. "I'm not going to give you a ticket, only a warning. Just be sure to get that light fixed right away."

"Thank you, Officer," he said.

She leaned down to his eye level. He could see her face, a blond woman in her late thirties, he supposed. "Have a nice one," she said.

I already have, he thought, laughing to himself.

4

On the night he was arrested, Bradley Davis had waited at home until dusk. He'd put on his bottle green poncho and walked down from his cabin through the woods with his grandfather's brass binoculars slung across one shoulder and a tripod balanced on the other, a sportsman on the hunt. There was no path on the steep incline. He made his way through the trees toward the house lights. He went down the darkening wooded slope, feet sliding in the dirt, holding on to tree limbs for balance. Small mammals scuttled in the leaves.

When rationalizing his behavior, Bradley never thought of himself as a voyeur, rather as an expeditionary anthropologist of sorts, a social scientist, even arguably an artist. He moved carefully to the familiar ledge where, concealed by the woods, his equipment could be put to best advantage. The tripod had telescoping legs and provided a stable platform for observation. The view through the twin lenses was keenly acute.

When a car arrived in the driveway, he realized that Nelson Hawkins and his wife, Maggie, were joining John and Grace Addison for dinner.

He watched the couples greet one another at the front door. They went inside. He saw them migrate in the house, through the kitchen and out to the deck in back. He watched. Standing on the deck holding cocktails, Nelson and Maggie Hawkins moved to the rails together with their hosts, the Addisons. The lake glistened. Long shadows and golden hues of sunset framed a firelit sky. Their faces glowed as they watched the lowering sun. Wakes of boats motoring homeward created a peaceful, somewhat stereopticon-like aspect at that hour.

Profile radiant at the rail facing west, a proprietary John Addison presented the sunset to his guests: "What do you think?" he mused, and then shared his inspiration. "Looks like Armageddon to me," John said and raised his glass to that notion. Nelson Hawkins saw in Grace an expression of private amusement. The sun slipped below the horizon. Vibrant colors in the sky at first got brighter and then began a fade to dusk. John Addison pointed to Nelson's glass. "Get you another?"

"I'm good for now," Nelson said as he covertly continued to study his host. Impressions came as wryly critical observations collected in the moment. Wearing a green polo shirt, black hair combed straight back, John Addison expressed that spruce look of limited excellence you might see in the local golf pro or a top car salesman. Social parameters more narrow than normal, the hale and successful real-estate speculator invaded your space ever so slightly, imputing larger-than-life schemes, smile agleam with untroubled greed. Grace had greater sophistication than her husband. Her understated elegance contradicted her husband's more flamboyant style. A calf-length powder-blue cotton summer dress with laced leather sandals expressed precisely her quiet, refined manner and a self-contained, ironic humor that appealed to men when it didn't make them anxious.

Nelson Hawkins was a writer of some note, a minor local celebrity as author of three novels, all moderately successful and optioned for film. Tall and fair-haired, with a chiseled face still youthful and unlined, he stood beside his wife. Facing away, Maggie followed the movement of a boat on the lake and the spreading out of its wake as it went. A marathoner, she had that taut physicality of the fitness adept and nearly yellow hair cut short as a complement to a lean runner's body. Voluble enthusiasm could at times retreat swiftly into dark moods when she became petulant.

"Well, are we ready to eat?" Addison said, clapping his hands to inaugurate the next phase. The two couples left the deck through a sliding door to the kitchen. Moving farther inside, John noticed Nelson observing the heavy timbers of the vaulted ceiling in the living room. "I designed it myself," he said. "What do you think?"

Nelson saw that the space lacked proportion. An architect would never allow the hypertrophied overelaborations his host found exalting. But since he knew Addison as a man comfortable with his assumptions, he said merely, "Nice." This pleased Addison, who nodded affirmatively to an understanding which did not really exist. Grace ushered them into the dining room.

As they went to their seats, a full moon rose low on the horizon through trees on the wooded shoreline, its silver light shimmering on the surface of the lake farther down. Maggie and John sat together. The table was set with linen and crystal. Votive candles flickered in glass orbs. Their tiny flames reflected in the convexity of the wine glasses made each setting seem alive with its own animating glow.

Grace served the first course, a tomato shrimp bisque with a glass of white Bordeaux. Nelson held Grace's chair as she took her seat next to him and, after she filled his glass, sipped the wine. It was tight, earthy, and exceptional. Darkening dusk made the candlelight soft, and Maggie's face seemed youthful to Nelson, her blond hair girlish, her blue eyes antic the way he remembered them at the beginning. She was in a happy mood. She had been humorous and bright all day, looking forward to dinner with the Addisons. John began to tell a joke, but Grace knew his humor typically disparaged with a wink and a nod, and this joke was no exception. "Two queers were standing—" he started to say, but Grace stopped him.

"Really, John, I wish you wouldn't. People don't think that's funny. It's like telling jokes about how women are stupid." He looked to Nelson vainly for accord and then shrugged. Not a fan of jokes at dinner, Nelson took the cue from Grace and changed the subject.

Bradley repositioned his vintage binoculars and adjusted the range and focus to effectively put himself at the table as an invisible guest. His absorbtion was nearly absolute, like a gambler who can't think of anything but cards. While knowing that peeping was marginal behavior, it summarized impossible aspects of his oblivion. But in rationalizations he saw himself rather as James Stewart at life's rear window, an audience of one with unique curiosity and appreciation for the extempore drama unfolding in front of him. From his place in the woods, Bradley could see their illuminated faces. The reason behind this odd interest was unclear. He experienced what he saw in different ways, but secrecy and risk gave him a thrill. The persons he watched were like characters in a silent movie performing their evening together, and he was able to imagine their conversation and at times read their lips.

After soup, Grace served the main course and John poured a rich Zinfandel. Its spicy aromas, bright fruit, and solid structure were a thoughtful complement to the lean, perfectly rare sirloin. The meat was tender as pudding, with medallion potatoes that seemed to float off the plate, and crisp, fresh asparagus. The conversation continued.

"I saw a show last week about latex plantations and logging in the Amazon," Nelson said. "It started as a film about corporate pillage. Corporate interests enslaved whole cannibal tribes to harvest latex. The film ended as a formidable documentary on the art of shrinking heads."

"Shrinking heads? For real?" said Grace, intrigued.

"They use boiling water, hot stones, and sand until the face is no bigger than a tangerine."

"Oh, stop it," said Maggie. "We're eating."

"Precisely," Nelson continued. "They were crouched around a cauldron probably preparing dinner, with little heads hanging from sticks over the soup."

"Nelson!" Maggie said.

"I'm fascinated," said Grace, leaning forward as she cut her steak.

His index finger pedagogically upright, Nelson continued. "We are taught technique. Hot rocks dry the product, and finally hot sand is applied for symmetrical shrinkage. Victorian collectors of curiosa wanted these artifacts for their trophy rooms, and this provided some additional income for the natives in the days before deforesting. The problem came at the end of the documentary, when it was far from certain what the viewer was supposed to conclude. Is logging the rainforest worse than shrinking heads, or is it the other way around? Furthermore, which group is more morally wrong, cannibals who shrink heads or Englishmen who collect them?

"Good lord!"

"Have you ever seen a shrunken head?" Grace said to Maggie, and then turned to Nelson.

"No," Nelson replied. "Have you?"

"I have."

"Really?"

"I've never heard that story," said John, frowning slightly.

"Two of them. In New Orleans," Grace continued.

"They couldn't have been real." Maggie said, disapproving of the subject but nevertheless curious.

"They *were* real. In a glass case near the cash register. It was one of those stores where you can find weird stuff, old swords, dueling pistols, and animal trophies."

"And human heads," Nelson offered.

"And human heads."

"What did they look like?" said Maggie, turning her head slightly as though away from the subject.

"The first thing you notice is how much hair they have. Their eyelashes are gigantic because everything shrinks, but not hair."

"How much did they cost?" asked John.

"They weren't for sale. I asked. The proprietor said he'd had three, sold one, and then realized they were pretty rare, so he decided to keep the other two."

Maggie's face expressed revulsion. "How morbid! How really just absolutely horrid and disgusting! Who are we as a species?"

"I wish I'd seen them." Laughing at his wife's distaste, Nelson was fascinated. "By the way, the steak is delicious." Lightning flashed and thunder rumbled in the distance. Grace popped an asparagus spear into her mouth.

When lightning flashed, Bradley squinted and looked up. A storm was coming. He returned to his binoculars. His lenses were trained on Grace, who ate an asparagus. In spite of his rationalizations, at bottom his peeping was finally about Grace. He had seen her at the library, where he worked. He had helped her to find books and DVDs. He was smitten the way a movie fan falls in love with a photograph. It was love to the sound of one hand clapping, unhappily, and he knew it. His head twisted at the binoculars as he squinted for a better view. He scratched his forehead, pinched the bridge of his nose, and resumed his reconnoiter of the couples at dinner.

John had the habit of augmenting conversation by brandishing whatever implements were at hand. Speaking through food, he waved his fork at Nelson. "Do you play golf?"

"Nelson isn't much for sports," Maggie intervened.

"I enjoy walking," Nelson countered.

Maggie's face gathered into a grimace. "Walking isn't a sport."

"Walking can be vigorous, and it's certainly healthy. I like that," Nelson insisted, rather resenting Maggie's smug dismissal. "It doesn't have rules, and it isn't competitive."

John, waving his fork again with his right hand, knife at the ready in his left, said, "What's wrong with competition?"

"Thinking in that way changes a stroll into a race."

"I've been training for November," said Maggie.

"November?" Grace looked at her uncertainly.

"The New York Marathon," John clarified, as he cut meat on his plate.

"Nelson won't even come to see me," Maggie complained—absurdly, petulantly, Nelson thought.

"You won't cheer for your wife?" John jabbed the air, this time with a meat morsel pierced on the tines of his fork.

Nelson looked up. "It is not my idea of fun." He shrugged and returned to his meal. Grace laughed, not sure if he was being serious or joking.

"What is not your idea of fun?" Grace said.

"Watching nearly naked bipeds acting out their fear of death."

Grace laughed uproariously.

"Fear of death!" Maggie harrumphed. She turned to address John. "He never has rooted for me."

"That's utterly untrue," Nelson said. "I can't chase you through the streets of New York whistling and clapping, can I?"

John, chewing earnestly and speaking through the sides of his teeth, said, "Try being there. Think of it as a Yankees game. You might enjoy it."

"A marathon involves dread," Nelson insisted, against John's absurd baseball analogy. Addressing Grace, he said, "One runs marathons to make a statement."

"To whom?" said Maggie.

"To oneself. To one's pride. To others. It's an effort to reclaim something: youth, confidence. Or to demonstrate immunity against aging, infirmity, and death."

"Fuck you, Nelson," Maggie exclaimed.

Grace put her hand to her mouth in a failed attempt to suppress laughter at Maggie, who ignored her and glowered at Nelson instead, and then turned to John for affirmative support. The grandfather clock in another room rang the hour.

For Bradley, watching other people in their living moments was compelling for reasons he could not say, precisely. Rationalizing, he imagined himself as a director on a movie set consulting storyboards, or a coach illustrating plays on a chalkboard. If he were to make such a diagram, it would chart two couples and himself with arrows of interest moving this way and that. Wind across the tops of the trees increased audibly in velocity. Navigation lights of small boats could be seen still motoring in the dark farther down on the lake. Another flash of lightning lit the landscape for an instant, and then darkness again. The party was festively highlighted, framed in window light. It really was all rather cinematic, he thought. But he was not a director or a coach, and he controlled nothing; this wasn't a film, and he wasn't in the game at all. These thoughts were muttering at the back of his mind as he watched lips move at a dinner party while bad weather was moving in.

John, attentive host, reached for the bottle and held it up. "Anyone?" He then forked another piece of meat and held it as a prop while he spoke. "But really, Nelson, what's wrong with competition? Competition takes pursuit to the next level and makes it a game."

"And in doing so makes the act less pure," Nelson countered.

Maggie squinted at her husband with aggressive incomprehension. "What do you mean, less pure?"

Nelson finished his wine. John replenished his glass. Nelson studied its color with appreciation. "Somehow, yes, less pure," he said. "Corrupted by agenda. All games have an embedded agenda."

John leaned forward. "But games are good. They're about clarity— winners and losers. Hell, that's life. Everything's a game."

"How do you win at marriage?" Nelson asked, a coy flash at Maggie.

Grace chortled. "I know exactly what Nelson means, though," she said. "Games imply that self-definition depends on defeating others, that excellence comes from without, not from within. Is that it, Nelson?"

"That's rich," Maggie said offhandedly, dismissively. "Nelson himself doesn't know what he means half the time."

The cheap shot fell with a dull thud. It pained Nelson. There was some deeper antipathy behind it. If marriage didn't mean something positive—growth, shared reality, a joining of hands through life's uncertain terrains—what did it mean? In recent months Maggie had grown distant, abstracted, evasive and excessively critical. He'd felt excluded from her thoughts. And unsettled matters had not yet been discussed. Their world was fragile for living too long on hollow assumptions. Soon candid conversations must take place with her. Clarification was the only weapon against phony togetherness and intimate decline. John began to talk about an old hotel in Rhode Island he'd bought to restore and sell. "It was in bad repair," he said, "but in a great location."

"How did you find it?" Nelson asked.

"The owners lost it in foreclosure. I keep tabs on bankruptcies."

"That's terrible," said Grace reflexively. John's look aggressively questioned her sense.

"The town around it is shabby, but that will change," he continued. "It'll be shabby chic; then you're on the way to gentrification. Cha-ching."

Nelson, who deplored clichés like *cha-ching*, asked, "What does gentrification look like?"

"Like a Starbucks on Main Street, Hoss. In my business a seven-dollar cup of coffee is the sweet smell of success." The sudden nickname invoked a cowboy hat, which to Nelson underscored how John's swagger had that pride of dollars which excluded him from a certain polish. Grace was put off by it; her smile tightened when her husband talked about money.

"Please pass the potatoes," she said.

In recent weeks, Grace had become important to Bradley in this way. He had observed her in private moments and had discovered that an intimacy existed between Nelson and Grace. His grandfather's powerful captain's binoculars (would his mother notice them missing?) allowed him to be an invisible man in her midst. Through the lens, his life touched Grace where she lived. Ocular penetration was virtual adultery (*rape* was a term foreign to his rationalizations). He had shared intensely private moments with Grace—in absentia, as it were—but what did they add up to? Peeping fed a fantasy of what intimacy would be like with Grace, and that was it, but it was a paltry thing. To truly have her love, to share her life, would be, of course, as he knew, impossible. Besides, as he dourly reflected, Nelson Hawkins seemed to have her dance card. Oh yes, he knew all about that. Bradley had become the keeper of secrets.

5

It had happened this way.

A week earlier, Nelson's mood had been as uncertain as the weather, and he couldn't concentrate. Nevertheless, he stayed at his work for the allotted hours. Afterward, thinking about Maggie, restless and frustrated, he left the house to take a walk and clear his mind, trying to add up impressions. He went down the drive and then over to the switchback, where he turned and, striding vigorously against the slope, went up the steeper road. The air was still, the sky monochromatic with mist. Clouds had thickened and sunlight thinned. Why was she so hostile? Or was it his own projected aggression? He could smell the damp corruption of long-fallen leaves. Maggie seemed withdrawn. In recent weeks she had become abstracted and remote. Taking drugs? Not the type. Perhaps an affair? Blue skies appeared intermittently as large, low clouds broke the overcast. He could feel his heart beating. Where sunshine began to warm the ground, it steamed. He barely noticed. Walking in energetic steps as though striding toward his own uncertain future, he thought:

their bickering, those vague explanations, the silence and outright evasions. Where did it come from? It haunted his confidence. Nelson had begun to believe in the possibility of his worst fears. Ghosts of his youth reconvened. After sterile years of high school, Nelson had fairly exploded with desire to travel. He had believed in that magic of unfamiliar places. He knew that youth had an expiration date. Driven to erase inexperience as a buffer against adversity, he traveled and read books.

Immediately following his high-school graduation, Nelson went to Paris. His first sight of the city came when he emerged from the metro at Sèvres-Lecourbe on a hot August night and saw a couple kissing under a tree. The man was wearing a blue beret and the woman a flowered summer dress that rippled in a gentle wind. He walked narrow streets and wide boulevards; he visited museums and cathedrals and tried to absorb as much of the city as he could. He met a family of Americans at the Musée d'Orsay, and he had lunch with them: mother, daughter, and two sons. The boys were approximately his age, and they invited him to stay with them in their suite of rooms at the Grand Hotel overlooking the Paris Opera.

After France, he went by rail to Italy. Arriving on the night train in Florence at dawn, he walked in early morning light to the Duomo and, with his back against the stonework of the church, read Manzoni, waiting for the cafés to open. Later, after a breakfast of bread and wine, he had walked tirelessly to see as much of Florence as he could. Those were days past.

In the present moment, Nelson walked on: the overcast was breaking up. He remembered with clarity the youth he was then: energetic, innocent, ravenous for experience that might serve his aspirations. Sadly, he could admit that the Nelson of today did not feel energetic, resolute, purposeful, or even wise. He did not feel accomplished. With his marriage faltering, life was coming apart at the seams. If Maggie had strayed, what would her infidelity mean? And recovering from betrayal is not a simple matter. Pride is at stake; identity; everything. Something must shore up adultery's damaged timbers, or the ship will founder.

Thus, inwardly absorbed and intensely abstracted, he walked on until, from out of the oblivion of his thoughts, unanticipated and therefore as shock, he observed the somewhat hallucinogenic and unreal figure of Grace Addison waving to him from her garden.

"Hi, neighbor!" she called, smiling and leaning on her rake, in the midday sun. Nelson abruptly stopped walking. He stared at Grace mindlessly with a puzzled expression, like an idiot unable to grasp the mundane. She took off her gloves and dropped them on a tree stump beside a small green tool shed.

"Cleaning up?" he said. Even as he spoke, his words sounded alien and foolish to him.

"I watched you come up the hill," she said, one hand now shielding her eyes from the hard, bright sun. "You seemed distracted. I thought you had music blasting through earphones."

He moved a few steps down the driveway to be level with Grace, who wore a white T-shirt, blue-jean overalls too big for her, and a kerchief on her head. Still abstracted, Nelson laughed. "No, no, I don't like earphones. I can't think if I'm wearing them. I was thinking. Walking and thinking. I don't like distractions."

"Alone with your thoughts," she said, smiling. "How nice." She had a face capable of infinite elocutions.

"Alone with our thoughts. That's all any of us can be, I suppose. Alone. With our thoughts." He doddered on. But her smile welcomed him with good humor. A film of perspiration caught the sun when she tossed her head to settle a strand of hair and came over to where he was standing. Her eyes were large and liquid under dark brows and focused on him. For the first time that day, Nelson forgot about Maggie entirely.

"It's been such a blah day," Grace told him. "I've been puttering. The weeds will not defeat me this year." She looked down at neat rows in furrows for lettuce. Her garden was cultivated with a farmer's pride. Nelson looked up and squinted at the sky where low, fat clouds had dissipated.

"The weather's been unresolved," Grace said.

Nelson nodded. "A good afternoon for—here, let me help you with that." He interrupted himself to push back a branch of wisteria from the fence where it tickled her neck.

"Thank you," she said. "Want to come in for a minute? Have a glass of wine with me." He was closer to her. Her smile welcomed him. "If I'm not keeping you from anything." He pushed at the branch again to be sure it was secure.

"Not at all. I could use it."

"Wonderful."

Nelson followed Grace up the stone path between larch trees noting how baggy pants highlighted her charms. When they got to the front door she opened it and ushered him inside. "I'll take you to my favorite place in the house and settle you there while I change my clothes and open a bottle of something." A flirty inflection in her voice established an easy familiarity, and they went down the hall to a room with books on three sides and a fireplace. The sun was bright outside, and zebra shadows broke from the window blinds. The shadows ran diagonally along the walls and across the floor, imbuing the space with the deep tranquility of Zen repose.

Nelson conspicuously admired the library. "Very cozy."

"Make yourself comfortable. I won't be long."

When Grace went out of the room, Nelson ran his fingers along the books, touching titles familiar to him. There were many. Pulling out a volume, perusing it, replacing it and pulling out another, he thus browsed for a number of minutes, happy to be in this unexpected place. In a short while, Grace reappeared, holding two glasses of wine. She had changed into slacks, and her hair was down on her shoulders. "Here you are," she said. Nelson reached out and took the wine. Its ruby color deepened when the glass caught a narrow blade of sunlight.

"Cheers," she said.

"Cheers." They touched glasses and drank.

Grace put her glass down on a side table, and they sat together on the couch facing the cold hearth. Nelson pointed to the books in front of them. "I didn't think John was a reader."

"He isn't. He's a practical soul devoted to business. Business and football. Business and football and golf keep him going."

"And what keeps you going?"

Grace smiled. "I don't like football, and I don't play golf."

Nelson laughed. In these moments, he chose to go with the flow of events as they unfolded, but the inference was not lost on him. Grace sipped her wine. The wine lubricated their mood.

"Do you like to watch football?" she said.

"I like to participate."

"A hands-on kind of person?"

"Well ..."

As silence grew between them, unbroken for an interval, tension grew palpable, requiring one of them to say something. Grace at last spoke humorously and ironically. "You know, Nelson, you have a unique way of being unemphatic." He laughed, and the ice was broken. Grace smiled. "When I saw you, I was hoping you would stop by. I'm afraid I shanghaied you."

"No, I signed on for the voyage. John's away?"

A cloud passed across the sun, and the zebra-like shadows from the blinds vanished all at once but in a moment reappeared.

"In Florida, at a trade show, something like that."

"Actually, Maggie's away too."

"Where?"

"She went to Boston to visit a friend. At least, that's what she told me."

Grace noted the dour tone. "Is there anything wrong?"

Nelson responded with a shrug, and Grace looked away, her brow furrowed slightly, struggling with a thought. When she looked up again, her expression had something peeled back and raw in it. She took his hand into hers, signaling intention, but Nelson stayed passive. After another moment, responding to desire, he leaned over, and their lips touched. Gently at first and slowly, and then more aggressively, their kiss was what a kiss should be, a crossing over leading the way to greater intimacy. Surprising himself, Nelson broke it off and said abruptly: "We can't do this!"

Grace, too, fell back confused and a little bewildered: "I agree," she said, though her voice was uncertain.

"Do you?"

"No," she answered, looking away. She cleared her throat and pulled a thread from her knee, sighed volubly, laughed once to herself, and then looked up at him resignedly and said, "I mean, yes. We shouldn't do this or even think about it. We're in agreement."

"Absolutely."

Nelson observed as they separated from their embrace that the properness of this felt falsely true, even as retreating from desire felt truly false. "Okay," Nelson said, attempting to relocate himself. "Okay," he repeated.

"And I agree, so we're resolved," she said. And after a moment, she added, "Let's seal it with a kiss." And so, as a way of certifying their commitment to avoiding further physical intimacy, they fell back into an embrace again, exonerating themselves with a second kiss as long and passionate as the first. The kiss had a particular thrill, given and taken under a guise of disengagement. Grace imagined it taking place in a honeymoon houseboat in Shalimar Garden.

In a short while they finished their wine. Nelson left to continue his walk.

This happened the previous week—Bradley standing on "his ledge" to try out his grandfather's wartime binoculars mounted on a tripod. Thus inserting himself visually into the lives of others, he soon realized that they have their own parameters and that peeping implied a kind of paralysis. Dormant feelings can emerge sudden and sore, and yet they can't be acted upon. Appalled and unexpectedly jealous, Bradley felt impotent, an involuntary sharer of the secret between Nelson Hawkins and Grace Addison.

Bradley wasn't deluded about his behavior. He knew his emotional life was uneven. The truth was that deep down he knew with certainty that peeping wasn't the answer to anything. This habit of his, and the visits to Mistress Angela's Dungeon, were traits of an existential eunuch. But it didn't feel that way all the time, and he supposed the larger question looming was, What did he hope to achieve? These behaviors offered no long-term plan. He adjusted the binoculars for a better view.

Meanwhile, a neighbor unloading groceries from her car wasn't sure what she had seen. Perhaps a surveyor. Once she went inside, she peered from her kitchen window and saw the man on the ledge. He didn't seem to be a surveyor. He appeared to be peeping. She picked up the telephone and called the police.

Dispirited as a lovesick teenager in deepening despair, Bradley made his way back to his cottage through the steep woods, binoculars around his neck, carrying his tripod. Once at home, he went to the kitchen and got a beer from the refrigerator. He sat at the table without seeing anything or having cogent thoughts. He scratched at the label on his bottle, making paper pellets on the table while staring out at the lake. Bradley had been unsure about his feelings for Grace. But Nelson Hawkins now added an accelerant of jealous petulance to his infatuation. She was a neighbor he would see from time to time in town or at the library. He didn't care for her husband, whom he rarely saw. A mere onlooker, an invisible man, he had no purchase on observed events. He felt himself powerless, wallowing in self-pity.

6

On the day of the dinner party at the Addison residence, Detective Mallory called Officer Garvin to his office. "Close the door," he said when she stepped inside. "Have a seat. We got a call a few days ago about a possible Peeping Tom up at the lake. I'd like to put some eyes on the site. Do you want to nose around there a little and see what you can learn?"

"All the plum assignments."

"Here's a copy of the report and the address of the house. The reporting neighbor wasn't absolutely certain. Have a look but keep it inconspicuous."

Officer Janet Garvin shrugged and took the report. She was a sturdy, some would also say pretty, five-year veteran of the Granville police force. Slightly shorter than average, she had shoulder-length bottle-red hair, white sun-shy skin, and zaftig charm lost beneath her uniform. "I'm curvy," she used to say. With a good-girl smile and a sturdy love of God and country, she looked like somebody boys remember fondly from junior high school.

Officer Garvin read the report, noted the address, and could mentally visualize the area. She knew the neighborhoods high and low where trouble might brew and flattered herself as being familiar with every part of Granville and nearby Wilberforce. In addition to the lake in the north quadrant, Granville was a town on a river where the mouth widened to a broad estuary and emptied into Long Island Sound. Policing its waterfronts presented safety challenges that swimming and boating bring to any town where recreation has special hazards.

In the hour before her shift ended, Officer Garvin drove up to the lake. She parked her cruiser in the driveway of a nearby house she knew was unoccupied and set off on foot through the trees, where she found a concealed area with a view of the road close to the Addison property. The area, built into a steep slope above the lake, was only one of two vantage points from the woods. It didn't take her long to identify Bradley as the peeper. He was on a stone ledge about forty yards in front of her, nicely concealed behind a cluster of young trees, peering through binoculars at a dinner party in progress at the Addison residence. A full moon in the eastern sky had been bright earlier, but the night had gotten very dark, as foul weather advanced rapidly from the southeast.

The storm approached with lightning and thunder, and it began to rain. As winds blew across the lake in sudden gusts, Bradley stood his ground like a war journalist, making a tent of his poncho to cover his head. Officer Garvin prepared to move in. Then a lightning bolt struck so close the smell of sulfur filled the air. Shaken to the core, Bradley packed up his tripod and binoculars. Rain was pouring down hard now as he turned to go through the woods up the hill. As he reached for a tree limb to give himself balance, a beam of light exploded in his face, blinding him, and biblically from the darkness came a disembodied voice that thundered into Bradley's consciousness.

"POLICE! PUT YOUR HANDS WHERE I CAN SEE THEM."

The sudden bright light confused his orientation. A woman's voice. His thoughts were frozen.

"YOU ARE UNDER ARREST. PUT DOWN WHAT YOU ARE HOLDING. HANDS AGAINST THE TREE."

Bradley, in compliance, dropped his equipment and put his hands on the tree. His heart was racing. He squinted into the light, which came at him from the direction of the woman's voice. Pouring rain fell in heavy sheets.

"I am Officer Garvin with the Granville city police department."

Bradley's mind began to whirl. Thunder sounded.

"You have a right to remain silent—"

"But my equipment," Bradley interrupted, his face illuminated by the beam of her flashlight.

Officer Garvin directed her light on the things he had put down and then on the path out of the woods. "Okay," she said. "Pick that up and go this way."

Bradley retrieved his binoculars and tripod.

Staying behind him, Officer Garvin marched him out of the woods to her parked cruiser. She sensed no threat from Bradley, but under department procedures she handcuffed him and put him and his equipment into the back seat of the squad car.

Humiliated, Bradley meanwhile felt swallowed into the belly of the beast. He was dizzy and had a keen need to pee. The squad car began to move. Lake roads gave onto the main way to town, ten minutes away. Shame in all its oppressive iterations engulfed him. He watched lights go by. When they got to town, the police station was lit up, waiting for his ignominious arrival. All things private were now suddenly public. The town would know. Miss Byrd would know. His mother would know. Another uniformed policeman met the squad car to escort him inside. The squad car door opened, and Bradley was unceremoniously welcomed into the next phase of his life.

7

Detective Mallory opened a folder. He shuffled through the pages while Bradley watched. "Officer Garvin observed you at the edge of the woods peering through a neighbor's window." The detective looked up at him. "Is that correct?"

"Yes, sir." Bradley, abashed, tapped his foot nervously. His face expressed restless disquiet.

"How long have you been peeping?"

Bradley cringed. Peeping: the word carried a reproach of something horribly perverse. "Not so often," he said softly, unsure if he could make his thinking understood. "I mean, not all the time."

"I see you are employed at the McAndrews County Library," Mallory said, scanning pages from the folder. The Phineas McAndrews was the largest library in the county. It had working fireplaces on the first and second floors, with large couches and fine old leather chairs throughout, the feel of an old-school club.

"Yes," Bradley said. "I'm an assistant to the librarian, Miss Byrd."

"Ah, Miss Byrd." The detective smiled and looked up again. "She's a fixture in the community. I often see her riding her bicycle through town." Miss Priscilla Byrd was the original librarian and for three decades had served the community energetically. People knew her by her prim, eccentric manner, precise intellect, and by her blue bicycle with a woven straw basket on the handlebars. She didn't own a car and rode her bicycle everywhere.

"Do you enjoy your work at the library?"

"Very much."

"How long have you been there?"

"Almost ten years."

"What sort of work do you do there?"

Bradley enumerated his duties, which included organizing the stacks, minor maintenance to keep the grand spaces tidy, and keeping the fires going during the winter. "It's not a high-paying job, but I enjoy what I do. I like books. On some nights, I stay late and spend an hour or two reading in front of the fire."

"Sounds like a perfect perk," Detective Mallory said and smiled. But then the detective leaned forward. "By the way, did you know Ann Wheeler?"

"I read about what happened to her. It was awful."

"Did you know her?"

"She was a regular at the library in wintertime. Nineteenth century English classics were her favorites, I recall. She also liked poetry and loved the fireplaces."

The detective looked down at the papers in the folder and moved a few of them, pursed his lips, and without looking up said, "Have you ever looked through Ann Wheeler's window?"

Here Bradley paused. It seemed now clear that his voyeurism—his peeping!—placed him among nefarious local suspects. If the detective's smile worked as a barometer of his thoughts, it was not predictive. Bradley was struck with fear

"I have never looked into her window. I can't even tell you where she lives."

"I've got to be brutally candid with you, Bradley. I've got a murder on my hands and no suspects, and then you arrive here under arrest for the freaky crime of peeking into windows. I don't think you have an appreciation for how close you are to becoming at the very least a person of interest."

"What does that mean?"

"It means that if I or anyone else can tie you in any way to Ann Wheeler on or around the time of her death, you are going to be fighting a battle to clear your name from suspicion. Innocent until proven guilty, of course. Are you hearing what I'm telling you?" Mallory watched Bradley closely and spoke simply and directly, trying to put the fear of God into him.

"Detective, I don't swat flies. I have never had a violent impulse that I can remember. I am absolutely not a murderer. I can't understand the sort of mind that could kill another human being." But even as he said these words the explicit indecencies of Mistress Angela's Dungeon came to him as an argument against his own claims.

Detective Mallory leaned back in his chair and appraised his charge with speculative eyes. Bradley met his eyes without flinching. The detective had a clear understanding of the young man before him. "Bradley," he said, "I've got a lot of discretion here. You've never been arrested before. Is that right?"

"No sir," he said. "I mean yes, sir, I've never been arrested."

"Look—here is what I'm going to do for you. I'm willing to drop this matter. For now."

Bradley's eyes got big as banjos with shock and relief. "You are?"

"But I'd like you to go into therapy, voluntarily."

"Therapy?"

"Do you have health insurance?"

"Through the library."

"Good. I have a therapist in mind, if this is something you can agree to do."

Bradley felt humiliation like arthritis in the brain. He thought it a fair request, however. If shame is pride betrayed, therapy seemed a way to come out of the shadows and broker some amnesty with himself.

"Yes, sir. I mean, what kind of therapy?"

"Here's the card of Dr. Caroline Singer. She's a psychiatrist, and a very good one." He handed the card across the desk. Bradley took it.

"Dr. Singer will help you with whatever is behind this. Do we understand each other?"

"I think so."

"Let me be clear, Mr. Davis. Bradley."

"Yes."

"No more peeping through windows. Dr. Singer can help you. I hope I'm right about this. I don't want to see your name on the blotter again. Is that clear?"

"Yes, sir."

"We'll keep this between us."

Bradley stood, and they shook hands. In the hall on his way out, he fingered Dr. Singer's card in his pocket. Then he opened his cell phone and called a taxi to take him home.

After releasing Bradley, Detective Mallory opened another folder and began to re-read an account of the discovery of Ann Wheeler's body. This was something real, unsolved, and the investigation fell directly to him. The notes in the folder brought him back to that day.

8

A cable man discovered the murder scene.

The driveway led to the back of the house. A car he saw parked there led him to believe that the house was occupied. "Cable company!" The man said cheerfully as he knocked on the door. The shades were down and curtains drawn. Leaning toward the window, he rapped on the door again. It was hot in the yard and humid from recent rainfall. Morning had been sunny, but now it was cloudy and the air was heavy and absolutely still. "Hello?" He rapped harder this time. "Anybody home? Hello!"

An odor issued from the porch, or from under the porch, something dead, a rodent or raccoon. Smelling the air, the man tried to identify the source of the scent. After a minute, he went back to his truck, paused a moment, and then walked around the house, peering into windows. But to no avail. The windows were closed and it was impossible to see inside.

"Hello?" The man rapped sharply on the edge of the screen door. "Hello?"

There were many reasons why a car might be parked at a house with no one at home, he reasoned. Also, sometimes people don't come to the door but rather, from the corner of the window, peer out from their silent oblivion. But the fetid odor, the sweltering day, the uncut grass, a sense of desolation about the property, and the story of Vermont contributed to an uneasy sensation. In the Vermont story, an installer dispatched to a rural home to disconnect service for unpaid bills discovered a year-old desiccated corpse. The corpse was lying on the couch in front of a television still on and tuned to an episode of Gunsmoke.

"Cable company!" he called again.

After some consideration, the installer decided to call the authorities. The call went through the police switchboard, and a radio patrol car was dispatched to the address. In less than five minutes, a squad car pulled up. It parked beside the cable truck. Two policemen got out of the car. The cable installer went over to introduce himself. A short discussion ensued.

"Let's move into the shade," the taller policeman said. The three of them went under a maple tree in the back yard, and the two officers interviewed the installer. The cable installer shared his apprehensions. The police went up to the screen door in back and opened it and knocked on the inside door. No response. After a few moments, they too circled the house. They knocked on each window. After that, they went back to the squad car and made a radio call to confirm permission to enter the residence based on the odor. The cable installer remained by his truck. Detective Mallory told them to enter the premises and that he would be out to check on the scene.

Police work was something Mallory had always wanted to do. At forty-one years old, he had no illusions about the capacity of human beings for wrongdoing, but he believed that the world was perfectible and saw himself as a Guardian of Good. Mallory was abstracted in the moment with that feeling of being trapped in a classroom on a warm, sunny morning. Gazing out the window for no particular reason, he experienced that rare, brief, whole comprehension, unexpected, intense, and sure: a moment of pure feeling. It faded slowly, but what lingered was a sober sense that the civic machinery had been running rather too smoothly lately. An old army warning came to mind: when the battle seems too easy, it's an ambush. Right after he had that thought, the radio call came in from the patrol at the Wheeler house.

"I'm leaving now," Detective Gerard Mallory said to his assistant. He stood and reached for his jacket. Murder, if that's what this was, brought a personal and professional challenge. The magnitude of it weighed on him. News of it would reverberate in the community, and, rightly, people would want answers. He would have to manage the response.

He drove to the site. His thoughts ranged on local murder cases over the years. The most memorable was the infamous wood-chipper case. The perpetrator had strangled his wife, frozen her corpse, and then dismembered her with a chain saw. Then he rented a wood chipper and in the middle of the night spewed her into the town reservoir. Without a body, the case relied on circumstantial evidence, and there wasn't much of that until an eyewitness remembered seeing a pickup truck parked at 2 am on an access road near a fishing area. The pickup was eventually connected to a receipt from a rental store where a wood chipper had been returned, but returned cleaned. Nobody did that. Ever. Eventually some hair and bits of fingernail were recovered near the shoreline. Not much evidence, but enough to convict.

Mallory pulled into the driveway and followed it around to the back of the house, where he parked behind the cruiser near the cable truck. It was hot in the sun. The grass was untended. White cabbage moths flitted among dandelions. The first-responding officers were standing in the yard with the cable man. They had just emerged from the house and stopped talking when Mallory approached. "What have you got?" he said to them.

"Lying on the couch. Naked from the waist down. Possible rape, strangulation, and maybe blunt-force trauma, we're not sure. She's dead, though. We're sure about that."

"You made the call?" he asked the cable man, who nodded affirmatively. "Do the officers have your information?" The other cops nodded to the detective.

"You're good to go. And thanks," he said to the man, and turned to the officers. "Secure the area and call forensics." Mallory checked his watch and, pointing to the back door, said, "That door?"

The officer nodded. "You're going to want to hold your nose."

Detective Mallory put on latex gloves and entered the house alone. Inside was dark but not grim, though the stench was overpowering. He put a handkerchief to his mouth while he looked around the house. Standing in the small kitchen, he could see the living room beyond. The living room was not large, but it had a fireplace. The furniture was plain but neat. Except for the flies, the house had that cottage feel of coziness and close comfort.

When he saw the murdered woman, Mallory was taken aback by the sight of her bloated corpse. She had been dead for at least a week, maybe longer. On the couch a white female in her mid- to late-thirties was lying on her back, partially clad in a T-shirt. Her body was nearly twice its size. Her head was hanging off the seat cushion, face upward, mouth agape, longish hair touching the floor. Sightless eyes looked heavenward in a ghastly lifeless stare. One leg was elevated. Flies swarmed the body. The stink of death and decay was nauseating. He examined her closely for abrasions.

Mallory was appalled as much by the indignity of the scene as by the crime that had produced it. Paying attention to the floor and to the walls, he went from room to room. In the bedroom he discovered what looked like a datebook or a journal. He opened it. An appointment book. It had been kept in pencil. He flipped through the pages and discovered an exceedingly odd thing—all of the dates and notes had been erased. On closer examination, it appeared that each entry had been written down and then carefully erased as a way of indicating that appointments had been met and calls returned, so that by this process there was nothing in the book at the end of the year! An uncanny system, Mallory thought: a record of life as an erasure.

In the kitchen, a teacup in the sink and a regiment of dishes washed by hand stood in a dish drainer. A single chair was positioned at a small drop-leaf table in the dining nook. An old Kodak photograph of what looked like a birthday party was fixed with a magnet to the refrigerator door. The deceased as a teenager sat beside a boy several years older in front of a cake. Mallory counted eighteen candles on it. Family resemblance suggested the boy was her brother. The detective opened the refrigerator and examined the contents. A carton of milk had an expiration date three weeks past. Yogurt was also weeks beyond its sell-by. He closed the door and went to the bedroom. There he noticed a metal crucifix above the bed, and a book on the bedside table opened to a poem of many verses, two of them marked with a pen stroke.

There's a stake in your fat black heart
And the villagers never liked you.
They are dancing and stamping on you.
They always knew it was you.
Daddy, daddy, you bastard, I'm through.

Mallory knew the poet but not the poem. Sylvia Plath had gassed herself at the age of thirty by putting her head into an oven. Passing through the living room, he paused to once more observe the corpse and then went out the back door. The two policemen were standing by the yellow-taped perimeter. He stood at his car and studied the small cottage house. "When the body is removed, tell the coroner I'd like his report as soon as possible." And death shall have no dominion, the detective thought, shaking his head at countervailing evidence. A peaceful home in a quiet setting, a sunny day, and the summer season ahead. Later, he learned that the deceased was thought to have been on vacation. She might have remained unfound a longer time.

Back at the station house, Detective Mallory made routine inquiries among patrolmen. Officer Janet Garvin detailed traffic nighttime stops she'd made in that area. "It's almost rural out there. Very quiet. Not much traffic at night."

"In the last three weeks, has anyone given you reason to be suspicious?" Mallory fiddled with a rubber band.

"Just the routine speeders, and some safety stops."

"No strange personalities?"

Janet shook her head. A rubber band shot across the room, where it bounced off the wall and fell into the wastebasket.

Driving home, Mallory shuddered at the horror of murder, of taking life from another. There can be no return from that degree of perfidy. He slapped the steering wheel as if to bat back bad thoughts. Such an inhalation of evil must be soul-destroying. He felt a keen need for his wife, Linda, for normalcy and the familiarity of her mind and heart, the comfort of her clarifying thoughts, the peaceable safeguards of his wife and his home.

9

"A smashed car can be fixed. Stolen property can be recovered or replaced. The toughest thing about murder is that nothing can be reversed. The crime might be solved, but the life stays lost, and the grieving doesn't stop." Linda poured her husband another glass of wine. Gerard picked it up and looked at the glass like a mystic contemplating a crystal ball.

"Nobody missed her?" Linda asked.

"They thought she was on vacation."

"How awful. Do you have any suspects?"

"I spent the afternoon asking questions of people who knew her. I get the same astonished response: Who would want to kill Ann Wheeler? It's a mystery."

"What about clues?"

"No clues, but there was a Catholic crucifix in her bedroom."

"How do you know it was Catholic?"

"The Jesus figure was on it. Other denominations don't have Jesus on the cross. I'm going to talk to the Catholic priest in Wilberforce."

"Was there a man in her life?"

"I don't think so."

"Gay?"

"No."

"A secret lover? Maybe a married man?"

"Anything is possible. She didn't date. Some women don't. She went to church. She had a job. She lost her life. Fade out."

Mallory and Linda had been undergraduates together at Indiana University. In the beginning he wanted to be a journalist. The School of Journalism published a daily newspaper, where they both worked. Mallory, on the City Desk, wrote a daily column, Police Blotter, and Linda organized the advertising pages. The paper had a 3:30 pm deadline, and while Mallory typed his copy, he could see Linda pasting ads on position boards across the aisle. She had striking copper-penny eyes. Her left cuspid slightly overlapped its neighboring incisor, the signature of her engaging smile. Working happily, she often seemed to be having an amused conversation with herself, which secretly had to do with a growing affection for the budding journalist in front of her every day. Linda would sneak glances at Mallory while he typed his copy; when their eyes occasionally met, it was with mutual unspoken interest. It was an ice-breaking gesture when he asked her out to dinner on Columbus Day. On that first date, he told her that she moved gracefully. She said watching him type was sexy. After returning to Linda's small cottage duplex, they fell into her convertible bed. By morning they were in love and never looked back.

His column at the newspaper gave him privileged access to the town. Each morning he went to the police station to read the arrests record from the night before. The police blotter logged local antisocial behavior and dark truths about racism. Homophobia indicated a stunning lack of sophistication about sexual matters, generally. Official accounts of a bar brawl, a domestic incident involving a knife, an Air Force colonel arrested for prancing around his hotel room balcony dressed as a woman— Mallory was drawn to the fervor of life around him. In time he realized how his reporter's love of secrets revealed a romantic relationship with the street. Slowly he began to be drawn more directly to the idea of law enforcement. As much as he enjoyed the power of the pen as a reporter, law enforcement's hands-on engagement with human realities made him see the kind of contribution he could make to the civic foundation. When he mentioned his interest in police work, twenty-two-year-old Linda did not respond positively to his shift in career aspirations.

"But why?" she asked him.

"I don't like injustice."

"Nobody does. You can write about it."

"The idea of preventing it appeals to me. I think I have the temperament for it."

"You'll have to have a gun."

"I'm not afraid of a professional relationship with weaponry."

"Relationship?" Linda said.

"Well, I don't have one at the moment." He shrugged, and they both began to laugh, but Linda had legitimate misgivings about police work.

"You could be killed. Is it worth the risk? And where will we live?"- Sensing that Mallory's reasons were altruistic and his desire authentic, Linda gave him her support. After college, he agreed to find work in New England, where she wanted to live. After scouring locations, they settled in Granville, where it was soon clear to his superiors that Mallory was thoughtful, diligent, and uncommonly astute. His integrity won their respect. He quickly rose in rank to detective. This was his first homicide case. Now he faced a different and serious matter. Murder was an offence against every decency in civilized society. It brought dread to a community. His emotions were churning. He was ready to apply every available asset to solving Ann Wheeler's death.

"It scares me that someone capable of murder is in our midst," Linda said.

"I am going to make a point to find every lead and pursue it. I take it personally."

"Don't take it too personally."

"Like it or not, there is a relationship between a killer and a cop, and it is personal."

Nothing was more unjust than the taking of life. It went to the core of his professional reason for being. The sight of her bloated body and the finality of death it projected screamed out for justice.

Linda believed that Fate was a projection made from inner needs and impulses, so that becoming yourself felt inevitable. What that accomplished you called Destiny. She knew her husband felt exactly the same way.

PART II

10

He wrote about his incarceration:

The cell block is a kennel, sometimes a bordello, often a drug den and always a dungeon of darkness and broken dreams. Men behind bars are beasts of blasted hope experiencing agonies expressed in constant imprecations, in crying, in screaming, in fighting, and sometimes in hideous laughter. At the beginning, I didn't know what was ahead. My first thought was that everything would soon be put right again. Surely someone would realize that a mistake had been made, and I'd be out of this hellhole. Being there is like having the wind knocked out of spirit so it can't breathe. You try to find a way to understand it. But this is a place of no choices, no friends, and no love. Anger grows inwardly like a cancer. But despair grows also, and you get numb. Numb means too overwhelmed to feel anything. Confinement is not reformatory. It is punishment. In taking your freedom, they have taken meaning and purpose from your life. And it gets worse as larger realities dawn. In prison everything comes at you from outside, and your choices are few.

Power demands favors. Toxic situations brew. It's sexual; it's serious. You get boxed in. Physical altercations are impossible to avoid and can add years to a prison sentence. And then there is the emotional isolation of hour upon hour in a locked cell, day after day, year after year. A cacophony of echoes fills the air. Mindless futile apostrophe, mindless endless chatter, and the shadow of constant threat is your living environment. Confrontation is a norm, and failure to answer disrespect marks a man as bait for further degradations. And more: losing freedom changes all assumptions you had about life. You have been rejected as defective, human garbage cast off from society; your soul is orphaned and unclaimed in a universe indifferent to pain and loneliness. You are an unaccommodated man. And yet come clarifying insights. From the pit of injustice, one can see how the righteous are villainous, the police criminal, the good suspicious, the virtuous conniving, the powerful weak, the weak overwhelmed, the wealthy dispossessed of spirit, and the impoverished blind to their riches. It could be my hallucination, but when you have known the belly of the beast, what people in The World call real life is a mirage, a delusion; most of them spend decades in a daze of oblivion. The unwashed are the un-self-aware, blissfully blind souls unable to see themselves in a mirror. All is bad improvisation, poor posturing, selling a personality profile not real or imagined well, like lawyers carried away with themselves, bad acting. The prison yard is a place of angry id, filled with bad actors and bad acting out.

—Parting Thoughts, by Russell Garner

Detective Gerard Mallory read this first-hand account of grievous wrong by the man sitting across from him. Russell Garner was a handsome, still youthful, and gentle-seeming former Assistant Professor of English. Until a week ago, he had been inmate 4357 at the Glendale Maximum Security State Penitentiary serving a twenty-five-year sentence for rape. He had spent twelve years in prison, until newly submitted DNA evidence exonerated him and he was released. Detective Mallory knew the basic facts of Garner's history.

At his trial, though the evidence was circumstantial, the jury returned a guilty verdict. Garner was sentenced. An appeal failed. After ten years served, his plight was brought to Proven Innocent, an organization dedicated to victims of possible failed justice. They took the case and learned that sperm samples collected at the scene did not match Garner's DNA, which convinced a judge that he had been wrongly convicted. But twelve years in prison was vile injustice. He was back now in his hometown in his first week of freedom paying a courtesy call to local law-enforcement authorities. His words chilled the detective with sorrow and regret. Some weak link had resulted in a miscarriage of justice and unimaginable, wrongful incarceration.

After so long, Russell Garner was free. Changes had taken place. To relearn the basics of daily living, Garner had been assigned to a voluntary release program to help him adjust to life on the outside. Mallory had been following the case. The mayor, who had been Garner's high-school track coach, wanted to show official contrition in any way possible, and Mallory was eager to help.

"Welcome back, Professor," the detective said. He stood and offered his hand across the desk.

"Nobody has called me that in a while, Detective." Garner shook Mallory's hand. The expression on Garner's face had a sanguine wisdom in it, like abstraction in the eyes of soldiers home after years of war. "Frankly I just want to put it all behind me."

"I'm sure that's true, Russell. May I call you Russell?"

"Of course."

"Please call me Gerry. Your situation was a failure of everything we try to stand for. Society owes you far more than an apology."

"Lawyers are negotiating a settlement." Life had swirled down a waste pipe of passing days when he was in jail, where the pure torment of *doing time* is eventually revised into its bitter truth: *time does you.*

What had happened to Garner contradicted everything Mallory had committed his life to improve. "How does freedom feel?"

"I don't know yet. I'll tell you when I do."

The detective in front of him was nice enough. His desk held a framed picture of his pretty wife. But Russell no longer felt inner warmth and security. Institutionalization had taken something from his spirit. He had not found immunity from loneliness. He could not imagine a favorite chair, fireside, or family life. He lived in a spiritual vacuum and ached with pangs of hunger.

"Thank you for the visit," the detective said. Russell stood and shook hands with Detective Mallory. "I want you to know that the whole town stands behind you in whatever you choose to do with the rest of your life. You've known the worst. I wish you the best."

Returning from the town square to his rented room, Russell stood on a corner waiting for the traffic light to change. He looked around. There was an unreality about freedom. Life on the outside seemed like everything was on television. Streets had the feel of a movie set. Maybe it had become his habit to feel imprisoned in his mind. Or society itself had become imprisoned, locked up in a virtual panopticon, with omnipresent TV screens—in restaurants, waiting rooms, and now even at gas pumps—making a spectacle of people's behavior. People were wandering around like actors taking direction from absent controllers through earpieces. Life had turned into a dress rehearsal for some other ultimate culmination. There was psychosis in it, expressed precisely in T. S. Eliot's observation on modernity: "Distracted from distraction by distraction."

People stared with blank expressions at advertisements insisting that life could be enhanced through pills, potions, new automobiles, or by vacations on cruise ships to cold climates. Awful music blared everywhere. It had taken him a while to realize that drivers in cars and people on the street were not talking to themselves but speaking into invisible cell phones. People lived in willfully corrupted translations of reality, legible but without grace, functional but without soul, active but without heart. Social habits had changed. The cell phone as fully capable hand-held computer was something new to him. Culture had shifted.

Ex (for exonerated) con and former Assistant Professor of English Russell Garner had rented a room in a house owned by an elderly couple not far from the railroad station. The room was on the second floor, with a private entrance. Each day brought him to a deeper appreciation of freedom, but freedom had challenges. If life in prison seemed to belong to somebody else, so did freedom. After so many years, choice caused him anxiety. Walking to the corner store for coffee could make him weep for the infinite possibilities ahead in a day. People and their phones were the changes that had come to daily life. It recalled to him a comment often erroneously attributed to Marshall McLuhan: *We become what we behold. We shape our tools and then our tools shape us.*

On the other hand, simple pleasures gave him joy. Later that evening, on the summer solstice, Russell sat at Cap'n Henry's bar having a vodka and tonic at happy hour. There he let life wash through him. As he wished for some insight or epiphany that could explain what had happened to him, he looked out across the estuary at motor boats and sailboats anchored there—great symbols of freedom, vessels of adventure. From his window that morning he had seen a boy on a bicycle riding fast down the street. He watched the boy riding, head down and pedaling fast, full of energy and thrill, unaware of everything but the ride, on his way to someplace else in a dream, Russell thought, but he doesn't know it's a dream. He's headed to someplace else, that land of rich promise just ahead of our average lives. Russell laughed. We're all on our way to that someplace else, a better life, tomorrow, the moon. We seek America the beautiful, the vague, the powerful, home of repose to the restlessly wandering expeditionary.

Even at happy hour, prison sounds echoed in him like curses in a madhouse. The waitress brought his drink. Her smile seemed incongruous—he still heard those voices moaning for unwinnable freedom. He sipped his drink and watched a cabin cruiser glide majestically like someone else's dream come true. In his mind's eye he saw jail cells within an hour's drive, where run-aground damned souls sat alone, stranded in a life without dreams.

Russell watched a sailboat leave its mooring and navigate the harbor to the channel, tacking with full sails. In the gumbo of daydream images, an idea materialized: I must have a bicycle. This notion came to him with the force of revelation. He couldn't buy a boat—he had no real money, only earlier savings—but he could find a bicycle somewhere and rediscover the thrill that the boy this morning had been enjoying. But it meant something else, he realized. By viewing options and making choices, he was finding a way forward in freedom. A bicycle will be my boat, my airplane, my personal expression of liberty, he thought.

Later, sitting at the window of his room on the longest day of the year, looking out at the scene before him, lit golden before the approach of dusk, he felt drawn into the poetry of it. For twelve years his world had been a cell and the prison yard. Now, free again, he was feeling freedom, as delighted to be contemplating a bicycle as a billionaire his new yacht.

11

While waiting for Bradley, Dr. Singer went over her notes highlighting moments of transference, those instances when the patient invests the therapist with ghosts of old fears he did not wish to share with anyone, including his therapist, including himself. These were precisely the key to his personal truth.

"Today I'd like you to tell me about the experiences you've had at the place you began to talk about at the end of the last session."

"You mean Mistress Angela's Dungeon?"

"Yes. Mistress Angela's. And you dress like a woman there?"

"Yes."

"Tell me about it."

There was never moral disapproval in Dr. Singer's tone, no shock or lurid curiosity. Resolved to be truthful, Bradley sighed. "I go there when I feel blocked up."

"How so?"

"I mean emotionally, I guess."

"Tell me about that feeling—the feeling of being blocked up."

"When frustration rises, and I can't get rid of it."

"Let's talk about that frustration."

"Sometimes I feel anxious and lonely, or else it's wondering if I've made the right choices about how I live, where I work, about mother and her problems. I think about the future. Those feelings can seem overwhelming. But I don't think it's unusual to feel that way."

"It's not unusual for you. Tell me now, Bradley, what is this place like, this dungeon, as you describe it?"

"How *are* you!" The ebullient proprietress walked around her desk and stepped down to greet Bradley. Mistress Angela was a diminutive woman of mannered effusions with the histrionic whiff of the impresario. Her mercenary sincerity welcomed you to her dungeon (on the sixteenth floor of an office building in Manhattan!), a place of wailing and gnashing of teeth, where an army of attentive specialists were ready to act on programs of abuse written by her clients. And Bradley had seen many empowered by means of submission and servile humiliation. These clients were money brokers and lawyers, judges, corporate executives, politicians, clerics, and venturing souls in pursuit of compulsive pleasures they could not understand. None seemed so exalted, however, when hog-tied, ball-gagged, and put into cages by young women issuing stern commands. There were other inferences, of course. Mortification had redemptive value in the guilty imagination. In this theater of the absurd, Bradley experienced masochism's worship and abuse as euphoria of exoneration. That first magic of his mother's underwear years ago had opened Bradley to other fixations at some distance from average. The formalized programs of self-abnegation had great appeal for reasons he did not clearly understand.

The outer office, despite the eccentric reception platform, looked like any place of business with a waiting room. Mistress Angela's desk was elevated behind a low barrier with a chair resembling something like a witness stand. In her forties, she no longer participated in what she called "The Show." She was primarily a businesswoman. She also had a liberal arts degree from Bennington College. Recently featured on a downtown cable broadcast on her enterprise, she wryly quoted La Rochefoucauld: "We are so accustomed to disguise ourselves to others, that in the end, we become disguised to ourselves."

Bradley sat thumbing through *People* until a woman of about twenty-five, dressed in black spandex, came into the waiting room and told him that his session was now ready. He stood obediently and followed her through the unassuming inner door which opened to an unlikely mélange of rooms and devices.

The larger main area was visible through a Plexiglas window along the hallway. It resembled a high-school gymnasium, but in place of parallel bars, gymnastic beam, and climbing rope were meat hooks, a whipping post, and wire cages. A thin, young, and bearded investment banker, chained to the post and caned by a sham nun, cried out with each painful assault. Farther down the hall on the right were small cells with windows that allowed a view of those who consented to being watched in their duress. Through one Bradley saw a naked man tied to a chair while a young woman holding a flog circled him, asking questions he couldn't answer, scourging him with each failure to come forth with information. In another room, set up to resemble a grammar-school classroom, a superior-court judge sat at a second-grade desk and wrote his ABCs while a "teacher" standing in front of him looked on. She held a heavy wooden yardstick and swatted him with great violence, ordering him to begin again, which he did—"Yes, Miss Buckley"—reciting each letter audibly as he traced it on paper like a schoolboy, until his orgasm, after which he whimpered like a boy who has wet his pants in class.

"Here's a note," the nominal Miss Buckley said at last in accordance with his script and handed it to him in a tone of disgusted resignation. "Give it to the school nurse."

The judge proceeded to the showers with this bit of paper, which he saved with other souvenirs and remnants of exoneration he kept in a special box.

Bradley's escort ushered him into the makeup/changing room at the end of the hall and settled him in front of a large rectangular mirror. "Put this on," she said. "And these."

She handed him a green cotton shift and red pumps. Bradley did as he was told and then took his seat in the chair at the vanity.

"Now relax. I'm going to apply your makeup." She worked for long minutes with brushes, powders, and blush, bringing out his features. She drew lines on his eyelids and applied mascara. She attached false eyelashes. "Red or white?" she asked, holding lipstick cylinders.

"Red."

"Put your head back."

She darkened his eyes and deepened his profile with the ease and artfulness of a theatrical veteran, and remarkably, through the magic of makeup, his unenhanced bland looks were transformed into the face of a starlet, but with protruding ears.

"Do you have the blond wig?" he asked.

"Of course."

She brought out a box with his name on it and withdrew a long-haired blond wig. She placed it on his head gently, almost formally, a royal investiture, making Bradley feel a tinge of keen excitement.

"I think I look stunning," he said with uncharacteristic self-assertion. "What do you think?"

"You look like a dream."

Bradley could hardly contain himself. "What's next?" he asked, though with too much eagerness, perhaps impertinently, and without permission. His mistress turned cold and rude.

"Brenda! How dare you, you cunt!" She reached for a black leather flog with many tentacles. "Get down on your knees!" she commanded. Bradley/Brenda slipped off the stool and on to the floor, eyes radiant with thralldom.

And so it began.

For the next three hours, he was manacled, scourged, forced to crawl on all fours and lick the boots of his mistress. He was caged in one of the smaller cells along the far wall, where other clients were also imprisoned while their respective mistresses joked and gossiped, periodically insulting them, finally releasing them for the next round of mistreatment, rotating through the various rooms and implements in a loosely improvisational cavalcade of torments. He heard one man screaming for mercy, his cries serving only as an occasion for amused derision among the dominatrixes who were chatting and laughing at private jokes. Only the safeword would end the role-play; all other expostulations were ignored as part of the eroticized general atmosphere of physical torture and psychological abuse.

In his final hour, Bradley/Brenda was led on a leash to have his snack: meat loaf in a dog dish, thoughtfully crumbled into bite-sized bits by his mistress. She filled his water bowl with white wine as a reward for obedient behavior. Then, like a spaniel, Bradley/Brenda put his face into the dish and ate until it was licked clean, partaking also of the wine. The template was orthodox, food at the end of his ordeal signifying consummation, a burnt offering meant to appease inner demons and cleanse the soul. Communicants here were no less troubled by primitive impulses than sinning Christians and, like most Christians, few understood the psychological underpinnings of their blood liturgies. Bradley/Brenda, sinner, unworthy penitent in search of expiation, flagellant, apostle of mortification seeking redemption, author of bleating petitions for mercy from young women he would never know, was a lamb among lost sheep of the biblical adage.

"Alright, Brenda. You are released."

"Thank you, mistress." Bradley/Brenda sighed.

"Go now."

"Yes, mistress." Bradley stood diffidently.

With head bowed, lightheaded, lighthearted, and weak-kneed, he walked out of the main cell block to the showers. There, un-bewigged, mascara running in black streams from his eyes, gripped by an almost paralyzing euphoria, he raised his head in elation. The showerhead rained on him like cleansing falls of holy water in Eden. He had learned a secret of saints and soldiers: when the sacred and profane occupy the same spaces in spirit, every emotion carries equally its opposite attribute. In the moment of ecstasy, pain is indistinguishable from pleasure, love indistinguishable from hate, certitude defined by vertigoes of doubt, and redemption discovered in extremes of self-abnegation.

He took the elevator down to the ground floor. He walked through the lobby door that opened automatically and emerged once again into the living world, where now everything seemed unreal in an atmosphere of tranquil joy. The faces of people in the street were filled with goodness and purpose inspired by benevolent intention. Automobiles and buses appeared free from gridlock and part of a great, happy ongoing carnival. A stranger's smile signified acceptance and love; the purposeful gait of pedestrians portended not frantic self-interest but resolute pursuit of public good. A powerful sense of new freedom made everything seem joyful.

As he drove the highways north, it felt like flying. When he turned off onto country roads leading to the lake, the houses nestled in the hills seemed somehow to exemplify perfection. That special euphoria lasted almost a whole day after these sessions.

"Well, our time is up," Dr. Singer said, ending the session. "We'll leave it here."

Bradley sat up and turned to look at her.

"Understand I make no judgment about the behavior, Bradley. But as I've said, I want you to think about what you're getting from these episodes. Everything you do in that place stands for something else. What you find there is not what you seek. You are going around in circles. That is what I want you to think about."

12

Nelson Hawkins paused at the typewriter, had a sip of coffee, and read what he had written.

Night fades. Gaunt outlines of the world are redrawn. When the warming sun rises, mists ascend in vertical columns and animate the lake while, in shaded treetops, patches of fog lie motionless like ghosts dying of daylight. On the waters farther down, diamond coruscations of sunlight dance on the surface. We have lived through winter's cracking ice thundering like gunshots in the night, chilly shut-in nights jewel-lit with stars across the frozen horizon, bald eagles hunting from the ice shelf and sportsmen fishing through holes in ice inside tiny tents that make long shadows in low sun. Spring comes, and days get longer and warmer and the birds return. Mornings are paradisiacal again. Buds appear and flower, and summer arrives. Lush, sunny, identical days with sultry afternoons. Alive nights echo laughter in the dark followed by murmuring voices of lovers huddled in hidden places. And then autumn's red-and-yellow-painted hills shine with their own light, and the smell of the earth permeates in cool air. A diminishing sun followed by bright stars appearing at dusk, and clear, cold dawns with morning frost on browning grasses. Then winter once more, life rhythms turning inward again after leaves are gone, every new cycle of renewal, every season retaining something infinite about impermanence.

Writing was the only activity that transported his intellect to spirit, where experience could be felt and understood in more exalted and meaningful ways. He wrote on his old Corona Standard portable typewriter, a typing machine—a writing tool that accessed imagination at a clarifying place in his brain. A musician friend had told him how trance-like muscle memory was, when fingers found notes without thinking. Typing at full speed was like that, with its special staccato intensity of striking type making words. He had another sip of coffee and studied the view. A gentle wind rippled the waters, chasing off ghostly patches of fog. Maggie was still asleep. Thinking now of her, Nelson began to type.

Our brightly-lighted lives ran like trains on parallel tracks that abruptly diverged, torn from shared illusion. And then one day I awakened to find myself living with a stranger, and the stranger was my wife, and I was a stranger to myself . . .

He stopped typing and walked to the rail on the deck overlooking the lake. It was impossible not to acknowledge that he and Maggie were at a crossroads in their marriage. Maggie expressed anxiety in predictable ways. She wore earphones all day and trained for the marathon. She texted compulsively, tweeted, or otherwise deflected reality as a way of coping with depression. Nelson knew that, but did she? They needed to clarify feelings and make some decisions. Sunlight on the lake sparkled farther down, where the surface was rippled. Closer in, the surface was glassy and mirrored the shoreline, quite beautiful and serene, with vivid inverted recapitulation. He leaned slightly forward into the morning air, trying to absorb something profound from the scene, when all at once Maggie herself appeared behind him in her robe. She sidled up to where he was standing at the rail. Nelson turned and smiled at his wife. She smiled back: a counterfeit, he observed. He could not locate her emotionally. At that moment, a V-flight of geese passed low overhead, honking volubly, nature's living brushstroke on a morning scene. He watched their formation fly down the lakeshore. When he turned to see Maggie, for an instant Nelson's mind flashed to their first night together seven years earlier. He had walked from Maggie's car to the back door of her house and waited with her in the dark while she scratched through her purse to find her key. The door opened into the kitchen, and eventually to London, Rome, Paris, Nice and Venice, Martha's Vineyard and Cape Breton Island, where Maggie insisted on riding bicycles over long courses that Nelson found exhausting but gratifying afterward. Their time together seemed like a daydream. But now, like colors in fading photographs, their affections were vanishing. He had to face the truth of that soon. He would not put it off. It must be addressed. But just as he was about to speak, Maggie preempted him: "I'm leaving you, Nelson. I don't know how else to say it, but there it is."

"This is sudden," he said, though it wasn't really, somehow. Her eyes shined with some lovely secret feeling he could not reach or know or share or change. He saw nothing in her eyes for him.

"I'm in love with someone else. I thought you knew by now."

He did not. "Not just having a fling?"

"I'm sorry."

"Sorry? That's an apology. Apology implies regret, and I'm not getting that." He turned to face her profile. "How long has this been going on?"

She looked at him briefly. "A year," she said, then looked away.

"A year!"

He felt dislocated. She wouldn't meet his eyes. "It's been living hell for me, if that matters."

"It doesn't. You certainly kept it a secret."

Her eyes narrowed. "You are incredibly insensitive!"

"Insensitive? How am I insensitive? You're the one with a boyfriend."

"How do you know it's not a woman?"

He sighed. He could feel his lips bleed into a thin smile of acid appreciation. This was painful. Maggie could pull a notion out of thin air and hurl it at assumptions like a fastball that you couldn't see. It was her limited gift. "A woman, then," Nelson said, with more bitter sarcasm than he intended.

She shrugged. "It's a man." And then added a rapier thrust: "You know him."

"Who is it?"

"John Addison."

"John Addison!" The name landed on him like an anvil. Another revelation Nelson didn't see coming. The dazzling lake view was growing in depth and color, but the rising sun now depressed him. Maggie's expression was coldly bland. "You've always said you liked John."

"Let's go inside," he said, his tone like a sigh, disconsolate, chagrined.

She shrugged. As they went in, Nelson thought how a shrug summarized their marriage. He sat on a stool opposite his wife at the kitchen island. He rotated the stool to look at the living room behind him, where symbols of togetherness did not add up. They never had. Maggie's movements were tense. Her fingers fidgeted in small experiments with a teaspoon. Nelson said, "So what are you telling me? Are you saying that our marriage is over?"

She raised one eyebrow defensively. "I suppose so, yes."

They sat wordlessly. Neither had anything else to say.

Nelson felt instinctive sympathy with her distress, yet if part of him felt bad about her discomfort, another less worthy part of him was happy to make it more difficult for her. After an excruciating full minute of silence, Maggie spoke. "I'm leaving for a few days."

"With John?"

"I'm meeting him, yes."

"Has he told Grace about this?"

"As we speak."

"You two really have this figured out."

Nelson felt numb. Fast-moving thoughts furrowed his brow. The situation was awful. He had a sip of coffee. Reality acknowledged is better than truth denied no matter how unpleasant the facts. He tried to see a bright side but found it hard to imagine the future. Life is better taken in small bites.

Maggie had a different idea. "I'll call my attorney," she said, abruptly, almost merrily.

Nelson glowered at her. "Why don't we take this a step at a time?" His tone was darkly disapproving, dismay devolving into silence and anger.

Shrewd enough to know that further discussion might break a fragile accord, Maggie stood up resolutely, eager to go. "I better get ready, then," she said and quickly disappeared into the bedroom. She returned with her suitcase almost immediately. Already packed! Nelson found this pre-planning untoward. She put her bag by the front door. He continued sitting in the kitchen while she got ready to leave. Her mood visibly improved, Maggie now seemed positively perky; she was all sensible concern, fluttering through the house collecting a few odds and ends while Nelson finished his coffee. She called from the other room: "Don't forget they're coming to fix the wall this morning."

A stone wall on the driveway she had backed into last month returning from a boozy tryst with John Addison, he could now guess.

"What time?"

"Eight, I think. It's written on the estimate in the kitchen by the toaster." Mundane chores of daily living continue in spite of upset. She checked her hair and makeup one last time and then rummaged through the hall-table drawer looking for a stamp. She found one and put it on an envelope which she first put into her purse but on second thought went with it into the bedroom. Returning, she crossed the area of the living room twice, turning her head from side to side, trying to find or remember something she was not sure she had lost or forgotten. Before leaving, she came over to where Nelson stood. He received her poignantly insincere embrace, which she held deceitfully longer than necessary to conceal an urgency to leave, all of which was perceived. Nelson looked at her as though for the last time.

"I'm sorry, Nelson," she said.

But she was not sorry. Her expression had that greedy expectation of a spoiled child for an undeserved treat. Cheerful readiness to run from unpleasantness was a virtue to weak character. She turned and got her bag, checked herself in the mirror one last time, and in moments she was out the door. Nelson went to the window to watch her get into the car, saw her settle into her seat. Then she put the car in gear, checked the rearview mirror, and drove away. He watched once more with a sense that this was his last sight of her. The house was empty, and he was alone.

Putting aside his own misgivings about their marriage, Nelson felt confused and disoriented by Maggie's departure. Experiencing an emotion akin to failure, he wondered how Grace was responding to this coordinated disclosure. Finally, it seemed unworthy and cheap. Nelson's familiar emotional landscape lay in ruins, and who could say what damage existed below the surface? When her car was gone, he looked at the clock: 7 am. Perhaps under the circumstances not too early for a belt of whiskey. He took a swig out of the bottle.

13

Meanwhile:

John Addison rubbed his knee as though to smooth the moment over. He sounded like a bad boss mishandling the wrongful dismissal of an exemplary employee. "We've reached the end, can't you feel it?" He was speaking to his wife. Grace sat stone-still, staring incredulously at her husband. He wanted to sound strong, but he knew Grace saw through him.

"Is that all you have to say?"

"I've been feeling it for a long time." He paused, and then added, "Since Sheryl's death, I'd say."

Grace hated him for saying that.

They had no language for what they felt about the loss of their daughter. Words were meaningless; silence was all they could share. They rarely spoke about it. And it didn't seem to be anyone's fault, but how do you define success after the death of a defenseless child? Sheryl's death happened at an age when they were unequipped to help each other through something so emotionally shattering. They grieved differently. John disappeared into his work and into trivial pursuits or worse. He measured recovery in dollars made; she in tears shed. When their daughter died, their hearts broke. What was anything worth after that? Grace looked at her husband with contempt. His insipid lusts were an embarrassment, his fear of intimacy a farce, his inability to address emotional issues lame beyond understanding, and now running off made him an absurdity. Thinking about it depressed her. Maybe he was right, and their relationship had foundered years ago, but this was weak of him. And wrong. And why did he bring up Sheryl? The loss of a child leaves you so you can't feel anything. She could remember months of no feelings at all, nothing. She remembered thinking how soldiers feel no pain sometimes, only shock and dull wonder while contemplating a leg nearby and blood from the place of its severance. Grace had a daughter, born of her body but severed from her soul. It took many years to feel again.

"You're really not much of a man, after all," Grace said abstractly.

Acutely pained by his wife's insult, John Addison clutched his knees. "Maybe I deserve that."

Grace sighed. "No, John, those are just words to you. You don't believe any of it, not in your heart. If you want to divorce me, fine, but let's be clear on why." Her head throbbed. She put her fingers to her temples and then raised her eyebrows and shook her head at private thoughts. She looked down at her coffee cup for a few moments, tapped the table, and, looking up again, caught his eyes suddenly. "Shadows are beginning to get longer. That's what this is about." She laughed as a bitter rebuke. John was not self-aware. His emotions were vague, and he was full of regret. He had a spiritless life, and what he felt was missing in him he blamed on her.

"I don't understand."

She spoke slowly, with a measured tone. "I don't take it personally, I really don't. You're weak, I've always known that. If you want a divorce, fine, I'll be fair with you. But you will never know me again." Grace looked at her husband, and all she felt was disgust. Confronted by a past that had no meaning and a present of mere endurance, her marriage was extinct. But she could face it now, and maybe it was better this way.

He stood in front of her, mute. God damn him, and all of this, and everything, she thought.

14

For the next hour, Nelson Hawkins sat on the deck and watched the moving forward of the morning. Two barn swallows cavorting in the air swooped though the trees right over his head, then chased each other over the deck and flew down the hill. Squirrels loped along the rocks; bumblebees hovered to sip nectar while butterflies jittered in the sunlight. Nelson sipped his whiskey. Well, well. His wife had left him for a neighbor—a squalid, banal, humiliating, emotional inanition. A large, low cloud shaped like a giant rabbit drifted into view, reminding him of a pet Maggie once kept but neglected in her yard. She returned from vacation and discovered the starved corpse in its cage. Bunny had been forgotten to death. Death terrified her, but Maggie managed her feelings in the modern way, by sharing them with "friends" on social media, a deluded narcissism which itself existed in a farther falsity.

A blue heron stood on a rock at the edge of the woods and scanned the area. It leaned forward, extended its wings, and took flight with three massive strokes that seemed to work in slow motion. Nelson watched as it flew just above the water, leaving a slight wake from displaced air. Wondering vaguely how blue herons fit into the scheme of things and continuing a theme of flight, he uncharitably imagined Maggie as a bat and typed out a poem:

> Bats have little leathern wings
> With nasty tiny fingers on them,
> Vampire teeth, rat's ears, and they are blind.
> A creature that flies and yet is blind!
> One's wife might take blind flight
> With another of her kind.

The sun was stronger. Nelson went inside and made another whiskey, in a proper glass with ice this time, and then went out again to the deck, but as he sat down, the front doorbell rang. Through sidelights on either side of the door, he could see a young man opening the back of a pickup truck. Holtzman Masons was written on the door panel, and below the name their motto: "Walls 4 U. Get that walled-in feeling." He opened the door to DEBBIE, her name embossed in bright yellow lettering on her blue Holtzman Masons polo shirt.

"Mr. Hawkins?" she said. She held a clipboard with a pen sensibly taped to a string attached to it.

"Good morning," he said.

"We're here to repair your wall."

"My wife backed into it last week," he explained. Debbie turned her head, and they both contemplated the damage. "Without the wall to stop her, she might have gone off a steep ledge backwards into the lake." He indulged in that thought with momentary zest but then put it aside as unworthy. He signed the work order, and Debbie rejoined her partner at the truck. The wall was made from flat stones fitted without visible mortar. They started the repair in an artful, precise rhythm to reestablish "that walled-in feeling."

While the Holtzman masons worked, Nelson stared out at the blue lake waters. Literally and symbolically, walls keep things in and keep things out, and there are different kinds. Maggie had never been emotionally available. Even her name, Maggie, a foreshortening of the more formal Margret, was in some way a rejection of self. She thought of herself as precocious, but there are limits to precocity. She had traded too long on potential. Her projects got lost to distractions, and after a while she blamed him for her inadequacies. His steady working habits held a mirror to her indiscipline, and she came to resent the very qualities in Nelson which at the beginning she claimed to admire. He could comprehend how someone like John Addison might bring her temporary satisfaction, but, if past is prologue, it wouldn't last—he saw the arc of this affair with the clarity of a psychiatrist who knows a patient's complexities after a few minutes. In his analysis, Maggie's relationship with John was everything and nothing at the same time and seemed an impossible attempt to establish an imagined perfection, a grab at youth again, or a way to feel freshly relevant. Maggie and John would slowly enjoin a drab process of bewilderment and blame. There would be that inevitable decline into bickering, venality, and recrimination, until blandishments were replaced with acid silence. Eventually, John would bore her. Then she would blame him for suffocating her aspirations and thwarting her dreams … wall him out of her life, so to say …

"We're finished, Mr. Hawkins."

Debbie was standing at the open door.

Nelson rose from his chair and went outside to inspect the wall, which was indeed restored to fullness and symmetry. They had done a good job in a short time. It was now 10:00 am. He took their invoice, and they left to provide some other client with their oddly reasoned antidote to dread. Nelson put the invoice in a pile of bills near the telephone and watched them drive off. Cheerful in their work, they yet depressed him for some reason. Their merry lack of irony disturbed him as callow. Or perhaps it was their innocence? What was he projecting? He sighed volubly.

Back on the deck again, he sipped his whiskey, and an odd thought dawned—a vague notion like a radio message fading in and out from a great distance, a weak and barely readable premonition: Maggie and John would not last, they had no hope, they could not be. Somehow there was hollowness in the very idea of them together. They had no future. He felt it in his marrow. But what fresh dismay made these impressions? He wondered.

After the wall repair, there was nothing keeping Nelson at the lake. After getting married, they had kept Nelson's apartment on Central Park West for a footprint in New York. He decided to drive into Manhattan. He threw some clothes into a bag and lobbed the bag onto the back seat of his car, put the top down, and headed to the city. He needed solitude, not isolation, and in any city of eight million people, it is easy to be alone.

15

John had left the house. Everything was very green after the night's rain. Grace imagined she could hear the cellular torrent of fecundated plant life as she stretched her legs out and sat back under the yellow umbrella while cotton-white clouds drifted above in a blue sky. In fact, all colors were vivid and looked unreal. The sun through the trees was bright, and the smell of moistened earth was sweet. She had a sip of coffee and tried to grasp more fully what was happening. John is gone, she thought. My marriage is over.

Grace analyzed her feelings.

She deplored but did not despise John. Though tawdry and despicable, his affair with Maggie was not surprising. He was weak. But in spite of his crudities, she believed he was a decent man. She did not fault Maggie Hawkins. Maggie was needy and wasn't sensible, but that describes many people. She wasn't stupid; she was just disconnected. As Nelson had remarked at that dinner not too long ago, she was literally running to or from something, but what? Maggie and John would be together in their illusion, but it would not last. They were not comfortable in their skin. Exulting in the fool's gold of infatuation, writhing in hollow optimism and mistaking pleasure for passion, the relationship was doomed. Grace was certain of one other thing: she herself would survive. She would clarify her future and resolutely go on. Twenty years of marriage was nearly half her life so far, but she would be unwavering, she would not fall apart, she would evaluate her situation, examine her options, and go forward. But to begin with, she needed to understand what had happened and what role if any she had played in the debacle. Unconsciously, she put aside her interest in Nelson as irrelevant.

Grief is intensely personal. The death of their daughter, Sheryl, fifteen years earlier, had begun the slow decline of her marriage. After the funeral, John became untethered, drifting slowly away from her, like a boat slipped from its mooring, Grace suffered acutely, but differently, and separately. Suffering became their marital bond, unshared separateness their unspoken way of coping, which, at its very core, felt like never-discussed human failure.

Her thoughts were racing in all directions at once. Motionless and silent, Grace stared ahead at flowers in her yard while every emotion in her boiled with contradiction. She had never imagined leaving her marriage, but what did those years together mean? It was not all waste and failure. Struggling to find footing, she felt vulnerable but strong, betrayed but ennobled. Confronting new freedom, she was frightened to be alone. In the same way that the silence of the deep night is made up of a million tiny sounds, her mind was teeming but blank; she felt empty spirit as sorrow in the soul. Suddenly she needed to occupy herself. With that thought, she jumped to action and went into the house.

Driven by impulse, she spent the next few hours cleaning out her closet and rearranging the bedroom. She removed framed prints of John and replaced them with photographs she had taken of the lake. She moved the chair away from the television and put it near the window. She changed the bedspread and put candles in the bathroom and took a bath. After bathing, she went out in her robe to the small back yard again, aware that there was some hysteria in these activities.

Relaxing with a glass of iced tea, she felt her depression lift and thoughts of Nelson reemerge. Was Nelson so fanciful an idea? A notion once forbidden was now possible. Could she and Nelson have a chance together? The prospect excited several streams of possibility. Sunlight moved into her shade. She was free, after all, and so, presumably, farcically, was Nelson. Their afternoon together had been a joyful secret. She conjured his intelligent eyes, smiling face, circumspect manner, coy humor—his derriere! The thought made her laugh, her first laugh of the day.

16

"Murdered. I can't wrap my mind around it. Murdered! She had a big heart and a beautiful soul. She was a good person, a private person." Alice Carpenter was incredulous. Alice was the bar manager at On the Beach and had known Ann Wheeler as well as anyone.

"I know how you feel," Mallory said. "I do." News of Ann Wheeler's murder had reverberated through the town on a whisper. People didn't want to be loud about it. They were frightened.

Alice confided in the detective. "I'm an ex-army master sergeant. I've seen a lot of violence and death, but that was Afghanistan during war. This scares me." Alice Carpenter was blond, tough, and smart about people. She had served during the Iraq invasion and ended up in Kabul before retiring. She poured a glass of Pellegrino for the detective and invited him to sit.

After his session with Dr. Singer, Bradley pulled into the parking lot of On the Beach. Locals called it simply the Beach. The building was a repurposed hat factory beside a brook with a railroad track close by on the other side. He parked under the big elm tree and got out of the car. He closed the car door. The sun felt hot, and it was getting hotter. Dust rose from the gravel as he walked. Bradley could hear the gurgle of the brook. Sunlight sparkled on the surface where it turned to the right. Blue wisteria hung clustered on a trellis between the windows near the entrance. Wafts of warming air carried fragrant blossom scent mixed with the occasional reek of creosote from track ties. Bradley opened the screen door. A rusted spring stretched with an audible groan, and he stopped the door from slamming behind him with the heel of his shoe as he went in. Once inside, he saw Detective Mallory speaking with Alice Carpenter. Mallory saw him and gave a short wave of his hand without interrupting his attention to Alice. The jukebox over by the pinball machine was playing Little Richard.

The interior of On the Beach was located somewhere in the 1950s. Atom bomb Armageddon and Beach Blanket Bingo were represented equally in a decorative time warp. Movie posters of *The Incredible Shrinking Man, Attack of the 50-Foot Woman, The Blob,* and *The Thing* hung on the far wall. In homage to the rails that ran nearby, pictures of locomotives by O. Winston Link hung on the track-side walls, and bobblehead dolls of famous deceased baseball players stood against the mirror on the bar. It was a large inside space. Old bicycles, snowshoes, and fishing rods hung from rafters. A small child's pedal car rested on top of the refrigerator. All of these oddities worked to a very successful effect expressing the weirdness of that "duck and cover" Cold War time. It was a favorite local place, cozy in its atomic nostalgia, in its casual celebration of alien invasion and sudden extinction. Five men on the other side were drinking beer and playing pinball.

"What was Ann like? What kind of employee?" Detective Mallory spoke discreetly, so as not to be heard by others. Alice took him to a table nearby, where they could speak privately.

"Ann came to work, did her job, and left. She was good-humored and well-liked."

"Friendly?"

"Yes. Always friendly. But she kept to herself. She lived at a certain distance from others."

"A solitary type?"

"I wouldn't say solitary, exactly. Not a recluse. Rather a private person."

"Gay?"

"No. She was definitely into men. She resisted relationships though."

Of everyone at the Beach distraught by news of the murder of Ann Wheeler, Alice Carpenter was spooked more than she wanted to admit. Mallory could see it. He had a lot of respect for Alice Carpenter's military service and knew she had at least a working relationship with the deceased that might shed some light on the case. He needed more information.

"Everyone seemed to think she was on vacation when it happened."

"She told me she was going to Florida for a week. That's why I didn't miss her."

"To meet someone there?"

"She didn't say. She kept her private business private."

"Anywhere else she traveled to on a regular basis?"

"The Caribbean."

"Do you know where in the Caribbean?"

"She liked a place in the Dominican Republic on the north shore near Puerto Plata—Sosua, I think. Inexpensive. A lot of Dutch and German tourists. Men were available too. You can rent them for the week, she told me."

"Rent them?"

Alice smiled. "Men rent women everywhere, Detective. They call them escorts. But men are reluctant to forgive in women what they allow for themselves. Wouldn't you say?"

"Fair is fair," he said. He shrugged and pursed his lips to conceal a smile. Her logic was worldly and true.

"Anyway, Ann didn't have scruples in that way."

Mallory liked her candor. Certain lifestyles could be dangerous. He wanted to know if Ann Wheeler might have had a secret life. "Did she see anyone regularly, a friend, lover, family member?"

"She had a brother, a couple of years older, but he died young, about fifteen years ago, in his early twenties."

"Accident or illness?"

"Someone sold him bad cocaine. It poisoned him along with nine others on the Fourth of July weekend that year. Ann took his death very hard."

Mallory had a vague recollection of that incident. He made a mental note to do further research. "Did she have anyone romantically special in her life?"

"She rarely mentioned her romantic life. She told me her parents had an abusive relationship. Her father was a drinker. She left home at eighteen."

A couple arrived for lunch. Alice acknowledged them with a nod and turned to the detective. "Excuse me a moment. I'll be right back." She went to greet the new arrivals.

Bradley approached the table where Alice and Mallory had been conversing in low tones. The detective greeted him jovially. "How are things, Mr. Davis?"

"Pretty good, Detective."

"Do you see Dr. Singer regularly?"

"Twice a week now," Bradley said, standing at the bar.

"Good. Very good," said the detective.

"I enjoy our sessions. I didn't think I would, but I do, very much." Bradley felt an unexpected affection for the detective as he said this.

"Well, that makes my day, believe it or not. Is everything else okay?"

Bradley nodded. The detective gave him a smile, and they shook hands, and Bradley stood by the cash register waiting to be seated.

Alice returned to her place behind the bar, and Mallory finished his glass of Pellegrino before walking over to hand back his glass. "Call me if you learn anything or something else occurs to you about Ann," he said, then pushed his card across the bar. She took it but refused his offer to pay for the drink. With a word of thanks, Mallory left the bar, nodding to Bradley as he went out.

"Heineken?" Alice said to Bradley, remembering his brand.

Standing at the bar where the detective had been, Bradley watched as Alice, in one continuous motion, pulled a bottle from the cooler, opened it, and handed it to him. Bradley took the bottle. "Thank you," he said and went to his favorite table by the window in the corner on the tracks side. When trains went by, they were close and fun to watch.

He sat down, and, looking out from his table, the Beach came alive to his solitary attention. Chimes of pinball play echoed in the wide room. Bradley had a sip of beer. His notice fell to the pinball player, who was wearing a football shirt and working the flippers aggressively while his friend, a fat man in overalls, stood watching with beer in hand, amused. Bradley was glad he'd had a chance to tell the detective that he enjoyed his therapy. Psychiatry seemed meaningful and mysterious, and he looked forward to his clinical hours with Dr. Singer. The requirement of absolute honesty was liberating, though not as easy as it seemed. Dr. Singer's moderate, even-voiced authority carried subtle guidance. Slowly, layers of repression and denial were peeled back. He began to see his mother as a person that, like other individuals, had problems, fixations, and challenges which, precisely because she was his mother, he could not fully appreciate.

One among many interesting things about psychoanalysis was how the seeds to the next session were often planted at the end of the clinical hour, when Dr. Singer said something like "We'll take that up next week," or "Why don't you give that some thought?" Her words functioned like a command to the unconscious. Sure enough, his mind would process whatever topic had been left dangling. In the time between sessions, certain memories would emerge, and insights would come. He was aware of being subtly led to them by Dr. Singer. Mistress Angela's Dungeon was, quite clearly, a symptom of an issue with a deeper cause.

On the subject of cross-dressing, something he rarely gave thought to, Bradley began to probe his memories. By the time he was thirteen, awkwardly tall, he felt acutely alienated, a stranger to his mother, to the world, and to himself. He retreated to his room and to pubescent mis-apprehensions where, in that wellspring of id, guilt, and bewilderment, he made wholly unanticipated discoveries about his mother's shoes and clothes. It began as a normal child's curiosity. One day, while she was shopping, he went into her bedroom looking for matches. Opening her dresser drawers to continue searching, his attention fell on her under-wear, folded neatly. For the first time, he took a pair of pale blue panties into his hand and felt the fabric. It was silk. He draped the garment over his fingers and held it up as a scientist might, examining it from every angle. The idea of panties, even the girlish word itself, seemed to have a magical power that made him feel suddenly keenly alive. Pivoting to notions of girls, a distinct tingle emanated from the hand and spread into him as a kind of thrill never before experienced. He removed them from his hand and put them on top of the dresser, and then opened a second drawer, where his mother kept her bras. He took one out and held it up, inspecting it. Magic was in the bra also. He went with the bra and panties into his mother's bathroom with clear intent. As he closed the door, he realized his erection was strong. He undressed. He studied himself in the mirror, holding his mother's articles of clothing. He put on the bra. It didn't look ridiculous: *fetching* was the word that occurred to him, which later in life he recalled as evidence of a kind of precocity. The magic of the panties was almost overwhelming as he stepped into them. The sight of slowly raising them above his knees made him ejac-ulate spontaneously. Curiosity and confusion ensued over the sudden mood change. Where excitement and thrall had been, shame and guilt now reigned. Bradley cleaned the bathroom copiously and hid the bra and panties in a corner of his closet, after which he felt bereft, like an actor when a performance is over and he is returned to whatever bland reality exists for him in the street.

This magic was potent with the unvarying message of fairy tales: secret powers always involve danger. The danger was not specific. Within keen pleasure came a generalized dread. Something in him was changing.

As a teenager, Bradley, a natively intelligent boy with a sensitive nature, read books beyond his age. In a teenage world fraught with confusion, dread became acute. He believed himself morally marginal, an outlier having something in common with the pedophile priest, the busted gay-bashing politician, or the family values proselytizer caught with a prostitute. He retreated into books and his computer; browsing animatronic pornography also gave him solace.

In analysis, he quickly grew to understand how obsession involves, unconsciously, two selves, one sexually ambitious and the other fiercely admonitory. Most recently, apropos of sin and guilt, the topic of God had emerged in analysis. Bradley had mentioned classes of religious instruction he'd attended at the behest of his mother when he began high school. Intrigued, Dr. Singer said, "You don't strike me as very religious."

"I'm not."

"How did you come to be in a religious instruction class?"

"My mother, of course. She's not very religious either, but at that time she thought I'd be better off with exposure to religion."

"Do you think you benefited from the experience?"

"I was only fourteen. It wasn't bad. We did things like help out at a soup kitchen in New York. That was fun. The priest was weird though."

"Really? How was he weird?"

"Aren't they all a little strange?"

"Many of them do good work. After all, they are in a community-leadership position. Let's explore that area next time."

And so Bradley had come to On the Beach after his session, knowing that the unconscious was starting to process memories of Father Capehart, a person he had not thought of in years.

The pinball players' verbal truculence was ongoing and indicated close familiarity. Amused at their antics, Bradley watched them and sipped his beer while abstractedly scratching at the bottle label, thinking of psychoanalysis. His therapy was making him ask questions: Do I compare myself unfavorably to others I see when I look through windows? Do I think my life is worse than theirs? He was working toward some central insight. What exactly is the thrill in it? He felt the answer was in front of him, but he could not yet see it.

Compartmentalizing cross-dressing by limiting it to Mistress Angela's didn't feel wrong. There must be something wrong, however. It was strange, and it labeled him as strange. The gratifications were keen but unsatisfying and unsustainable. His finger scratched at the label. And then he made a psychoanalytic connection: I am removing a label! An act meaning one thing with significance for another, and no denying the connection. Freud's modest promise fulfilled: that a little bit of what was unconscious would become conscious. Amused and surprised, he laughed. This is how the onion is peeled. He arranged and rearranged the torn paper bits unconsciously in various patterns on the table as he daydreamed. He could see how his undertakings at Mistress Angela's were pleasurable but ultimately solitary. The initially powerful euphoria later turned to a deeper sense of alienation followed by spiritual emptiness. Is my life small? Is it morally wrong or simply wayward? In any case, I am an outsider, he thought grimly. Dr. Singer's words echoed like a song he couldn't get out of his mind: *Everything you do in that place stands for something else. What you find there is not what you seek. You are going around in circles.*

He began to see with awakened insight. Happy curses of pinball players revealed messages from their id. The messages involved the usual sexual impossibilities, expressed in terms whose casual references to incest and homosexual abuse exposed tantalizing latencies and fears. Images of Grace began to sweep in free associations through Bradley's daydreams. He had seen her breasts! He had seen her canoodling with Nelson Hawkins (but did that mean anything?). And his mother was drifting further from him into drink and isolation. Was his response proper or correct? Where did his responsibilities begin and end? Some questions had no answers, or if they did, the truths they revealed were unwelcome. These were his thoughts, and they made him dizzy.

But he liked his job and his house and reading books and so many other things that were normal. He did not have the easy confidence of someone like Nelson Hawkins, who could walk down the street into Grace Addison's arms, while he, Bradley, could only watch from the woods. Then this occurred to him: if peeping established him as an outsider, it also risked discovery and humiliation, which in fact had happened. And so self-loathing was involved. Was peeping for him mainly a device to invite episodes of punishment at Mistress Angela's? Could it be so? Bradley took a deep breath. Is this what Dr. Singer calls insight? He twizzled bits of paper with his fingers, making small pills that he arranged with other remnants in rows. If I am completely honest with myself, he thought, I must acknowledge that I am chronically and somewhat expertly inept at life.

A deep-throated whistle meant an approaching train. The pinball players stopped playing; the flippers and chimes fell silent. Alice leaned from behind the bar, and Bradley turned his head. It was an Alco Century 425 diesel, large, black, squared-off, powerful and heavy. They all watched as the big engine passed. The engineer waved, as if from a strange dream. He was pulling a mile of freight cars, one and then another, passing like a procession of identical thoughts. The building trembled as this went on, until the caboose passed. The whistle sounded again but at a distance now, fading on its way, the click-clack rhythmic tattoo fading also, fading as memories fade, diminishing, evoking loneliness and pathos.

Bradley finished his beer and swept the little bits of exorcism into his hand and then brushed imaginary crumbs from his leg. He rose and went to the cash register, where Alice gave him the check.

"Thank you," Bradley said and handed her a twenty-dollar bill. She made change swiftly while he stood in front of the register, abstracted. Pocketing the change, Bradley left, careful not to let the screen door slam.

Alice watched him cross the parking lot. He had the look of a mathematician working through some complex problem indecisively. I like him though, she thought. She watched him get into his car and drive off.

17

Maggie parked her car beside the tractor shed in the gravel parking lot. The shed had once been a stable for horses. You could still see troughs along the front of it. It had been part of the Granville Country Tavern Inn, a stagecoach stop on the way to Boston during the Revolutionary War. Nowadays the inn had a large restaurant with an outside deck in back that overlooked a pond fringed with weeping willows. Maggie carried her bag across the gravel parking lot to the porch entrance and went into the lobby. The main building was a rambling wooden affair.

Inside, the staff was setting tables for lunch. The manager, Mrs. Sullivan, came out of her office behind the lobby desk. When Maggie identified herself, she was able to check in right away.

Mrs. Sullivan smiled approvingly when the reservation appeared on her computer screen. "The suite has dormer windows and a fireplace. I think you'll like it. It's one of our best. Martin will take you upstairs." She tapped the desk bell, sounding a sharp pinging ring.

Presently, a diminutive man with a limp appeared. Dressed in gray flannel with red piping, he bowed slightly and took up her bag. Maggie followed him up wooden steps from the lobby to the second floor. Leaning to one side, he shambled down the long corridor, reminding her of old exhausted ponies at those woeful carnivals in summer. At the corner suite, number 12, Martin opened the door and Maggie went in.

"This is wonderful," Maggie said, performing a pirouette in the middle of the main room. Martin put her bag on a rattan caddie near the closet, and Maggie surveyed the wide living room. The ceiling was vaulted, with dark timber beams and book shelves on either side of a fireplace.

Martin opened the suite's connecting door. "The bedroom's in here, ma'am. And the master bath."

Maggie went in. The bedroom fan turned slowly above the bed. The bathroom was large, with an antique tub. All aflutter and excited to be there, she tipped Martin liberally as incentive to leave.

"Thank you, ma'am," he said, handing her the key.

When he left, Maggie began to unpack. Alone at last, she felt exuberant. But she remained restless. A new life was ahead of them both. She kept checking the time. She knew that her leaving had been a shock to Nelson, and she felt bad about that, but at least she had left him a letter to soften the blow. She was eager to hear from John how things had gone with Grace. Having unpacked and stowed her bag, she felt more relaxed, less guilty, more at liberty to enjoy her first day of a new life with John, who as it happened was arriving that moment in his red Cadillac.

She saw him turn into the parking lot and get out of his car with an overnight bag. He strode across the road to the main entrance, and when he appeared in the hallway upstairs, he was carrying his bag in one hand, a bottle of champagne in the other. Maggie was standing at the door to their suite, vogueing in a silver chemise, head to the side with one arm raised and the other on her hip. Wearing khaki slacks and a dark blue polo shirt, John looked fit and younger than his forty-six years. He stood back to behold her.

"You look good enough to eat."

"You ought to see me in my special sauce."

At last she had her John. Once inside, they kissed deeply in a tight embrace. After an hour of fierce lovemaking, sitting on the couch in white robes, they were in a new world, with no going back.

Maggie felt indefinite about the sorrow they had caused. She asked John, "When you spoke to Grace this morning, how did it go?"

He took a deep breath. "It went," he said without enthusiasm.

"Was she surprised?"

"Surprised? Maybe relieved, I don't know."

Maggie mused. The tedium of dreary marriage was over. Nelson's inattention and abstraction, his making her feel small, were things of the past. She felt closer to John and within reach of what they both thought they wanted. John picked up the bottle of champagne and led Maggie back into the bedroom and into bed again, back to that sweet universe of two souls who have found the secret to life. The ceiling fan turned lazy circles above them.

18

Dr. Singer was sitting with Detective Mallory. The memorial service for Ann Wheeler was later that morning. Their waitress poured them both another cup of coffee. "Even in admirable persons one discovers infantile obsessions and repressed sexual desires which may have been changed by what we call reaction formation."

"What is reaction formation?"

"Think of it as an opposite claim to true disposition."

"Such as?"

"The latent sadism of the surgeon comes to mind. The pyromaniac interests of firemen, the lawless tendencies of policemen, the sexual obsessions of celibates, or the lurid voyeurism of psychiatrists."

Mallory inquired, "Speaking of deeper inclinations, how is our Peeping Tom doing?"

"Very well. He's willing and responsive. Without getting too deeply into it, there are some family issues that need to be clarified and turned

to constructive ends, but I think that's already happened. Most important, he's not a threat to the community. You made a good call, Gerry."

Mallory leaned forward with greater seriousness. "On another front,
I'm struggling with the Ann Wheeler case. I have a few ideas, but they're
vague. Can you give me any insights if I share with you what I have?"

"What can you tell me?"

For the next ten minutes, Mallory detailed what he knew about the
murder site, what he had seen there, the appearance of the half-naked
body, the missing cell phone and computer, what he had learned about
the victim's family and background. That the photograph on the refrigerator door was of Ann's older brother, Bobby, at his eighteenth birthday
party. He told her how Bobby had died, poisoned. He told her about the
coroner's report.

"She was strangled but not raped. And I think that the photograph of
her brother is significant, simply because it was on her refrigerator. And
finally," Mallory told her, "there was a book of poetry by Sylvia Plath,
open to a poem called 'Daddy.'"

"I'm familiar with the poem."

"Ann was a reader. According to our friend Bradley, she was a regular
at the library, especially in the winter." Mallory turned his head slightly
sideways, eager to hear what the psychiatrist might say. "What's your
sense of it?"

Dr. Singer put both her hands face down on the table. "From what
you've told me, I would guess that the killer was a male, probably in his
forties. He is either overweight or visibly muscular, quite intelligent, or
at least above average, and probably has a job with a certain amount of
status."

"Why do you say that?"

"He made it seem like a sexual assault, but he didn't rape her."

"There was no forensic evidence to indicate rape."

"It wasn't about sexual assault. He seemed to reason that the appearance of assault might disguise his true motives. Which were …?"

"That's the big question."

Dr. Singer leaned forward in her chair and continued. "He might not even have intended murder. He might have been appalled at his own behavior. In other words, in a seizure of violence, Dr. Jekyll became Mr. Hyde. Also, anxiety and violence and the murder itself might have caused spontaneous ejaculation, after which Dr. Jekyll was truly appalled at Mr. Hyde. The cover-up, ironically, was pulling off her pants, meant in some way to imply what was not in fact accomplished."

Mallory sat back, deliberating. "He went there wanting something."

"She let him into the house." Dr. Singer held up her finger to underscore a point. "We can assume she knew him, or at least she didn't feel threatened."

"She had bruises on her arms and legs." Mallory tried to put himself in the room. "They talked, they argued, and then they fought."

"She might have been angry at first, then frightened as she watched his manner change, then terrorized. She didn't or couldn't give him what he wanted. He might have snapped. By that I mean reverted to an infantile state. He became enraged when he couldn't get from her what he came there to get. Narcissism is likely—his needs foremost. He thinks of himself as superior. He doesn't think of himself as a rapist or a killer, however. Quite the opposite." Dr. Singer moved her head slightly and pursed her lips. "Also, you may know him. If not now, soon."

"Why do you say that?" Mallory was instantly intrigued.

"He has a relationship with you because you are investigating a murder he committed. And Gerry, you have a relationship with him. You are the hunter, and he is the pursued."

"Does he know me now?" Mallory knew Dr. Singer was correct in this.

"Maybe, maybe not. Maybe not yet. There is a deeper side to this killer. He's a psychopathic thrill seeker. He'll get close to you in some way, if only to throw you off the scent."

"Do you think he's a local?"

"Unless there is reason to believe he is not."

"All very interesting, Caroline. Many thanks." Mallory looked at his watch. "Got to go. I'm meeting Linda at the memorial service."

"Where is it being held?"

"At her church in Wilberforce. The Catholic church."

"Who is the pastor?"

"Father James Capehart."

19

Back from his beer at the Beach, Bradley stood on his deck and looked at the lake far below. He continued to ponder his psychotherapy. He was becoming aware of psychological subtleties, how denial, repression, displacement, and projection struggled in him. Dr. Singer predicted that insights would emerge in the way an ebbing tide reveals slowly what was not previously possible to see. Comprehension was deepening. Complexity, contradiction, and overlapping aims did not seem odd to him: peeping, driven by guilt seeking punishment for cross-dressing, might not be far-flung from fact. He existed at the center of a Venn diagram of conflicting impulses, unsure.

Meanwhile, the sky darkened. At first the wind blew from all directions at once, with gusts that launched whirlwinds. One umbrella tumbled into the water and wheeled offshore. People at the beach grew restless. Mothers beckoned to children still swimming. Beachgoers looked up at the ominous sky to decide whether to give up for the day. The defining moment came when lightning flashed and thunder volleyed like a battle begun. Boats headed to shelter. Bathers scrambled in the blowing wind to pack up their blankets and towels, coolers and chairs. Rain started to fall.

The lake disappeared into an advancing curtain of mist. Bradley went inside, but he stood behind the closed sliding door to watch as the deluge came. The skies opened up, and high winds on the ridge shook the trees dramatically. The driven rain made an opaque Impressionism of splatters and smears on the windows. Bradley turned on the radio for a weather report. A religious program had begun. The rain distracted him, but when he began to hear the broadcast, he turned to look at the radio, amused for the impression it gave him of a senseless, raving homunculus trapped inside a small box.

"Do you think the Almighty wants you to live a life in poverty?" the voice said. "No, dear friends, He is called Almighty because He is almighty, and the Bible says we are made in his image and likeness. Consider what you can do to honor His greatness. Make a prayer offering, brothers and sisters, and your dreams will be empowered by the will of the Supreme Being. You will begin at once to have the life He's aching to give you. God is your ally in this journey. He's on your side. God wants you to succeed. Beware the place of howling and gnashing of teeth. Beware the depthless pond of roaring fire, the Wrath and Lamentation. Heed the Ten Commandments: they are not the Ten Suggestions. Get ready for the shroud and the box, brothers and sisters! God is waiting to judge you. Prepare to meet your maker."

Bradley turned the radio off. Even while God and greed were somehow intertwined, evangelism's message had also been the voice of fear speaking to spiritual impoverishment. Rain was pounding on the roof and against the windows. The beaches had cleared, and there were no boats visible on the part of the lake he could see. When Bradley went to get coffee, he inadvertently caught his reflection in the window and did not recognize himself. Realizing this gave him pause. Not to recognize yourself in a mirror—what does it mean? He had begun to ask himself questions. Have I changed, or have I just become a stranger to myself?

He saw the notice for Ann Wheeler's memorial service on the side table where he kept his mail, sighed reflexively, and began to dress for the service.

20

The signboard announced:
REVEREND JAMES CAPEHART, PASTOR.
MEMORIAL SERVICE FOR ANN WHEELER 11 AM.

Mallory took Linda's hand as they walked from the parking lot to the stone steps of the church and up to the tall, impressively carved wooden doors at the entrance. Inside, the church felt like the hall of a castle, haunted when the organ played, and populated with all manner of unseen angels and ghosts that communicants believed were benign. Mallory and Linda sat together in a rear pew.

"I haven't been to church since Uncle Webster's funeral," Linda whispered. "Was Ann Wheeler a practicing Catholic?"

"I don't think so," he said. "But she kept ties. I'll learn more from the priest when I see him."

As an atheist, Gerard Mallory could not comprehend why the Catholic imagination relished images of extreme pain. Wood carvings on the walls depicted scourging and public humiliation on the way to crucifixion!

Above the altar, a twice-life-sized bleeding Jesus stared upward from the crucifix with a petitioning expression of acute agony and mortal dread.

High mass was already underway. The church was crowded. Among those in attendance, Mallory recognized Bradley Davis. Also, to his surprise, Mallory saw wrongly incarcerated and recently released Russell Garner enter and sit in a pew beside Davis.

After a reading of the Gospel, Romans 6:3-4, Mallory watched Father Capehart assume the dais. His handsome, somewhat epicene good looks, suited the stage. As he stood stone still and silent at the pulpit, allowing tension to build, his eyes roamed the congregation and seemed to study each face individually. The altar was a proscenium of sorts, his vestments a costume for this starring role in a long-running performance. Still silent, he leaned forward, his hands grasping the edges of the lectern, projecting authority to those before him. Celebrating mass was an apt default for an actor manqué of his qualities and instincts. When satisfied that all eyes were attentively upon him, Father Capehart began to speak in a slow cadence punctuated with rhetorical pauses for emphasis before a checkered audience of the faithful and the nonbelievers.

"Ladies and gentleman," he began. "Welcome to this memorial for Ann Wheeler, our friend and neighbor taken from us too early into Heavenly Peace. She now resides among angels in joyful communion with God for all eternity. But we lament the manner of her death and mourn her loss from this world. In our humility before God, we can say with assurance that her death was part of His plan, for He is all-powerful and all-knowing, and our faith decrees it must be so. But that does not diminish our grief at her loss or make less our sorrow for her manner of death. We here are given only a small part of whole understanding. God alone holds the answer to questions we have. What we can do, what we are gathered here to share, what we celebrate in this House of Christ the Lord, is the life of a young woman of grace and good character, known to us, loved by us, and now no longer in our midst ..."

The nave was bathed in light. The large crucifix hanging from cables seemed to float above the altar.

"In conclusion," said Father Capehart, holding his arms wide and palms upward, petitioning the divine while also offering his body as a priestly antenna for God's response, "we ask for mercy as we grieve our loss of Ann Wheeler while taking comfort in the assurance that she is with You for eternity in heaven, happy at last and smiling down on us forever and ever, amen."

When the priest stepped down from the pulpit, he moved to the altar at a liturgically formal pace. Now came prayers, incantations, and ablutions. Bowing over the paten, Father Capehart converted bread into the flesh of Christ by means of transubstantiation, a feat of divinity impossible to science. The consecrated host was broken into pieces and then consumed by the priest as the Flesh of God. Wine was taken as Blood. Who but a cannibal or Christian seeks to eat human flesh, even as a metaphor? But priests were literal in their belief, making the detective wonder what other flights of fancy might afflict them. After partaking, Father Capehart bid communicants form a line to receive the sacrament. All rose. Those receiving communion came forward. Organ music filled the church with a cascade of calamitous notes portending glory while sounding like the End of Days. Altar boys and priest exchanged bows signifying the finish of ritual housekeeping.

Detective Mallory was a rationalist. To him, there was a lot of mumbo jumbo here. Reflecting on Father Capehart's recitation, he could not imagine murder as part of a larger divine scheme for human beings on this speck of cosmic dust. Also untenable was an image of Ann Wheeler smiling among angels in some celestial utopia. Mallory had seen her body in its deathly state. As he watched and listened to Father Capehart, the detective marveled at infantile images of afterlife put forward as valid to credulity. It seemed amazing. Did the priest really have the sort of faith he wholesaled to his congregation?

At the conclusion of the communion ceremony, sacerdotal cleanup commenced and sacred articles were returned to the tabernacle. Mallory later learned that Father James Capehart had attended Catholic schools exclusively and was deeply religious. Soon after college, under the urging of an influential admiring bishop, he had attended a first-rate seminary in Chicago. His eyes were pale blue. Boyish good looks and the lean build of an athlete were convincing to any theatrical purpose. Mallory learned that, in fact, the priest had once been an actor, and his love of theater never left him. Celebrating Sunday mass redounded to his love of histrionics. He wore a silk chasuble of garnet and black with impressive gold piping that fell with a clerically distinguished flair over his lace skirts. The mass was a pageant he enjoyed immensely, his communicants had great affection for him, and he appeared lucky to have become precisely what he was suited to be.

Wilberforce was an upper-middle-class, white-collar, largely homogeneous town adjacent to the less ostentatious, more democratic, Granville. These churches were social centers. A friendly rivalry existed among the pastors, each of whom enjoyed a good living afforded by their congregations. Father Capehart was chided at times by his peers for his extravagant services. His instincts were those of an impresario.

From his pew at the Church of the Incarnate Word, Detective Mallory tried to fathom Catholic references to reality. By the look of it, Catholics relished pomp, more than Episcopalians and far more than Lutherans. Liturgically, Catholics appeared to link prayer to expiation, penance with redemption, and the Christian metaphor of sheep obtained. Their creed required punishment in purgatory for most transgressions and submission as path to adoration.

Father Capehart's preaching style was a balance of opposites, at once innocent and clever, thoughtful and impulsive, antic and coy, capable of blessings or imprecations equally. He could be dominant or submissive in his outreach, guided by the source of ebb and flow of what he felt in the room. He projected God as a stern Father Figure of Wrath but also as the source of Grace, an authoritarian guarantor of Eternal Life in trade for praise. Mallory knew that off-duty (if one may ever say that a priest is off-duty), Father Jim (as he was known to familiars) rarely wore the clerical collar, opting instead for the stylish garb of the suburban grandee. He had a "knife and fork" membership at the golf club in Wilberforce; on Saturdays in summer he raced sailboats on the Sound.

When the mass proper ended, Father Capehart bid the congregation remain seated. He had arranged for a guitarist to play. A pretty, blond student came forward and sang affecting hymns known to all. As she began to sing "Amazing Grace," Mallory was wondering how religious Ann Wheeler had been as an adult. By all accounts she was someone independent who loved life but did not view death as the gateway to "a better place." The priest bowed his head to the souls gathered before him and the congregation repeated: "Our Father, who art in heaven …"

After the Benediction, the organ once again erupted in a cascade of notes that seemed to scurry in different directions like hidden creatures in sudden light. Mallory and Linda watched the priest lead a procession down the center aisle to the steps outside the church. The detective and his wife followed the others to the bottom of the stone stairs. There they paused to watch the farewell. Standing with his deacons, Father Capehart bid farewell to his departing congregation. "God be with you," he said as they filed by. The men nodded and the women smiled. Preadolescent children, pushed forward by their parents, were respectful but had little interest in an "old" man in funny dress who tattled their sins to God. One young girl, squirming with impatience to be free, was forced by her mother to greet the priest. When he put his hand ecclesiastically on her head, she grimaced, abashed, like a twelve-year-old pinched by an uncle.

21

"If you don't know where you're going, you might end up someplace else." The words of the great Yogi resonated as they so often did. Nelson Hawkins swung through a sharp turn with a certain amount of satisfying aggression. Life was shaping up like the final chapters of a failed novel, he mused. We're all orphaned bastards of something, abandoned bastards of love, bastards of fate. As he picked up speed, heading southbound, he could not fathom the future. Strangers at the beginning and strangers at the end; I can't remember what was in the middle. Life with Maggie had been like starving to death. Where will I be in a year? he wondered. Nelson stepped on the accelerator.

Driving through horse country near Bedford, New York, along the state border, racing with the top down for the first time since October, he savored the earth scents rising up from the wet, warming ground. After downshifting for the hairpin by the French restaurant, he accelerated on a straightaway that ran beside a horse farm. A camel-colored stallion, interrupted from grazing by the insolent whine of his motor, raised its head with mild rebuke. Wind in his hair, bright sunlight, flickering shadows as he drove, he continued beyond the state park entrance farther down, through thicker woods to where the sky opened up suddenly at the reservoir. Nelson could feel the sun and see it shining brightly on the mirror-perfect surface, where reflections doubled the natural beauty of an uncorrupted shoreline.

He passed a small church. It conjured the past. He saw his first wife's face, pretty as a poster for perfect teeth: vibrant, engaging and charming—until she drank. After two cocktails, she became maundering and vituperative. Soon it was clear she had never come out of her own closet. After their divorce, she dried out in the 12-step program and found Jesus. She achieved a tattoo. She developed a new interest in weaponry and moved in with her friend from the pistol range, a butch lawyer named Happy. And so, sober at last, confident, newly spiritual, tattooed, armed and resolved, she went off to live contentedly with her eponymous girlfriend, happy at last in her own private something or other (where she began to speak in baby-talk). Nelson laughed out loud. Life can be complicated. He downshifted and roared up the entrance to the parkway.

He crossed the Henry Hudson Bridge into Manhattan, where the parkway goes south along the river and becomes the West Side Highway. River traffic was bustling. He saw tugboats, barges, ferryboats, helicopters, and yachts. It all stood for something, a spectacle of life taking place, of things going on. He needed that positive energy and wanted the city's intensity. Manhattan has everything you want, and everything you think you want. If frustrations don't crush you, and you can hold on to your dreams and swim against the current, anything can happen. You can be young at eighty in New York, and there is no sell-by date on possibility. It is all there for you.

Exiting at 96th Street, he drove east to Central Park West, where a car was just leaving a parking spot in front of his building. Finding a parking space always felt like finding money in the street. It was legal for three days. He pulled into it. When he got out of the car, he saw an earphone-wearing couple pushing a baby stroller. Two smartly dressed older men were holding hands. A small woman with an enormous dog on a leash was standing at the curb texting on her cell phone, waiting for her beast to defecate. The city in motion, Nelson thought, endlessly in motion. He greeted the doorman, got his mail, and then took the elevator to the tenth floor. Inside the apartment at last, he paused to take a moment to appreciate the view of Central Park. He opened the window. The tops of trees swayed slightly in a gentle wind. He could see people running on the footpath and hear dogs barking while a bongo drummer beat a frantic tattoo. Schoolchildren were laughing in the distance.

There was much to consider. Surely Grace had received the bad news from John by now. What was her response? Was she angry, shocked, saddened, or worse? Again, he was tempted to call her, but restrained himself. Better to wait a day for privacy's sake and connect tomorrow. The irony of this affair between Maggie and John had remarkable aspects, not least of which was the attraction he and Grace had been fighting to contain. He got up to go into the bathroom to shower. When he unzipped his bag to fetch his toiletries, he noticed an envelope tucked into it beside his shaving kit, where Maggie had placed it before she left. It was addressed to him, and it had an uncanceled stamp on it but no return address. He unfolded the letter and began to read.

Dear Nelson:

I am writing this on the night before leaving you. I know I won't be able to say what I want to say tomorrow, and you wouldn't hear me if I could. I'm not an expert on emotions; I know only what I feel. And what I feel is that life is too short for unhappiness. You'll say we should have talked more about our problems. That may be true. But I think it's also true that you didn't listen to me when I did talk, which I felt as a lack of respect and concern for me. You blame me, not all the time, but often enough to ruin my confidence in us. Our relationship was running on empty, didn't you know that? When a marriage turns against dreams, what's left? Nothing is left. Couldn't you feel that? Didn't you know that?

I don't have bad feelings about you, Nelson. You're always looking for what you call meaning, but I don't think there can be meaning without happiness. Or happiness without fulfillment. And none of it matters if love isn't part of it. Without love, there is just existence and bewilderment and disappointment and all of those things that hurt us or make us feel bad. That is not happiness.

I'm not saying you're not right about how the world is, Nelson, or where you fit into it. It's just not my world. Your outlook is different from mine. We should have known it earlier. It's my fault too. For too many years I felt I was living someone else's life, and I wasn't having fun anymore. I felt unloved. I felt like a ghost. It's a feeling of emptiness, Nelson.

When I leave tomorrow, I am going to a new life, a new future, a future that never could be if we stayed together. It will be better for both of us, please know that. I don't know if I've gotten across my hope for your happiness. You are a good man, and if I've hurt you, I'm sorry, but the way things are—the way they've become—I have to try for something else. My best hope for you is to find what, at last, I've found.

Good luck,

Maggie

A painful but honest letter. She's right, he had to admit, suddenly sad about everything. He let his hand drop to his knee. Marriage was something we tried, but something we never had. He looked at the letter again and then stared out the window. Clouds were moving in rapidly. Overcast skies lowered. The buildings on Fifth Avenue were disappearing in mist and thickening fog, and his mood felt like that. There was nothing to say, even to himself. Looking out across the park, he noticed a large bird upright on a limb near the top of a tree. Vigilant as a general, ruminative and alert, it stood stone still. It looked like a falcon. Nelson watched the bird for several minutes until it spread its wings and rose up like a seraph in swift ascension. It hovered a moment and then with

great speed plunged into the misty woods. Agitated by the airborne intrusion, a flock of pigeons flew up suddenly, hundreds of them, in tight
formation going this way and that, slavishly following their leader to
some doubtful destiny.

At 2:00 pm he left the apartment and walked over to the Mexican
restaurant for lunch. He sat at a small table in the corner. His thoughts
were agitated—*the marriage turned against our dreams*. Maggie wasn't
wrong in her analysis; what she had written was true, yet he resisted it
as too facile. It's more like *early promise faded*, he revised. Her life was
unfulfilled, he thought uncharitably. She had become a joiner of caus-
es, a signer of petitions, a walker, a marcher and wearer of ribbons for
chronic diseases.

He finished his lunch and went back to the apartment. His thoughts
circled in a stream of rationalizations, condemnations, justifications and
speculations—she was getting older, and she blamed me for her dread.
But, he thought, I withdrew from the marriage unfairly. She hid from
herself, true, but I didn't care enough. Life, he thought, is a series of
mistakes, reevaluations, and recoveries, after all. She was entitled to her
blame. He was having precisely this thought when the phone rang.

"Hello?"

"Mr. Hawkins?"

"Speaking."

"My name is Detective Mallory at the Granville Police Department."

"Yes?"

"I tried to reach you at home."

"I'm in New York."

"I'm calling about your wife."

"Sorry, what is your name? Detective who?"

"Detective Mallory. Gerard Mallory."

"What can I do for you, Detective Mallory?"

"It's about your wife, Margret Hawkins."

"This is about my wife?"

"A Margret Hawkins with an address in Granville, on Sunline Drive?"

22

Running was Maggie's metaphor. Staying fit was her religion. She had run in three marathons, and each time improved. Running made her feel good, mind and spirit, something she could not communicate to Nelson. John understood it. Satiated and full of vigor, Maggie put on her running shorts and shoes. In the mirror she could see John sitting in the pink chair by the dormer window. As he tightened the laces of his running shoes, she pulled her hair into a ponytail through the size strap at the back of her baseball cap. When she finished, she turned, at the ready.

"Come on, John, hurry. It's a gorgeous day!" It had rained the night before, and now the air had that springtime smell of earth and flowers in it. The sun was shining brightly on the ground. She yearned to be outside. "If we run past Silver Hills, it's a big circle of about four miles."

"I think I'd rather have another glass of champagne."

"There'll be plenty of time for that later. We'll have lunch on the deck when we get back."

"Something to look forward to."

When he finished lacing his shoes, John Addison stood, and Maggie went up to him, smiling like a shy schoolgirl. He put his arms around her and pulled her close to him. She giggled and mussed his hair. "Let's go," he said.

Maurice Jenkins pulled out of the loading dock at the cement factory with ten yards of concrete. First a delivery in Granville, and another in Wilberforce, and afterward he had plans to take Jimmy fishing in the new Boston Whaler. Jenkins had begun hauling freight coast to coast after high school. But after he met Irene, driving cross-country became burdensome. When they married, he continued driving the big rigs for a year, and though he loved the road, he grew to hate the long haul. After their Jimmy was born, Irene wanted him closer to home. Then a job came up locally driving a cement truck, and he took it. He kept his independence and was home every night. He didn't mind the work, and if he'd never be wealthy, he could easily provide.

His mind was on the new Boston Whaler, sweet, with a snappy 95 hp Johnson outboard: he and his son would be fishing on the Sound by late afternoon. The thought of that put a smile on his face. Jimmy was thirteen now, and he loved the boat. Maurice was a responsible man, and he knew the boy would soon be going out alone or with friends, and that girls would be in the picture. Since opportunities for father and son to be together would be fewer, he savored the moments left to them, and he wanted to be sure his son developed safe and responsible operating practices.

The truck moved slowly under its heavy load. The barrel turned at a rate calibrated to keep the concrete liquefied. As he moved through the gears, the truck gathered speed. The stoplight was green at the intersection, and he entered the on-ramp at Exit 8, downshifting to climb the grade. He went through the gears again rapidly, building speed for the merge into highway traffic. Traffic was light and moving fast. He stayed in the right lane, and when he exited he turned right at the T-intersection onto the Granville Country Road northbound.

Maggie led, and that was fine. John enjoyed trailing her strides, admiring her strong legs and fitted shorts as she kept a steady pace. Pockets of cool air hovered invisibly along the side of the road. They could feel it as they ran. Through ear buds, guitar licks of the Allman Brothers played to John's stride, making his mind a stadium concert.

The mixing barrel turning behind him made a grinding hydraulic clatter, preserving the liquefied concrete to be poured into the first stage of a building project. Maurice Jenkins downshifted. What a beautiful day, he thought. Maurice loved his son. A good boy, who played little league baseball, Jimmy was a natural shortstop, scrappy and fast on his feet, with a quick eye. It was a thing of beauty to watch him field a line drive and fire the ball to first base, or call for a pop-up to make the final victorious out. Because Maurice himself had never been a natural player, he loved to watch his son perform on the field with accomplished grace. And Irene loved nothing more than to see Jimmy and his father at work or at play together. Their marriage of eighteen years was strong and sound. When Jenkins drove past big houses in expensive neighborhoods, he wondered what those people could have that equaled what he went home to every night. Life was rich and rewarding, satisfying and good. He envied no one. He turned the corner and passed the Granville Inn. Continuing on, as he approached the joggers, Maurice Jenkins was thinking of the evening's fishing, that if they caught fluke or flounder, Irene would make them a dinner of fish and chips. She was a great cook and had a number of seasoning rubs in tins purchased last year at outdoor markets on vacation in Cape Cod.

Music's thunderous tumult absorbed every sense, and the quicker beat made Maggie increase her pace unconsciously. She was high—high on the scream-like voice of Aerosmith's front man, high on the day, and high on John and their new freedom, a beginning and a brighter future with every possibility renewed. John also had something that Nelson would never have enough of: money. Not that she thought much about money. She didn't want to think about it at all. Nelson thought what money they had was enough. What was enough? Maggie's notions were different.

Joggers ahead. The road was damp with last night's rainfall, and the pavement steamed where sun shined through trees. Maurice was thinking that he needed to tell Jimmy how operating a boat was a responsibility. He knew how boys take risks, and he meant to give his son some safety tips. He'd tell him about the time a few years back when three couples went out in a motorboat late at night half drunk, and whoever was driving pushed up the throttle to go faster, and one of the men, father of three small children, fell off the back of the boat without anyone noticing. His body washed ashore on Long Island later in the week. Maurice watched the figures in front of him, a man and woman running along the right side of the road, and debated whether or not to sound the horn.

John turned up the volume on his iPhone. When running, music deflected his attention from pain and fatigue. They rounded the corner, intending to face traffic, but there was a moving van parked on the street, so they stayed to the right. John was focused on Maggie in front of him. She lowered her head to check her GPS, but when her head came up again, she saw the bloated carcass of a large, dead possum lying on its back directly in front of her. All of her phobias exploded in terror and disgust. Maggie screamed and sprang sideways from her unbroken stride to avoid the dead creature. John then saw the animal, and he too, as if in slow motion, followed her lead with that weightless agility music gives to motion. John didn't zig or zag but rather pivoted, executing a leap worthy of a running back sidestepping to gain the down, a comparison he himself made even as he performed the maneuver. It was his pride to have a young man's speed and reflexes.

When Maurice saw them jump directly into his path, he gasped. He stood on the brakes and sounded the horn. He tried to turn the cab but in this sudden moment realized he would run them over. He braced for the dull thud and sickening bump. In their last moments alive, John and Maggie might have understood how a shadow registers an object advancing the way an eclipse tells a story of celestial bodies in motion.

When John made his leap to follow Maggie, he could see his shadow beneath him, a circular disk with legs, or so it seemed in that noontime airborne moment. But in the next second his shadow was swallowed up by a larger encroaching shadow behind him. The last thing he heard in this life was a full-throated A-flat blast of sound like an ocean liner signaling the beginning of a long voyage. John Addison realized that his life would be over in a split second while insisting it couldn't be true. Retreating into denial, he entered that infinite instant where the doomed mind comprehends its end by flashing a final judgment. Every emotion went white hot, lighting up a world orgasmic with facts and truth. He saw how life had no death—he saw how death had no light. He saw himself at the beginning of his memories—becoming once again a child on a sandy beach jumping from rocks to assert super powers—becoming the boy who loved to climb trees and ride bicycles—becoming the adult stranger to himself—girls fascinating him, girls lifting up their skirts for a lark, pulling down their pants on a dare, the new world of sex, love, and heartbreak as part of the flux. And then true love, and finally marriage, becoming then the young husband, becoming the provider, becoming a father until, with the sad horrible death of Sheryl, becoming John the grief-stricken not-parent, and then John the workaholic, John the philanderer and bad husband to Grace who suffered in silence, becoming finally John the infidel deserter, broken-hearted breaker of broken hearts.

In this split second stretched already outside of himself, he could look down and see a man swimming in a swift current of pleasures and confusion, eddies of lust and loyalty, whirling moments of getting and having, of easy assumptions and tedious argument, backstroking toward oblivion as a vortex of moments already lived and the tragedy of everything lost: his life, his wife, Grace, their child, Sheryl—ah, mysterious as the moon was she, who came into being without the capacity to hear, and in her perfect features all the love that made her; watching her grow day by day, fierce intelligence of baby eyes blinking wonderment and delight, laughing with hysterical joy, crying in acute misery, banging objects with scientific curiosity, her silent world alert to vibrations, covetous of attention, vigilant, fascinated and hungry for food and love. And she grew out of her first year into her second, gloriously unafraid of the backyard, crawling, and then walking, venturing forward to follow the family cat, pausing, reconsidering her distance from mother, retreating in a gaining toddle, tumbling forward onto her face, crying, and then laughing at the whole adventure from the sanctuary of mother's lap and her warm, enfolding arms, all the while keeping a continuing sharp eye on the stealth movements of the pet. Toddling, pointing to flowers taller than herself, imagining them as equals while determining a policy of engagement. Her petulance, her stubborn assertions, her insistent demands! A little whirlwind of directives, determined to have her way. And that pure parental joy of issuing a stern rebuke for bad behavior and laughing behind her back. But, oh God, the great grief of losing that little girl. And the doctor's diagnosis, and our stupefaction at the loss of a child who gave us her love, but we could not give her our protection. She disappeared from us into the unanswerable Why? And then the loneliness of grieving, the deep private sorrow and alienation from Grace, yielding to selfishness and anger, unable to stop the slow, unfixable hemorrhage of joy out of life. Grace, who did not deserve such callous behavior from me. But how can all that was and all that is collapse into this ear-splitting horn blast? It is the Gabriel trumpet sounding from on high, the fierce swift advance of doom—gone the illusion of forever. *And yet, no! No!* There must be a way back to unsay the smug words so absolute about so many unknowable things: where the path to redemption, what the importance of love and truth, loyalty and faith, and the necessity for reconciliation and shared commitment with Grace? What a fool I've been, how blind and callous, selfish and insensitive, how limited in understanding—ready to throw off eighteen years of marriage for false hope and foolish expectations! How did I take life itself so for granted? How could I make plans for tomorrow and the day after and the day after that except in deepest denial, and why did I not know how swiftly and unexpectedly the end can come? The horn's declamatory blast of sound also a funereal lament, encompassing regrets of a lifetime, decades of mistakes, lost opportunities, the squandering of time, trading days for dollars; the horn blast as Last Judgment's denial of amnesty for wrong choices; the horn blast as summary dismissal for procrastination and petty self-indulgence and the putting off of ways to be a better man: everything now belonged to the horn blast. And he tried to comprehend all that he had known, alpha and omega, though even as it seemed to imply a greater purpose, it remained a mystery, there was no answer—all he could do was scream in a voice from within, unheard against the overwhelming sound: I'M NOT READY YET! I'M NOT READY! I'M NOT—

23

When the police arrived, the driver of the truck was sitting on the side of the road in front of his vehicle, weeping and muttering disjointed phrases at the scene's implacable horror. Neighbors moved into the street from their yards to see the spectacle but regretted their curiosity. One man farther down, describing the scene into his cell phone, was an exception. The curious appeared but quickly retreated back into their homes in shocked revulsion, this stark sight to haunt their lives forever.

After a second patrol car pulled up the area was cordoned off. Sirens announced the arrival of the fire department. The police went about their duties silently, grimly, making measurements and taking photographs. The ambulance arrived and medics moved swiftly to put the human remains into body bags. One policeman went into the woods to be sick. The driver was inconsolable. Stunned by the collision, overwhelmed by incredulity, sadness, guilt, and fright, he wept. A second driver had been dispatched to take the cement truck on its deliveries.

When he arrived in the company car, a manager along with him waited for Maurice Jenkins to finish his business with the police and took him home to his family.

"Have you got their identification?" one of the policemen asked his partner.

"A key to a suite at the Granville Country Tavern Inn was lying in the road. Evidently they were staying there."

"We better go to the Inn," said one of the responding officers to his partner, who had been speaking with the firemen preparing to flush the scene with water and disinfectant. They got into their patrol car and drove off to notify the hotel management of the tragedy. Four hours after the accident, the area was cleared, the road reopened, and life continued as before.

She watched as they came through the entrance and walked up to her at the registration desk They looked like extras on a casting call for some dreadful police drama. Mildred O'Connor sensed no good was behind the arrival of these policemen.

"I'm Officer Joe Howard," said the taller policeman. "And this is Officer Alvin Crumb. We need to speak with the manager, please, ma'am."

She looked at them with circumspect appraisal. "I'll get Mrs. Sullivan. Just a moment."

Mildred O'Connor went through the door behind her into the office, and in a moment a middle-aged woman with gray hair and an inquiring smile appeared. "I'm Ann Sullivan," the manager said. "How may I help you?"

The two women listened while Officer Howard explained what had happened and gave descriptions of the deceased. "They were carrying this key." He withdrew it and handed it to Ms. Sullivan. Mildred O'Connor put her hand to her breast and appeared to falter in shock when she realized the attractive couple she had seen only hours earlier had perished. Officer Crumb, the shorter and younger policeman, caught her arm.

"Mr. and Mrs. Addison were in Suite 12," the manager said.

"We'd like to see their room."

"Of course," said Mrs. Sullivan

Mildred stayed at the desk while Mrs. Sullivan led the officers up the stairs and down the hall to the suite. Their task was to make a positive identification of the victims, establish the permanent address of the deceased, and see what they could learn from their personal effects. She lifted the Do Not Disturb sign and unlocked the door with her master key. When she and the officers entered, she stood back while they performed their duties. The officers moved through the rooms. The deceased had left their suite as any couple might, with the usual examples of habitation left behind: shampoo in the bathroom, travel kits open on the bath counter, a hair dryer. Officer Crumb photographed clothes flung over chairs, books and magazines lying about, and other personal items to be catalogued and included in a formal report. It was Officer Howard who found Maggie's purse and discovered her driver's license.

"The name here says Margret Hawkins, 8 Sunline Drive, Granville, Connecticut. The photograph matches the deceased." He turned to Mrs. Sullivan, who was standing by the kitchenette. "I thought you said the name was Addison?"

"Here's John Addison's wallet," said Officer Crumb, displaying his driver's license and address, "39 Alpine Road, Granville. Same neighborhood." The two officers looked at each other. Mrs. Sullivan sighed. Police business was deeply unpleasant.

"We'll check their license plates and find their cars," Officer Howard said.

"We have that information on the room registration." In spite of her misgivings, Mrs. Sullivan wanted to be helpful. In a short time, the officers had finished their duties. The belongings of Maggie and John were catalogued for removal and the suite released to management.

The two policemen walked to their patrol car. "They say most people who die violently don't know their life is even threatened until seconds before the end, if at all," Officer Crumb said.

"That's a cheerful thought, Alvin."

The officers drove back to the station house to make their report. Detective Mallory assigned himself to the case. When he confirmed the phone numbers of the deceased given to him by Officers Howard and Crumb, he drove up to the lake to notify the spouses. The Hawkins house was empty, so he continued to the Addison address. It had rained earlier, and the weather was humid and uncertain. There were periods of bright sunshine and moments when low clouds darkened the skies. He parked his car in the street above the driveway and took a deep breath before walking to the front door. He rang the bell. He heard movement inside. When Grace Addison opened the door, he was face-to-face with one of the difficult duties of his job.

24

A knock on the front door.

A slight breeze washed through the yard. Grace Addison, meditating new freedom, looked up at marshmallow clouds floating low and unreal on their swift passage to nowhere. She envisioned sailing on windswept seas, slicing through waves and passing out of sight of land to new horizons. Nelson appeared once again as a presence in her daydreaming. There existed between them mutual attraction, but, wronged also in this, they shared a common outrage. If intimacy was something they wished to explore, there was nothing to stop them now. Grace was about to go deeper with this when she heard knocking on the door. It crashed her dreamy reverie. She went to the door and opened it to a man quite tastefully dressed in a yellow tie, khaki pants, and a blue linen jacket. He was in his late thirties or early forties, she estimated, pale blue eyes, generous but with a look of consternation written into their expression. She thought he might be someone who had lost his way. The lake roads were a labyrinthine network of steep and narrow paths to properties that traversed the shoreline. It wouldn't be the first time someone had come to the door for directions.

"Hello," the man said. "My name is Detective Gerard Mallory of the Granville Village Police. I'm trying to reach Grace Addison."

"I'm Grace Addison."

A fly jittered around her face, and another appeared. She swatted at them as Detective Mallory showed her his badge. "I'm here about your husband." The detective's voice had that professional concern of a schoolteacher speaking to the parent of a failing child. They stood at the door in the shade, facing each other.

"My husband?"

"Your husband, John, was involved in an accident early this afternoon," the detective said.

"What kind of accident?"

"He was hit by a vehicle while jogging."

A stab of cold horror flashed through Grace. A long pause ensued.

"Ma'am?"

"Is he badly hurt?"

"He was a casualty, I'm afraid."

"A casualty? Do you mean John's dead?"

"I'm sorry to have to bring you this news."

All at once Grace couldn't breathe. Genuinely astonished by this sudden physical reaction, she reached for the doorframe to keep her balance.

Mallory stepped forward. "Ma'am? Are you alright?"

She found it impossible to speak.

"Ma'am?"

"Yes," she said at last, the message sinking in. "Was anyone with him?"

"He was running with a neighbor. A Maggie Hawkins. Do you know her?"

"Of course. I mean, she's a neighbor. But you said that."

"I'm afraid that she also—"

"Are you saying they were both killed?"

"Yes, ma'am. They were jogging together."

"Maggie is dead too?"

"She also perished." He paused a slight interval for decency. "Mrs. Addison, we need you to identify your husband's remains. Would it trouble you come to the Granville hospital?"

His remains? John's remains! She put her hand to her mouth to cover a gasp.

"He's in the hospital morgue. Is there someone who can drive you?"

"Thank you, Detective. I'm, I-I'm sorry."

"Will you be all right?"

"Yes. I-I'll—thank you. Do I need to go now? I'd rather . . ."

"Later today, anytime. But only if you're up to it."

The detective assured himself that Grace was all right, and he gave her his card and told her to call and they'd meet at the hospital. When he left, she closed the door and stood motionless for a minute, trying unsuccessfully to have a coherent thought. Her mind raced in circles, and she wanted to cry but could not. She went back to the deck overlooking the lake. This is surreal, she thought, but it was much more than that. Her mind struggled for some explanation. She took several deep breaths and became aware of something like a weight on her chest, recognizing it as that sensation she'd had when Sheryl died. Measured deep breaths freed her from the pressure of shock and distress. Under the umbrella again, with great conscious effort, she organized a sequence of necessary steps to be taken in the next several hours.

25

The Granville hospital was a nondescript building. It might have been an office building or a school. There was nothing distinctive in its appearance beyond a suggestion of cold utility. Indeed, it was so uninspiring as to be nearly invisible. Nelson Hawkins had come up from New York by train and had walked from the station to clear his mind. The clock on the wall said 7:10 pm. Nelson identified himself to the woman at the information desk. She made a phone call while he stood by. The lobby smelled of industrial solvents and plastic.

A minute later, a man in a blue jacket with a name tag on it appeared to escort him to the morgue. He was tall and thin, with long hands and a measured manner with slightly hypertrophied inflections. "We've been waiting for you, Mr. Hawkins," the man said. "I'm William Childs."

Childs led Nelson to a bank of elevators nearby and guarded the elevator door with his arm while Nelson entered. The morgue was at the basement level. The door closed and the elevator descended. When the doors opened, the men stepped out into a long hallway. Their footfalls echoed on black and green checkerboard tiles overscrubbed to a dull, flat, functional shine. It had all the charm of a military installation. At the end of the hallway was a double door leading to the main room of the morgue. Childs ushered Nelson in.

"This is Dr. Boyd," Childs said, introducing Nelson. "And this is Nurse Robbins and Detective Mallory." The doctor wore glasses low on his nose and looked over them with kind eyes. The nurse had short blond hair and small blue eyes and looked vaguely familiar.

"We spoke earlier," the detective said. They shook hands. "My sincere condolences."

In Nelson's shocked state, everyone seemed overemphasized and distorted, strangers moving in slow motion seen through a fisheye lens. He followed the detective and the doctor to the wide aluminum drawer that held his wife's remains. Nelson heard the handle turn and the sound of the sepulchral drawer opening. When he looked down, Maggie's corpse was covered in a blue plastic shroud. Due to massive disfiguration, the doctor discretely uncovered only her face.

When Nelson saw her, he felt a sharp stab of disbelief. There she is, he thought, but where is Maggie? This face frozen in final repose—skin translucent, eyes closed, motionless, inert, tragic, silenced forever—did not seem real. Where is the woman of this morning, who left our house and got into her car and drove off to meet her lover, the woman by whom I was betrayed, at whom I was angry, with whom I have enjoyed love and company over the years (and frustration and hurt)? Where is the person I knew? She's is not there; her animating spirit is gone. He stood looking at death and saw it was nothing. Not a thing. The doctor and detective waited for his declaration.

"That is my wife," Nelson said in a voice he did not know, speaking to a fact he could not absorb, his head turning away as if to avoid his own confirming statement. "That's Maggie—Margret—Hawkins." His voice echoed in the cold metallic room. Echoes are ghosts of words in this place of ghosts, he thought. Nothing made sense. The doctor noted the time and then gently covered her face. It was the last sight of Maggie Nelson would ever have.

"I'll need you to sign some documents," Dr. Boyd said as he led them to the elevator.

When they got to the lobby, Nelson took the detective aside. "Detective Mallory, may I have a word with you."

"Certainly," the detective said.

"I want to confirm with you that there was no foul play."

"None whatever," Mallory said, his expression somber. "It was death by misadventure. The driver made a statement of what happened. They were running along the right side of the road and suddenly saw a dead animal in front of them. They evidently tried to avoid it without realizing the truck was behind them. They never saw it. They were wearing earphones, so they didn't hear it. They leapt into the road in front of the truck, and the driver had no time to stop."

Mallory escorted Nelson to the doctor's office on the first floor, where the identification was officially recorded, signed, and notarized for the death certificate. "I have a list of funeral homes," Dr. Boyd said, opening his desk drawer and a folder with brochures. "You can take a look at these unless you have a preference."

Nelson gazed at them with a stupefied expression. Brochures! Necessary, he said to himself, absolutely normal and reasonable, and yet strange and repellent, fantastic and grotesque.

"I'll be leaving you now," said Detective Mallory. "Oh, one more thing," he added, turning, his eyes meeting Nelson's again. "Your wife's car is at the parking lot of the Granville Country Tavern Inn. Management asked me to give you their card. They said you can leave it where it is for a few days if it's an imposition."

Nelson took the card from Detective Mallory, thanking him. They shook hands.

Dr. Boyd pointed to his prescription pad. "Is there anything else I can do for you?" He was willing to prescribe sedatives.

"No, thank you," Nelson replied. Dr. Boyd nodded good-bye and left the room. Nurse Robbins had some additional papers for Nelson to sign.

"You look familiar to me," Nelson said to her.

"I'm Brenda Robbins. We're sort of neighbors," she said. "I live on the lake, by the beach not far from you."

"Yes, the little red house," he said, placing her at once. "I've seen you in your garden."

"That's me. I'm very sorry for your loss," she said, looking up at him with honest blue eyes and sympathy. For some reason, in this fraught moment, she seemed to represent all goodness in the world, and for that reason Nelson suddenly felt a wave of sadness about life. Sadness permeated his emotions, a dismal helplessness about events. Pain and suffering and terrible things could happen, and that was reality. And Maggie, so alive only hours ago, was now dead. He felt close to weeping as he filled out the paperwork Brenda Robbins put in front of him. These tasks completed, he said good-bye, thanking her for her attentiveness.

"One of the strangest days of my life," Nelson said out loud, mostly to himself, as he sighed volubly and sought the exit with a staggering gait and many confused and overwhelming feelings.

26

When Nelson left the hospital, the sun was low in a clouded sky. He had no sense of time, he couldn't think or breathe, he needed to walk, and he wanted a drink. Feeling lightheaded, vulnerable, and vaguely paranoid, he quickened his pace down the long hill toward the outskirts of town near the harbor. He came to a bend in the road where a sea breeze harped ghost notes through a fence. Beyond the trees, he could see boats at anchor. The sight of boats lifted his spirit.

A decade before, Nelson had lived with his first wife in a rented house at the mouth of the river not more than two miles from where he now stood. At that time, Granville was changing rapidly. Parts of it had been rundown. But in recent years, a rising generation of young professionals had moved into tattered neighborhoods, injecting them with cash. Soon new restaurants and shops on the main streets were gleaming with that prosperous halo money brings to wherever it flows. Pockets of poverty still existed though, and he walked on a narrow street through one of those neighborhoods coming down from the hospital. On either side, a row of small wooden houses shared a common neglect; untended yards imprisoned a gritty essence of life. Cracked sidewalks and dirty windows told of lost lifetimes and broken dreams; there are places inside myself like this, he thought. In the harbor, sailboats and motor yachts at anchor seemed to belong to a good and prosperous existence, and he belonged to that too.

As a boy, Nelson had sailed, an activity he enjoyed and wanted to revisit. Sailing taught him about tides and currents, and wind and weather, metaphors for thinking and being. Sailing was a laboratory for self-reliance that put him in touch with adventure. He sailed in pursuit of visions and found them; he sailed to experience beauty and saw it. With these thoughts, descending the hill, he looked beyond the harbor where gray waters gleamed in gratifying late sunlight and the wider estuary came into view with its animated scene.

At last Nelson could see Cap'n Henry's Bar and Restaurant, built on a wooden barge moored to the pier. A southwest wind swept through high salt grasses growing along the seawall, making reeds sway in furious articulations, alive to some unheard music. Sailboats rocked at their moorings. Indulging fantasy, he stopped for a moment to contemplate the scene.

There were many moods here unique to the harbor. On fog-blind days ghostly mists shrouded this view entirely. The foghorn sounded from the channel rock at the end of the breakwater. Invisible halyards chimed on masts that seemed to answer it in codes of an unseen world searching for itself. In a moment when his mind seemed empty, the normalcy of the view overcame him suddenly. He leaned against a nearby tree. He stood there for a moment as though about to be sick, bowed his head and, overcome, wept. He wept at the spectacle of a world he felt suddenly so separated from, and he wept for Maggie and for John, and for Grace and for himself; he wept for the young man he once was and for the old man he might one day be; he wept at the certainty of his own demise and the death he must face; he wept for the loss of all fleeting wonders of this strange, brief, self-consciously awakened interlude on earth. Weeping threw open floodgates of catharsis; he felt it as expurgation. Caught in this whirlwind of all emotions at once, betrayal, shock, grief, guilt, sorrow, sadness, anger, and even hope, he felt a dull stupefaction. Then he saw himself from above, disconnected from all of it. What he sought from the world was truth in all things, but on this day of horrendous revelations, it was hard to accept truth. Their marriage, the logic in her last letter, Maggie's abandonment, and her death, these were matters he had to accept. Recovering himself, he spent a long time looking over the harbor.

27

At 7:50 pm, Detective Mallory returned to the hospital to greet Mrs. Addison. She had arrived to identify her husband's remains. When he got to the basement, he encountered a scene. Grace had faltered in the elevator. She was in a small room off the main corridor, sitting to recover herself and attended to by Nurse Robbins, whom the detective had seen less than an hour before, when Nelson was there. He knocked on the door. The nurse said, "She's all right," signaling with her eyes for a few more moments of privacy. The detective nodded and, closing the door, retreated to the hall.

"Finish this glass of water," Nurse Robbins said to Grace when they were alone again. Grace took the glass with great appreciation.

"I felt suddenly dizzy. I'm very glad you were with me on the elevator. Thank you so much."

"We don't know each other," Nurse Robbins said. "But we're neighbors." The nurse had a familiar face, though out of context. Grace looked at her more closely and then recognized her.

"You live on the lake in a cottage by the beach," she said.

"Yes." Nurse Robbins nodded and smiled. "I see you drive by sometimes. I'm Brenda Robbins. I'm terribly sorry about your husband. If you need anything, call on me. Please. Anything, I mean it. Or if you need to talk to someone. I'll give you my card."

"You're very kind. I feel better now. Thank you."

Even in her distress, Grace evinced a dignity and presence that Nurse Robbins thought admirable under the circumstances. She handed Grace her card, and they both stood. When Nurse Robbins opened the door, Grace recognized the detective, waiting in the corridor. Nurse Robbins introduced Dr. Boyd, who drew out the body of John Addison. Mrs. Addison identified the remains of her spouse. The moment had a deeply personal horror, and it threw her into a state of breathless shock. She left the hospital to seek anonymity among people.

Nelson reached the parking lot at Cap'n Henry's restaurant. The afternoon tide was ebbing, and the air smelled of creosote and salt. Low clouds continued to sweep the skies. Occasional sunshine broke through, illuminating boats in the channel with late light. A giant rusting anchor marked the entrance. The anchor was surrounded by a bed of roses that looked like a memorial to sailors lost at sea. When he went inside, the smell of seasoned wood and salt air mixed agreeably with the odor of food and beer. Colorful burgees, lobster traps, and mooring buoys decorated the bar. Oars and fishnets hung from the rafters. Looking around at the decorations in this place he had not visited in a while, Nelson felt that kind of disorientation when the familiar seems alien and the alien familiar. In this setting he began to shake off what had begun at the hospital, like experiencing a kind of trance.

Patrons had gathered at Cap'n Henry's on the deck outside, but the main bar was empty. Nelson took a seat there. He knew the bartender from his former life. Roy Middleton had been a neighbor. Roy was a balding, middle-aged man with a large belly and bright but defeated eyes. He was that American familiar, a local high-school star footballer with all manner of promise at the beginning. But homosexuality in a less tolerant era had demoralized his pride. Unable to fully accept his nature, he lived half in light and half in darkness as half the person he might have been. He spoke with a familiarity that Nelson welcomed. Nelson didn't want to mention Maggie or the situation. There was nothing to say about it, and its horror would take oxygen out of the moment.

"Howdy, Nelson."

"Roy."

"Vodka tonic?"

"Thank you, yes."

Roy swiftly returned with his drink, and Nelson spent the next twenty minutes lost in thought. He forgot himself watching boats come and go in the channel, a pretty sight. Nearing sunset, an outbound sailboat raised its spinnaker. The big sail rose and fluttered and then caught the following wind and billowed nicely with a snap. At that moment the sun came out. The boat seemed radiant with full-sail splendor, a soothing vision to Nelson's seared nerves.

When nothing makes sense, everything makes sense.

Out of the corner of his eye, Nelson saw Grace come into Cap'n Henry's. She sat down and ordered a glass of wine. Her eyes were swollen. "Grace," he said. She turned and recognized him with startled eyes, at first unbelieving. When she knew it was really Nelson, her shoulders dropped as though unburdened and relieved. She came over to where he sat. Her eyes pleaded for something complex from him.

"Are you … all right?"

"I can't begin to understand it, Nelson. *They're dead*. Maggie and John are *dead*." She took a deep breath. "This morning I hated him. And now this. It's too much. I don't know what to do. I don't know what to think. I don't know *how* to think."

Nelson put his hand on hers. He thought it odd but right that he and Grace were together in this moment.

Roy brought Grace the wine she had ordered. She took a long sip of it. Her gaze fell on the sloop, farther out now, spinnaker still set. Boats and houses took from late sunlight an aspect of glowing richness and splendor. Grace studied an oar on the wall painted white and green. "They didn't deserve to die," she said at last.

"It's just something that happened."

"I don't understand it. It's too horrible …"

They talked about their feelings of the morning. The shock of being abandoned. Nelson described what Maggie had said; Grace told him about John's awkwardness. For more than an hour they lingered and spoke. A roar of laughter went up on the deck outside, and Nelson turned to look briefly at the people standing there.

Grace finished her second glass of wine.

"Do you want another?" Nelson asked.

"No, I don't think so. I have to leave here," she said, suddenly anxious. "I'm sorry. I don't feel I can be around people." The ambiance of Cap'n Henry's seemed now oppressively frivolous to them both.

"I drove into the city this morning to stay at the apartment. I took the train out this afternoon after I got the call. Do you want to come with me into New York?"

"No, I—" Grace looked down. "I, um … actually, I booked a room at the Granville Country Tavern Inn." She looked away.

"But why would you want to go to that place?"

"I don't know." She was silent for a few moments, and then said, "I didn't want to stay at home alone." She turned her head to face Nelson directly. "I don't know what I'm doing or why—that's the truth of it." After a pause, she said, "Did you get Maggie's car? Their cars are still in the parking lot."

"The detective mentioned that."

"You can come with me. I'm glad you're with me, Nelson." Her brow furrowed slightly. "I've got to use the restroom. And then we can go."

"I'll meet you up front."

Nelson signaled to Roy and gave him his credit card. After he paid the bill, he went to the entrance to wait for Grace. As he stood there, Bradley Davis came in. Bradley recognized Nelson, but Nelson did not greet him. When Grace reappeared, they walked together to the door. Nelson saw their reflection hovering in a large window, a fleeting portrait in the moment. It showed a man and a woman together—a couple, clearly—their reflection in a dark glass, transparent, ghostly and somehow occult, trapped in time and waiting for release from something.

They stepped out of Cap'n Henry's to a slight chill in the air. The sun had set, but the sky still held visible light above high clouds in the west. The ebbing tide gave up muddy odors. Grace found her keys, pressed the unlock button, and the car horn beeped, the lights flashed, the doors unlocked, and the motor started automatically as they approached the car. The Granville Country Tavern Inn was ten miles away. When Grace made a left turn out of the parking lot, they were on their way, quiet as soldiers together after battle, frightened as children after watching parents fight.

After a few miles, they drove on a dark, narrowing road that ran beside a creek, winding through thickening woods. They were on that road for about fifteen minutes. In another few miles the brightly lighted Granville Country Tavern Inn loomed ahead through the trees. Isolated, wooden, rambling, and anachronistic, it seemed to hover in the night.

When Grace parked the car, they both got out. The doors closed and locked. She opened the trunk. Nelson took up her bag, and they walked across the street to the entrance.

28

Detective Gerard Mallory was idly twirling a rubber band in his fingers. He twirled it and then cocked it on the tip of his index finger and thumb and let it fly across the room, striking a framed citation from the mayor dead center. As he was privately congratulating himself, a familiar voice called to him.

"So, this is how you spend your days?" His wife, Linda, was standing in his office doorway.

The sight of her lifted his mood. "This is how I distract myself while I'm having deep thoughts."

"Deep thoughts about what?"

"Life, liberty, and the pursuit of happiness."

"I better leave you alone then."

"No, I've got it figured out. Come in."

Linda made his soul smile. Whenever he saw his wife unexpectedly, he fell in love with her all over again. She was his bulwark against menace and confusion. His work fascinated her. While she sometimes found his duties disturbing, she felt civic responsibility relevant and important and believed her husband exampled active thoughtful citizenship.

"A couple was killed this afternoon."

"I know. I heard," she said. "That's why I'm here. I thought you might want some company. What have you learned?"

"Maggie Hawkins and John Addison were evidently having an affair and met at the Granville Country Tavern Inn in the morning. They went jogging, wearing earphones and listening to music as they were running. A dead possum lying beside the road seems to have spooked Maggie. The truck driver said it looked like she was startled and jumped suddenly into the road. Addison followed, right in front of a truck they never heard or saw. It happened in an instant."

"Truck?"

"A cement mixer. Not terribly maneuverable. They never had a chance."

"Good God, Gerry."

"It literally tore them in two."

"How old was she?"

"Forty-two. He was forty-six."

"Are you all right? I mean really?"

"Accidental deaths happen, I understand that." Mallory picked up another rubber band and fired it at the wall. "It just seems a waste, that's all." Linda caught the rubber band and shot it back at him. He grabbed it on the fly and looked at his watch. "I'm done here. I'll take you to dinner."

"How about I take you?"

"Better still."

"Italian?"

"Why not."

"Alfonso's Trattoria?"

"Of course."

Mallory grabbed his jacket, turned out the office light, and together they went into the warm early evening.

They took the corner booth at Alfonso's Trattoria, the one Mallory favored. It functioned as an alternative to the office and a good place to conduct unofficial business. A waitress brought their menus, and they continued to talk as they perused the choices before them.

"I know Grace Addison slightly," Linda said.

"How?"

"We were in the Garden Club together a few years ago. I liked her."

"What about the others?"

"I know Nelson Hawkins to say hello to. He spoke to our group once about writing."

"Maggie Hawkins?"

"I didn't know his wife, but I knew she ran in the New York Marathon. She was written up in the Sentinel last November, and maybe I also heard it from Grace."

"The two couples were neighbors on the lake," Mallory said. "They were friends. And then, lo and behold, John Addison and Maggie Hawkins were lovers, registered together at the Inn. They checked into a suite in the morning and then went for a run before lunch. A couple of our officers gathered up their personal effects."

"It sounds way too incestuous up there," Linda said, waving her hand to fan imaginary heat.

"It gets better. Do you recall our friend, the Peeping Tom? He also lives close to the Addisons. We had a complaint on him peeping through their windows."

Linda sat back in her chair, shaking her head. "My God."

"He has a thing for Grace, evidently. Or did."

"A peeping thing?"

"Yes." Mallory's expression grew serious. He put his thumb under his chin and rested his index finger against his temple, a tell when an unsolved problem hovered. "There's something in front of me, and I'm not sure what it is."

"About the dead couple?"

"No, the Wheeler case. Something in the air. Facts will appear eventually, I'm convinced of it. I just don't know when or how." Linda knew he had an uncanny nose for these matters. He loved his work. His thrill in it was expeditionary, alive in the wilderness of human interaction, seeking secrets and motives. He gazed at the menu on the table in front of him. "Do you know what you want?"

"You don't think sex was the motive?"

"She might have been silenced—I think I'll have the penne pasta— I'm going to see the priest."

"The one from this morning?"

Mallory nodded. "He knew Ann Wheeler from her high-school days. He might be able to shed some light on her life. We'll see."

"I think I'll have the veal," Linda said. "Shall we order a bottle of Chianti?"

29

Tree canopy blocked the moonlight, making the kind of dark that frightens children. Nelson spotted Maggie's car by the shed as they went. Their footfalls on pebbles made a crunching sound until they crossed the road to the front entrance. "I made reservations under my maiden name," Grace said.

"What is it?"

"Fisher."

"Grace Fisher," Nelson said. "A nice name."

"Thank you."

The porch lights shined on them as they emerged from the shadows. Nelson began to realize that he didn't want to leave Grace in this place. They approached the lobby entrance, went up wide wooden stairs to the broad wraparound porch and through the front door to the lobby. The registration desk was on the right. A fire was blazing in the anteroom, but nobody was sitting there. Nelson thought that whatever her initial motives for coming to this place might have been, Grace did not want him to leave her alone. He did not want to be alone either. Even if it was strange considering circumstances, he wanted her company tonight. The woman at the registration desk, her head tilted slightly, smiled broadly, expressing that earnest wish to know to whom she was speaking.

"Mr. and Mrs. Fisher," Grace said.

The woman queried her computer, and her expression brightened when she found the reservation. "Here it is. Grace Fisher." Looking up with that professional smile again, she said, "For two then?"

"Yes," they said simultaneously.

Grace glanced at Nelson and saw an understanding that they would pass through these howling hours together. The woman, looking over her glasses, smiled and said, "I see you requested an upgrade if possible." After a few keystrokes, the woman opened a drawer at the desk and handed them a key. "I've put you in the number 12 suite for the regular room rate. We don't normally do that, but we had an earlier …" The woman's words faltered, and she looked away. "We had a cancellation. But it's available and it's charming, with a fireplace. Very romantic. I think you'll like it."

"Thank you. That's very kind of you," said Grace.

"How many days will you be with us?"

"Just tonight," Grace said.

"Cash or credit card?"

"Cash," Nelson said and gave her the cash amount. She gave him a receipt and then tapped the call bell beside the telephone. A man in a maroon uniform approached.

"Martin will take you to your suite."

They followed the limping bellman up the stairs. At the top, Martin turned left and went to the end of the hall. He opened the door to suite 12 with a brass key and stood by while Nelson and Grace went in. Martin put Grace's bag on a caddy near the small kitchenette. He opened two windows for fresh air.

"Is there anything else I can get for you, sir?"

"No, thank you," Nelson said. He gave him some bills. Martin handed him the key, made a crisp turn, and left. The door closed, leaving them alone in their future for the first time.

Nothing was clear to intention. Grace stood motionless by the fireplace, abstracted, absorbing the atmosphere. "Well, here we are," Nelson said. Under the enormity of events, Grace laughed in spite of herself, surrendering to a state of mind, a dream, or a dream within a nightmare, something neither fully understood.

"Would you like a drink?" she said.

"Why not?"

"I'll make it."

"Whiskey and soda," he said.

She mixed drinks with small ice cubes from a tray at the mini-bar and handed Nelson a glass while her eyes continued to scan the space in silent meditation. Grace brought the drink to her lips. "This was their room. I can feel it."

"In fact, you're correct." Nelson had noticed an earring on the floor behind the leg of a chair by the fireplace. He picked it up. "This is Maggie's," he said, and showed it to Grace.

She smiled tragically, then glanced at the bed, visible in the other room from where she stood at the window. "Less than twelve hours ago they were here. John and Maggie in this room. And now Mr. and Mrs. Fisher have taken it over." Her words were dreamy.

"Do we know them? The Fishers?" Nelson studied his drink.

"We're beginning to learn about them."

"Did we ever think a day like this was possible?" Grace said, words that trailed off from the world of reason to straddle an unhinged parallel universe. Nelson was her husband now, and she was Nelson's wife. Something secret shined out when their eyes met. Nelson got up from the couch and went to the wing chair by the living-room window, watching Grace as she stood staring into the bedroom. She was examining art on the walls, the bedcover's quilted design, the area carpet where it was frayed below the foot of the bed, and a lacquered room-service tray on top of the dresser. A chill came into the air.

"I'll make a fire," Nelson said.

Grace looked up. "That would be nice."

He stood and went to the fireplace, where some papers and kindling had been arranged. Crouching at the hearth, he lit a match. Grace came over and sat in the chair beside his. The dry wood lit easily. For a while they sat silently. Outside, skies had cleared. The bright full moon was visible just above the trees and cast a blue light through the window. Flames grew in the hearth.

"I'd find it more credible if it weren't so absurd," said Grace. The fire, cracking and popping, threw frantic shadows on the wall that seemed to summarize the day's alarm and fright. In a soft, measured voice, she began to tell Nelson about a dream she'd had that morning.

"I was in a large, empty house," she said, also talking with her hands. "The house was a ruin, an empty, cold, and disheartening place. The shutters rattled like bones in a box. While being in the house, I was also outside of it, looking at its front door like a princess contemplating a castle and feeling afraid of something inescapable about her fate. Somehow, I understood it as meaning many things: my marriage, my soul, my present circumstances, my unknown future, my daughter's coffin, her mother's womb—all of these things at once. And I can still feel the strange anxiety at waking."

"And this was before John told you he wanted a divorce?"

"Yes. I must have perceived it unconsciously. I seemed to know that the house in the dream was my life: past, present, and to be. And then in the morning, when he said he was leaving me and left, I started rearranging furniture."

"Dreams have meaning. I believe that." Nelson's mind whirled. He shifted in his seat, had a sip of his drink, and told Grace about his nightmare of the week before. She listened.

"In my dream," he said, "a number of ventriloquists were standing mute and downcast in a large room, all wearing tuxedos, but without their dummies. I woke up understanding that my marriage was over."

"How did you get to that interpretation?"

"The dream wasn't terribly fair to either of us. She often accused me of putting words in her mouth. Hence, my dream was her portrait of our marriage. There were clowns in it somehow too."

"I hate clowns."

"A clown is an exaggeration into caricature. A clown stands for collapsed identity or some flagrant inadequacy."

"Sheryl never liked clowns."

"Anything exaggerated contradicts normal understanding. This is scary to a child. References to reality are undermined."

Grace was quiet for a moment, and then she began to talk about her daughter, something she rarely did. Nelson listened intently. Her voice softened. "I thought about my little girl, Sheryl, today, after John left. Sheryl was a sacred miracle to me. She was born deaf."

"I didn't know that." A further dimension to Grace, Nelson thought. And to John. He listened with great interest.

"When they told us she was deaf, in one sense it didn't matter: it would never be a loss for her. But it would be a challenge for us. John and I were determined to make her disability an asset. We learned to sign. We signed from the beginning so it would be natural to her. And she was so smart, her little fingers answering mine—talking at two with her fingers! Nelson, I can't tell you how she made us laugh, how cute she was. Any honest parent will tell you that children are the funniest creatures on earth. They look at something, and then their expression asks you for some answer to what they see. She loved bugs. Bugs and flies. They were like toys to her. And you laughed out loud at her curiosity. She tried to catch flies in her hand, and I swear she had a relationship with them. A fly would buzz around her, and she pointed to it, giggling. She was deaf, but she saw the world, felt the world, with astonishing clarity. Her visions came from vibrations. Nature makes compensations. Colors, shapes, and percussive sensations is how she experienced life. She delighted me, and naturally I imagined a brilliant career for her. But then she got sick. I didn't think it was serious at first. Children are prone to catch whatever germ is in the air. But she continued to weaken. And then we got the diagnosis: leukemia. It was so sad, and so profoundly painful. My little girl, my Sheryl. We loved her dearly, and she was so special, and it seemed to me that she should get well on the strength of love alone, that some rule of the universe must sustain that notion simply because children are the tender force in a hostile world. In just a few months, she was gone from our lives forever. She had appeared and disappeared, and we knew her for so short a time—all of that love and joy—and now John—" Grace put her hand to her mouth to contain what seemed like a gasp. "I will never see him again." Her head went down, and her voice whispered. "He wasn't a bad man, Nelson. I accept my part in the tragedy of my marriage, how it faded."

"We're all guilty of hiding in distractions."

Grace looked up and spoke through sorrow. "I'm sad, Nelson. Is sadness what my life with John amounted to? I cried this morning after he left. He had abandoned me, and I was alone. I felt cold and cast-off."

"We're together in this, Grace."

"Women believe they are being most valued in the moment when their depreciation begins. How do these things happen? I lost my baby. I lost Sheryl. And John left me, and now he's gone. I'm unprepared for this."

A mother's love, the death of a child; perhaps only women can know profound tragedy. Nelson had not been tested in those tortured ways. He felt deeply touched by Grace, humbled before her humanity. The fire was well established now. Firelight on the beams across the ceiling gave the room a new animated warmth of spirit. Nelson turned off the lamp so that moonlight flooded the room with a blue dreamlike lumen. Flames danced like little emissaries from the sun. Grace extended her legs to rest her feet as each took comfort in the other's company.

A bond between them grew through sharing these deeply private emotions silently: they understood each other. Togetherness instead of loss and dread—being together—was all they could think of to do. As one, they rose and went into the next room to lie down side by side. The curtains breathing night air rippled, and, turning circles, the ceiling fan counted moments. For a long while they lay silent. But slowly, in the ambient moonlight, Nelson found her hand, and Grace responded to his touch, answering long-felt desire. She was alive to him. They shed inhibition, and when Nelson turned, he saw her eyes were brimming. They kissed in the blue moonlighted darkness. Slowly at first, but following rapidly steepening contours, they submitted to desire, premature and also overdue, right and also wrong, blessed and also cursed, and if sacred, somehow also profane. They had what they wanted but not how they wanted it. Nevertheless, the next few hours belonged to that desire. Spent and exhausted and dazed, they lay naked on the bed, sharing in blessed silence the peaceable resolutions of sexual exorcism. The fire had gone down. The minutes passed. There were no further observations to make on events of what was now yesterday. Whatever reasons Nelson and Grace had for being there faltered. They seemed to decide simultaneously to greet the dawn freshly together in this new freedom borne out of the night's emotional upheaval and sexual intensity. Nelson turned his head to Grace. "Why don't we go to my apartment?"

"In New York?"

"Yes."

"Go now?"

"Why not? There's nothing for us here. Dawn is coming. We don't want to sleep here. The drive will take us an hour."

It was dark when they left. It felt like leaving a war zone. But birds were beginning to sing, and the first faint traces of daylight soon appeared high on the eastern horizon. When they got on the parkway heading south, the way went swiftly. Pockets of fog in the woods hovered in the cooler hollows. The Connecticut Merritt Parkway turns into the Hutchinson River Parkway at the state line until the Cross County Parkway cuts west at Eastchester to the Henry Hudson Parkway, which runs along the river in Manhattan and becomes the West Side Highway. Grace found driving a relief. By the George Washington Bridge, morning sunlight brightened the Palisades on the New Jersey side. They exited at 96th Street and drove to Central Park West. They couldn't find a parking spot on the street, so they put the car in the West 95th Street garage and walked the half block to where Alex, the Ukrainian doorman, greeted them with a smile. They took the elevator up to Nelson's apartment on the tenth floor. Nelson unlocked the door. They were weary but not sleepy.

The living room was wide, with a stunning view of the park. Grace sat on the leather couch and examined the wall of books opposite the window. They sat in silence, recovering from the drive and also from the night and from the day before. Day rhythms began again as life awakened. Someone was yelling in the street as horns of cars at the park intersection sounded their impatience. Grace went to the window to see dog walkers and early risers jogging in the park. The sun was still hidden behind buildings along Fifth Avenue. Grace remained by the window, soon with daylight on her face, silent, looking out, feeling safe and relaxed but emotionally drained.

"Shall I put on some music?" Nelson said.

"That would be nice."

"Coffee?"

"No thanks. I'm beginning to fade."

Grace left the window and went to the couch again. Nelson drew the blinds. With the blinds shuttered, the darker room felt cool. He lit the table candle and moved over to the couch. He put his arms around Grace, and they lay there together silently, private in their thoughts, until at last, holding each other, Mr. and Mrs. Fisher fell asleep, plunging into one of those deep comatose hibernations that follow extreme emotional trauma.

PART III

30

Earlier the previous day, after returning from the memorial church service, Bradley had taken a nap and dreamed of a girl stuck in a well. She could not be saved. In the dream, he paced around the well distraught, wishing for a solution, unable to do anything. He woke with relief that the dream wasn't real, but the content had troubled his mind. He felt the need to go out. Cap'n Henry's was a ten-minute drive, and he went there. As he walked in, he noticed Nelson Hawkins. Nelson did not see him. Bradley did not see Grace. He went to the bar and recognized the man beside him as the one he had sat next to in church. He reached out in a friendly way to the stranger. "I'm Bradley Davis. We sat together this morning at the memorial service."

"Oh, hi, yes." Russell Garner extended his hand to the amiable stranger.

"Did you know Ann?" Bradley asked.

"I did. I knew her in college," Russell said. "But I've been away, and I didn't know anything about what had happened to her. I was riding my bicycle through town and saw the church notice for a memorial service with her name on the sign outside. I was surprised to learn she had died but shocked to hear she was murdered. Did you know her well?"

"She used to come into the library where I work. I liked her."

"Which library?"

"McAndrews County."

"Is Miss Byrd still there?"

"She's my boss."

Russell turned in his seat. "Does she still ride that blue bicycle with the basket on the front?"

"Rides it to work every day."

"I just bought a bicycle. I haven't known such freedom in years. I'm really enjoying it."

"My father rode a bicycle all his life," Bradley said. "They've made a big comeback."

"Did you know that the bicycle as we know it was not invented until 1885?" Russell enjoyed little-known facts.

"I don't think I knew that."

"About the same time as the typewriter was invented. Just after the telephone and a little before the airplane. But think of this: it took the entire history of man to understand how Archimedean energy exchange could apply to the creation of a useful vehicle for personal transportation, fast as a horse and you didn't have to feed it. They called it the *safety bicycle*. You could travel five miles as easily as walking to your mailbox. It changed everything."

"The bicycle was clever, but the automobile was the game changer," offered Bradley, who, as a librarian, was no stranger to arcane information and also enjoyed social history. "The first horseless carriages appeared about 1895."

"The automobile was transformative, of course," Russell agreed. "But the bicycle is pure poetry in its simplicity, and we can't underestimate how remarkable it was in its broad appeal at the beginning. The freedom it allowed to ordinary people was extraordinary." Russell was experiencing that freedom.

Engaged in conversation, Russell and Bradley didn't immediately notice two women come in until they sat down where the bar cornered, making conversation easy and natural. They appeared to be in their early forties. One wore a long blue summer dress and a shell necklace, slightly more formal than her friend, who wore white shorts and a blue cotton T-shirt. The two men introduced themselves.

"I'm Bradley. This is Russell."

"I'm Mary, and this is Susan." Mary had fair hair, nearly blond and shoulder length. Susan's was short and dark, cut at a fashionable pageboy length. "Do we know each other?" Mary said to Bradley, speaking across Russell.

"I work at the McAndrews library."

"That's it!" she said. "That's where I've seen you." Then, turning to Susan, she said, "You know that library. It's the old mansion."

The bartender took their drink order. Bradley was willing to include them in their conversation, and said, "We were just talking about bicycles. Early bicycles."

"Mary rides a bike," Susan said.

Russell's head turned to Mary. "After the bicycle rage in the 1890s, women's fashions began to change rapidly," he said. "Women went from bustles and bloomers to sportier jodhpurs. Their clothing morphed into what was called *rational* dress."

"Is that what they called it?" Mary said, amused.

"The bicycle was a catalyst for social changes of all kinds."

"I have a new bicycle," Mary said to Russell. "I just got it, and I love it." Her eyes were humorous and curious.

"I love mine too," Russell enthused. "It makes you intimate with the road, with neighborhoods." Russell had a pride of possession that valued virtues of objects. "It puts you in a storybook world."

"I agree completely." Mary noted how Russell's well-spoken comments inferred a good mind, genial nature, and boyish enthusiasm eager to share. "We should ride together some time," she said with the barest hint of wile as she fingered her shell necklace. She sent him a message, and he received it.

"That might be fun."

"I've wanted to travel the country by bicycle," Mary said. "It's something I've thought about. But it would take a long time."

"Not so long, taken in stages." Russell, new owner of an old bicycle, meditated freedom's possibility. "A ride of about twenty-five miles per day would do it. On that schedule you could go on indefinitely."

"Stay in on bad-weather days."

The idea had great appeal. Russell was delighted by the easy way that he and Mary conversed. He realized in the moment that she was a litmus test of social graces long dormant. Mary did not sense it, but his nerves vibrated with anxiety. The question looming for him was how should he handle his past. What was possible after hello? Also, he thought, how do you confide twelve years in a federal penitentiary on a conviction of rape, even though eventually exonerated? He was terribly, painfully aware of having spent one fourth of his life in prison. It made him feel unclean and unworthy. He felt branded with slander, and he knew that with slander, people tend to split the difference (it *could* be possible).

Mary was attracted to Russell. She transmitted this in a myriad of small expressions, inflections, and gestures. Russell saw it, but his first thoughts were defensive: I must be careful in my reactions and relearn the art of appropriate comportment. I must control my feelings and steady myself. These and other cautions fired through him until he heard himself matter-of-factly ask Mary, "Are you and Susan sisters?"

"We're neighbors, actually," said Susan. She pointed to a complex of garden apartments visible on the far side of the channel. "We live in those condos. Over there. Mary has the view. I'm across the hall from her, so we have cocktails on her porch and watch the boats come and go." Both Bradley and Russell turned in the direction she indicated and saw a long, low residential building set back from the seawall.

"You are very fortunate to have a view," Russell said, who for twelve years had no view of anything.

It wasn't clear to her yet, but Mary's attention was drawn to something in Russell, a sense that she knew him in some nonspecific way. Soon she would be shocked to learn why it was true and how it was so. A few days later, they ran into each other. Russell was out for a walk when he saw Mary come out of a bakery near the train station off Main Street. He felt an impulse to wave to her or call out, restrained by an equal fear of presumption and embarrassment. But Mary saved the moment by recognizing him and then immediately crossing the street to say hello.

"Russell," she said as she came up to him. "Mary Simmons. Do you remember me?" Wearing sunglasses and a red and white striped summer dress, a wooden necklace, and leather lanyard sandals, she looked like an ad for good health.

"Of course, I remember you, Mary. I saw you come out of the bakery, and I recognized you right away, and I, er ..."

"And you weren't going to say hello?" She cocked her head back facetiously, reprovingly.

"No, I, ah, I mean, yes. I mean you beat me to it." And he laughed. Her social ease bewildered his anxiety. He had to keep saying to himself that normal people respond in normal ways for normal reasons.

"Well, it doesn't matter. I'm glad to see you again," Mary said, her sincerity bold, direct, and believable. "I've wanted to invite you to my home for a glass of wine. Is Thursday afternoon all right? Five pm?"

"I guess so, sure. Thursday's fine. I'll be there."

Mary smiled. "I'm so pleased. You know where I live, at the Harbor View Apartments across the channel?"

"I know where they are, yes."

"It's Simmons in 5C. At five. See?" She covered her mouth, laughing at her lame joke. "That was terrible." This slight self-deprecation was one of many becoming social reflexes on her part that put Russell at ease.

"I look forward to it. To seeing you. Really. Thank you, Mary. Thank you very much." I sound too grateful, he thought, too needy. He was hard on himself. In fact, his demeanor was genial and appropriate. Mary had an antic side. She smiled as she walked off, then turned once to see him again with a big smile on her face.

Since his release from prison, Russell felt like an escapee trying to pass as a citizen of Granville, that soon he'd be found out, arrested, and sent back. It was irrational fear. He'd been through a lot. The jailhouse changes a person in unknown ways. He had no idea how to approach the subject with Mary, and this gave him much trepidation, though he distinctly looked forward to his date with her.

31

Anticipation gave new meaning to his days. They passed slowly until, on Thursday, in a joyful mood, Russell Garner rode his bicycle down the hill toward town and out across the channel bridge to a promenade along the shoreline. Mary's apartment building was wide and low, with outdoor porches overlooking the channel. He found her name on the lobby roster, "Five. See?" and rang her apartment. She buzzed him in. He took an elevator to the fifth floor, and as he stood pausing for a moment at her door, it opened before he could knock.

Full of good cheer, Mary was holding a glass of wine and handed it to him as she welcomed him into her home. "Let's have a toast," Mary said, closing the door behind him.

"How about: to health, happiness, and bicycles," Russell said, taking the wine from Mary.

"Health, happiness, and bicycles," Mary repeated, and they touched glasses.

Russell looked around. Her apartment was decorated with a theme of the ocean and sailing and the beach. She had a bookshelf in the living room, and a quick glance at her volumes told him that she read thoughtfully. Her decorative style was bright, colorful, and informal. There was nothing cheap in the room, nothing gaudy, incongruous, or overdone. She had some nicely framed etchings of harbors and boats. Amused, curious, and a little nervous, but happy to be in her company, Russell enjoyed the cozy comfort and unselfconscious character of Mary's apartment. Standing by the window, he admired her close view of the harbor and, just beyond, Long Island Sound, with Long Island's North Shore visible in the distance. "It's beautiful, Mary," he said. "Do you commute to New York or work locally?"

"I work as a legal assistant close by."

"How far away?"

"It takes me ten minutes to drive to work. I don't think I'm made for the city commute." Her face had an aspect of kindness and patience.

"Why did you invite me here?" He realized how stilted he sounded, almost aggressively abrupt and un-nuanced. Mary was without condescension, and her smile seemed radiant on behalf of his charm.

"I invited you here because I enjoyed our conversation at Cap'n Henry's and because you like bicycles." He smiled shyly and looked down abashedly. She saw in the man before her a wounded creature, but she was aware of the reason for this, though she wasn't sure how to address it.

"You don't know me." Russell's eyes were circumspect but defensive; he felt shame draining confidence. But Mary came to the rescue.

"I know about your time in jail, Russell, if that's what you mean. And your exoneration."

Russell could not have been more surprised. The brutal prison environment had given him the habit of concealing feelings.

"How do you know?" he asked with the innocence of an alien.

"I Googled you, of course. All the news features about the trial, conviction, the DNA evidence, and your release are there. And accounts of the Proven Innocent organization—the successful efforts they made on your behalf are detailed."

As she spoke, Russell's eyes watched the wake of a motorboat moving from the cove to the river channel. "Somehow it's not comforting to hear that. I guess there's no privacy in the modern world." He laughed grimly.

Mary shrugged at the truth of that statement. "Not much privacy if you've appeared in any form of media."

"Some people know themselves by what they are not, others by how they have changed, still others by what they've become. I'm rebuilding myself. If I can't return to the person I once was, I at least want to re-claim some of the qualities I've kept." Mary was bringing him out of his shell. He was not ready for her next disclosure, however.

"You were my teacher once upon a time."

"I was your teacher? Truly?"

"When I Googled you, I realized who you were. You are not entirely a stranger."

"How is that?"

"You taught me how to read."

"I never taught grade school."

"I mean how to read literature. Do you remember teaching *Wuthering Heights*?"

"Emily Brontë. I remember that lesson plan, yes. You were in that class?"

"Before we read the book, you told us it was important to understand 'the cognitive process of symbols in imagination and how they inform expanded understanding.'"

"That sounds a bit pretentious." He laughed at himself, but Mary wasn't having it.

"It wasn't pretentious at all, because you explained it in a simple way. Symbols, you told us, are things that stand for themselves and also for something else. You used the Statue of Liberty as an example. It's a statue of a woman holding a torch, you said. More abstractly, it's a symbol for liberty and enlightenment, but it's also a harbor beacon, and it can be other things too, so that there can be layers to meaning in symbols, and that's how art enhances what we see around us. You told us that great writing has meaning embedded in images and that sentences and paragraphs have a life of their own. When you began to talk about *Wuthering Heights*, I could see it. You made it sexy. I could feel it. All of a sudden, I couldn't wait to read the book and talk to you about it." Mary had a sip of her wine, not taking her eyes off his.

"*Wuthering Heights* is a rich novel."

"Remember how you asked us to interpret the characters and the landscape the way a writer would, through an article of clothing, a texture, a color, the weather? Heathcliff would be a muddy boot, a rough, torn blanket, the color purple, and a violent storm. Linton would be clean underwear and a meek complaint, Cathy the sound of swirling winds murmuring on the moors. Think like a writer, you told us. As I say, you taught me to read."

"I'm pleased to hear you say that, I really am." Russell was genuinely moved.

"You made a difference in my life, and I'm sure I'm not the only one. When we met at Cap'n Henry's, I didn't recognize you as my teacher. Then I read about you online."

A flash of emotions passed across Russell's features: his eyes expressed surprise, pleasure, pride, and also anxiety.

"Prison must have been terrible for you because you were innocent. You don't have to talk about it."

"Maybe I should."

"I can't imagine it."

Every compassionate impulse in Mary was felt on behalf of the person in front of her. She felt closer to him as a former student. He could see she was curious, and he hadn't talked to many people about the experience. He thought it might be therapeutic to share some of his feelings about it with her. He spoke candidly, in an offhand manner.

"The whole experience felt like it belonged to someone else," he said. "I was made a stranger to the facts of my own past. The world insisted I was different from who I was."

Mary felt him in her marrow as a mission: this man, Russell Garner, needed her. "It can't be an easy transition. Going from prison to freedom, I mean."

"It beats the reverse."

"I want to help you."

Russell struggled for a moment and then said, "It's good of you to say that."

"But I mean it."

In a flash, Russell's mind returned to the hopelessness of prison days, the deafening din, the freakishly psychotic inmates, and how he didn't dare dream of freedom again. Mary could read his thoughts. "You were in bad company, under psychologically impossible circumstances."

"Jail is the lowest tier, home to the social fuckup and criminal flunkout. I don't know yet how it's affected me."

"You don't have to talk about it," Mary said.

Russell took up the wine bottle and filled their glasses again. Mary was curious but attentive to his feelings. He wanted to answer her interest, and it felt liberating to talk to her about it. "If you want to know what jail is like, I'll tell you."

"I am interested. But only if you want to."

He paused for a moment to collect his thoughts and then began to speak slowly, as though telling a story. And it was a story, his story, and he seemed to see and hear the images as he put them into sentences.

"It's a place without a beginning or an end. Those forsaken who pray to God are mostly insane. The scene is piteous. The clamor is mind-bending. Men in cages. The daily cries for mothers, wives, children, lawyers, and revenge still ring in my ears. There is no higher abstract power than the law in this place of high howling. It's the sociopathic home of despair, where only hopelessness echoes. 'I'm innocent!' I maintained, to laughter and derision. The received translation: I didn't mean to get caught. Innocence is never to be creditably claimed, and yet one does claim it. But no matter the truth, if you have been convicted, you are guilty. There is no larger truth. Prison is punishment. What is lost is freedom. Rehabilitation is a myth. Raw and in pain, you have joined broken souls in the place of grinding eternal despair." Russell fell silent and seemed to study his wineglass as though it held an answer to something.

"Good Lord," Mary said. His prison experience horrified her. He was telling a story of entrapment, of mortal frustration examined from every perspective for years. Her imagination understood he had been wounded terribly. He seemed a hero of some extreme adventure, nebulous and obscure. That innocent prisoners did exist, betrayed and forgotten, appalled her. She sensed correctly that Russell was suddenly feeling claustrophobic. Realizing they both could use fresh air, she said brightly, "Why don't we go for a walk?"

"I'd like that." They finished their wine and left the apartment.

Once outside, Russell and Mary strolled together at a leisurely pace. After years of incarceration, Russell was not used to open spaces, and as a consequence he noticed things others did not, for example, that from a parallax view, the sight of sailboats and their tall masts moved backward as they walked along the quay. Mary charmed Russell immensely. He was delighted that she had once been his student. Her fair hair, golden in some lights, abundant and pulled back, and the cotton dresses she favored, projected a personal style he thought refined and smart. She put on sunglasses against the late sunlight and wore them like royalty on the Riviera. He felt proud to be walking with her.

"What do you see now that surprises you after being away for so long?"

"Women," he said. They both laughed. "That there are two or more televisions in every restaurant and bar, or so it seems, and bad loud music everywhere, and so loud you can't talk, you have to yell." He continued, shaking his head. "I counted thirty-six televisions in one sports bar."

The wash of waves splashed the side of the promenade. "What other changes?"

"People seem to do everything on their cell phones. They text continuously, holding phones close all the time, waiting for the next message or a 'like' for something They watch movies on them. They send out naked pictures of themselves to lovers and strangers."

"It would seem odd to witness that all of a sudden."

"They might write a poem instead."

The harbor horn sounded: one gargantuan note like a blast from an ocean liner rolled across the estuary, and five teenagers walked past them, each one talking on a cell phone. "There is a perfect example," Russell said. "Look at them. They're not in the moment with each other. They're psychologically elsewhere."

Russell talked about how GPS allows you to get where you're going without your knowing how you got there, and how ubiquitous pornography makes you a voyeur instead of a participant while stripping sex of mystery, and how Facebook answers the cult of celebrity with fifteen seconds of fame for everyone, while Andy Warhol had predicted fifteen minutes. "But, my God," said Russell. "If your life is digitized, advertised, corporatized, and merchandised, who does it belong to? How real is any of it?"

Sea grasses swayed in the breeze. Mary listened intently as they sat together on a bench along the quay. The lowering tide line showed on the pilings under mustaches of seaweed. Mary had admired Russell as a teacher and reached out to him as a friend. Now she thought of him in more intimate terms.

"How is your friend, Bradley?" Mary asked.

Russell gave her a questioning expression and then remembered. "Oh, yes. From the bar. I don't know him well at all, really. I happened to sit next to him at a memorial service."

"For Ann Wheeler? Susan and I were there."

Russell's expression moved into abstraction. "I knew Ann Wheeler. We knew each other from town, and we were friends in college the way people are friendly to others from the same place."

"It must have been a terrible shock for you," Mary said, turning her head to face Russell again.

He told Mary about riding his bicycle past the church and seeing Ann's name, how curious he'd been, and then how shocked when he learned she was murdered. "Murder assaults the logical world until it feels as though we're living under a curse of some kind."

Then, on some sympathetic impulse, as though reaching a conclusion together, they rose from the bench as one, hardly noticing the synchronicity of the event as they continued walking and talking.

32

Gerard Mallory had lunch at Cap'n Henry's on the broad deck over-looking the docks. He finished his lobster roll and was preparing to leave when he recognized the Catholic priest, Father Capehart, wearing khaki shorts and a green polo shirt, standing near the corner of the deck on the other side and sipping a glass of wine. On his way out, he went over to the priest and introduced himself.

"I'm Gerry Mallory, Father. Detective with the Granville Police Department. I attended your memorial service for Ann Wheeler last week."

"Jim Capehart, pleased to meet you." They shook hands. Taller than average and with a smile that turned up on one side in an engaging way, the priest said, "A memorial should be a celebration of life. I hope that came across in the service."

"It did."

"Beautiful day," The priest said, nodding toward the harbor.

"Spectacular."

"Is this one of your regular places for lunch, Detective?"

"It's one I prefer on days like this," Mallory said. Two seagulls swooped low toward the shoreline. The ebbing tide was showing its mud line where the salt grasses grew and seagulls harvested clams. Mallory watched them pluck shells from the mud and fly up almost vertically, drop them onto rocks to shatter the shells, then swoop down to retrieve the meat.

"Have you had lunch?" the priest said. "Would you like to join me?"

"Thank you, I've just finished." Mallory paused, and then said, "Father ..."

"Please call me Jim." He held up a glass of wine.

"Jim. I wanted to ask you a few questions about Ann Wheeler's brother, Bobby, if you can spare a few moments."

"Of course."

"He was a religious-instruction student of yours, I understand. We found a picture of him on Ann Wheeler's refrigerator door, an old photograph of a birthday party."

"He died years ago."

"Perhaps you can tell me something about him."

The priest turned and leaned against the guardrail to face Mallory directly. "Bobby was part of a religious-instruction class I taught for children who went to public schools. He was an impressive boy."

"Was he a particularly religious boy?"

"So few are at that age. Interest strays from God to girls at fourteen, or sooner." Father Capehart laughed. "My goal was to get them thinking about faith's connection to charitable acts and show them another side of life." The priest assumed a more serious aspect and held up his finger for emphasis. "I remember Bobby. He was an intelligent boy, like his sister. He was curious enough to ask provocative questions, I remember that. 'How can we say God exists if we never see or hear Him? How can God allow evil people to have happy lives?' That sort of thing. May I call you Gerry, if it isn't too sudden?"

"Valid questions." Mallory smiled wryly. "And please call me Gerry. Were you aware of any early interest in drugs he might have had?"

"I was not. Naively, perhaps unwisely, I thought him too young for that." The priest ran his hand across his head to take the wind out of his hair. "Bobby died about fifteen years ago. Poisoned with bad drugs. Case never solved."

"Was Ann close to her brother?"

"Very."

"Her mother?"

"Deceased. She died while Ann was in school."

"And her father?"

"Out of the picture."

"Divorce?"

"I'm not sure there was ever a divorce. He left the family. Disappeared."

"Tell me more about Bobby as a student of yours."

"I taught religious instruction on Thursdays at the church. For Catholic kids from public schools. Bobby was in the class for two years."

"You said he was thoughtful. What else?"

"Something of a scrapper. Smart and tough. There was a story about how he saved his sister from being raped in high school."

"True?"

"Yes."

"What happened?"

"Bobby heard Ann had gone alone in a car with a particular boy known to be sexually aggressive. Bobby went to a place where he thought the boy would take her, a lover's lane near the gravel quarry. And in fact, when he got there, she was in serious trouble. Bobby prevented an assault that was about to happen. His intervention was rather harsh, as I recall."

"Oh?"

The priest canted his jaw with amused approval. "Bobby ripped the boy out of the car and gave him a proper beating."

"No turning the other cheek?"

"He kicked the living daylights out of him is what I heard. Put him in the hospital. A brother's defense of his sister's honor. Bobby was a hero to her for real reasons."

"Do you still teach religious classes?"

"No, not in some time." The priest had a sip of wine, put down his glass and paused slightly. "I should start it up again though. Kids benefit from exposure to less familiar environments."

"Why did Bobby leave religious instruction? Do you know?"

Father Capehart shrugged. "The class was noncompulsory. He decided he didn't want to come. As I said, fourteen-year-olds have other interests."

"Do you know Bradley Davis?"

"Yes, he works at the library. In fact, Bradley was in class with Bobby, I believe. You should talk to him."

"I have."

"Oh?"

"He didn't offer much except to say that you and he were close at one time. You were a kind of surrogate father."

"Not everyone comes from a solid family background." Father Capehart assumed a serious expression. "Bradley was vulnerable. His mother was a widow and Bradley an only child with some problems."

"What sort of problems?"

"Teenage angst, mostly. His mother came to me. She was afraid he'd run wild. She felt he needed male guidance. He was very capable, smart. I made him a Tiger."

"Tiger?"

"Tigers did good works. They helped the poor."

"Was Bobby a Tiger?"

"He was. Bradley and Bobby were both Tigers."

"What distinguished a Tiger from a non-Tiger?"

Father Capehart shrugged and laughed. "Well, it was a loose distinction. Motivational, mostly. Tigers were the first team, the strongest students, open to larger experience as a path to leadership. I tried to expose them to Christ's message of social responsibility. I'd take them into New

York to work in the soup kitchens. The dioceses also did neighborhood cleanup work, that sort of thing."

"I'm sure they took a great liking to you."

"They seemed to enjoy the outings, different environments."

"You were influential then. They looked up to you."

"Sometimes yes, sometimes no. It's no small thing to be held in high regard by an impressionable teenager, but they are fickle." The priest pursed his lips and spoke seriously, "There is a lot of turmoil at that age, and you have to let a struggling mind deal with demons."

"Is there anything else you can think of with respect to Bobby Wheeler?" A gust of wind blew across the deck and drove ripples over the water.

"He was in my class for the good part of four semesters. That was nineteen, twenty years ago. I was young then. What is your interest in Bobby, if I may ask?"

Detective Mallory rubbed his forehead as a way of gathering his thoughts. "Well, I've begun to wonder if Ann Wheeler knew something about the source of the bad drugs. Maybe she learned who was responsible. If she confronted him, that person might have decided she had to be silenced. It's just a hunch."

"Gerry, let me know if I can offer further help in any way."

The detective smiled acknowledgment, but his brow furrowed, and some other thought occurred to him. "There is one more thing, but I'd appreciate it if you could keep this between us."

"Of course."

"Bradley Davis was caught peeping through windows in his neighborhood."

"Bradley?"

"You had a unique opportunity to observe early challenges or difficulties he might have been confronting. Is there anything you can tell me in confidence about him?"

A shadow crossed the priest's features as he considered this reveal. "I liked Bradley very much. He struck me as a very intelligent young man. His mother was earnest about his religious instruction, but she had a host of problems herself. She was an alcoholic. In addition, Bradley might have been traumatized by the death of his father. But I don't believe he is capable of anything criminal."

"Peeping is real, and peeping is criminal behavior. I didn't seek to prosecute him, because he agreed to enter therapy. Therapy might help him to identify the real problem behind that sort of conduct."

"The Bradley I knew doesn't have a mean bone in his body. I can vouch for that." The priest was adamant and sincere.

The detective smiled and extended his hand. "Thank you, Father Jim," Mallory said. "Father Jim is what your congregation calls you?"

"Yes, but Jim is fine."

"Thank you, Jim."

"Listen, why don't you drop by the rectory on Wednesday, say 2 pm. I'm intrigued. You've awakened some memories. We can talk some more. I'll see if I can come up with more about Ann and about her brother too, if you think it can help."

Mallory bowed his head gracefully, almost humorously. "I accept with pleasure your kind invitation," he said. "Thank you very much." They shook hands on the deck of Cap'n Henry's.

"By the way, do you know Les, Les Turner?" the priest asked. "He owns a sloop. I race with him. If you'd like to come along sometime, I'll put you in for crew."

"Absolutely," Mallory said. He and Linda had decided to buy a boat for next year's season, and this further excited his interest. Leaving the restaurant on this day, bright and warm with an occasional gust of wind disturbing otherwise still waters, he could see preparations taking place on a sloop getting ready to sail. Indistinct voices drifted up from the harbor as he watched the heaving of sail bags from dock to deck, the purposeful back and forth of the crew along the topside. Sailing had been an early interest. He knew the history of great navigators, Columbus, Vespucci, da Gama, and Magellan. As a boy, he'd learned the knots that sailors use, and in college he'd bought a sextant at an antiques bazaar and taught himself to use it.

33

On Wednesday, prior to meeting with the priest, Detective Mallory left his office at noon. He went across the town square to Donna's Diner for lunch, where, while waiting to be seated, he contemplated the bobble-head dolls on the window ledge there: Frank Sinatra, Dean Martin, and Babe Ruth. These notables of yesteryear, in farcical reiteration, gave him a rueful sense of time passing. He was shown to an empty booth, and after the waitress poured him a glass of ice water, he ordered the fish special.

Father Capehart was on the detective's mind. How does a Catholic priest spend his days? he wondered. He thought the prohibition against marriage of priests and the doctrine of celibacy unnecessary, emotionally barren, and absurd to modern understanding. Instincts could not, should not, and would not be ignored. The rule of celibacy could not be wholesome and must in some way account for sexual predation at the hands of priests.

During lunch, Mallory thought about sailing and sailboats. There were several types that interested him. Day-sailing in the Sound and racing appealed to his imagination. Each type of sloop was handicapped, and he thought that learning the rules of racing would be fun. Finishing lunch, he checked his watch and, after paying his check, stepped out into the warm, sunny afternoon, then walked across the square to his car and drove to the Wilberforce rectory of the Catholic Church of the Incarnate Word, James L. Capehart, Pastor.

Later that evening at dinner, Mallory described to Linda his visit to the priest at his rectory. She poured them each another glass of wine. Mallory's observant nature retained details, and he had that reporter's sense of scene, character, and story. "Tell me all about it," she said.

"The yard was small, but it had sun. In one corner stood a white statue of the Virgin with her foot on the head of a serpent—Catholics are especially fond of iconography. There was also an urn by the garden gate and a brass sundial near the entrance. It's a tasteful residence inside and out, except for the gloomy religious kitsch, which is all over the place."

Mallory described the Italianate limestone townhouse with journalistic specificity. "Three stories tall, with shoulder-high hedges around a very private property. The wood was dark Brazilian mahogany. His housekeeper opened the door and told me to come in."

"Housekeeper?"

"Someone has to cook and clean for the priest. Her name is Mrs. Reilly. She led me into the living room, where a large iron crucifix hangs above the fireplace. The room doesn't have much natural light in the afternoon. She turned on the floor lamp. 'The father will be with you soon,' she said."

Cool digs. The detective apprised the living room. Identity is embedded here, he thought. What do heavy furniture, fruitwood side tables, lace coverlets, and large lamps with shades that look like hats women wore a century and a half ago mean? Diamond-shaped panes with lead mullions, charmless religious artifacts decorating the walls, a bronze bas-relief of Christ carrying his cross, the Blessed Virgin surrounded by angels ascending through fluffy clouds, an Aryan Jesus holding forth his stigmata from a throne? To an atheist, they signified an illustrated mythos of faith and false promise.

The priest entered, dressed in black slacks, a white polo shirt and loafers. "Please don't get up," Father Capehart said, leaning over to shake Mallory's hand. He sat on the couch. "I'll have some wine brought out. White Bordeaux?"

"Thank you."

"Excuse me a second," he said and quickly sent a text to Mrs. Reilly.

Mallory was amused: cell phone as servant bell, a vicar's concession to modernity. The priest's casual style was a far cry from the vestments of high mass, but, because of his canonical good looks, informality also suited him.

Mrs. Reilly appeared at the door with a bottle on a silver tray and two Waterford crystal glasses. She set the tray on the coffee table.

"Did you know Ann Wheeler well?" Mallory asked the priest.

"She is—was—part of my congregation. I've known her for twenty years or more."

"What kind of person was she?"

"Smart, kind, shy by nature. Pretty too, in the way some girls have a thoughtful look."

"What kind of a family did she come from?"

"An average family. They lived on the rural route. She and her older brother, Bobby—we talked about him."

"You told me that Bobby was a Tiger."

"Did I?" A complicated expression flashed across the priest's features. He contemplated the glass in his hand, laughed slightly, sardonically, and looked up at the detective. "It was a time when I was young and idealistic. I had a sense that, through Christ's Word, I could change the world. Yes, Bobby was a Tiger. So many distractions these days," he said. "God is not dead, as Nietzsche proclaimed, but he has suffered a pub-lic-relations setback."

"Modern life has changed a lot in a short time."

"My worst fear is that future generations will be distracted from morality."

"I think people instinctively know the difference between good and bad."

"Without religion, what will keep people from killing each other?"

Mallory laughed. "Human compassion, Father. Empathy."

"I can't see how good can come from loss of faith."

"History shows that religion is the greatest cause for slaughter."

"You are not a man of faith?"

"I am a man of reason and accountability."

All at once, as though coming out of abstraction, Father Capehart put down his glass and placed both hands on his knees, ready to spring to action, which he did, and said, "By the way, would you like to hear some music?"

The detective watched the priest move across the room to the shelf of books beside the fireplace. He turned on an amplifier embedded there, and sultry sounds of a saxophone sailed out from invisible speakers. A saxophone's silky sexy sound from the fingertips of a brilliant artist. He knew the music. "Ben Webster?" said Mallory.

"Very good, Detective. Isn't the fidelity fantastic?" The priest pointed to the source of sound concealed behind the couch and announced speaker capacities. "Two discretely concealed 12-inch woofers and bass reflex port three-ways. They're good for everything from high-frequency rock and jazz to the deep bass of hip-hop and R&B. The music is all around you. You can't tell where it comes from."

Like God, thought Mallory. "Is that so?"

"Top of the line," the priest said, his hand sweeping air. "Listen to it."

Ben Webster, ghost of sound, floated invisibly from nowhere to everywhere in the room. Mallory admitted excellent fidelity while noting the peculiar conflation of sensual music and penitential depictions dominant on the walls.

Then Father Capehart had another thought. "I don't know if you'll like racing, Gerry, but I know you like to look at boats. You were admiring the J-class sloops as they prepared for the Wednesday races."

"As a matter of fact, my wife and I are going to buy a boat next spring."

"Sailboat?"

"A sloop. We're looking at different brands. So I'm in for it all."

"Listen," Father Capehart said. "I've got a proposition for you. I'm going to crew for a friend in the race on Saturday and there's an opening for an extra crewmember. Maybe you'd like to join us?"

"Maybe I would," said Mallory. "But I'm not knowledgeable."

"Doesn't matter. Another hand is helpful."

"If I can I will. Let me check with my wife, but thanks for asking me."

Linda listened to her husband's account of his visit to the rectory with growing interest and curiosity. She thought the image of a priest did not comport with high-end audio systems, sexy music, and sailing. But Mallory, nonreligious and practical, thought "normal" behavior a wholesome sign for a celibate priest.

"If you want to sail on Saturday, it's fine with me," Linda said.

"It will be instructive at the very least."

"So, what's your final impression?"

"Of the priest?"

"Yes."

"I liked the guy," Mallory said. "He's a man alone in a large house among angels and ghosts of dogma."

"With a surrogate mother looking after his needs! How old is he?"

"You saw him in church. Early, maybe mid-forties. About our age." Mallory held his glass up and studied its color for a moment, finished it, and then laughed, in response to her comment, so it seemed.

"What?" said Linda.

"I had the vaguest feeling, but it kept coming back."

"What?"

"It struck me that he's one of those likable guys who cheats at golf and beats his wife."

34

Dr. Singer thought Bradley's emotional isolation had roots in his formative years following the death of his father. Before his session, Dr. Singer reviewed her notes. Contours came into focus. His mother's alcoholism amplified Bradley's emotional isolation and erotic misapprehensions. Dr. Singer's next investigation would take in Bradley's relationship with extrafamilial authority figures. Her office door was open when she heard Bradley enter the waiting room. "Come in," she said, welcoming him with a wave of her hand that encompassed the couch, where he readily assumed the supine position now natural to him.

"You told me that you began to take religious instruction at age thirteen," Dr. Singer said. "How did that come about?"

Bradley, lying on the couch with his eyes closed, laughed at some private association. "He called us Tigers."

"Who?"

"The Catholic priest at the church in Wilberforce, Father Capehart. We called him Father Jim. Tigers were his favorites."

"What made Tigers favorites?"

"Tigers were his soldiers in training to do good. We went on field trips. He gave us special attention. He'd take us to New York to work in the soup kitchen on the Bowery. We rode bicycles along the river. He taught me to drive."

"Let's talk about that time in your life."

Bradley now found it easy to speak honestly with Dr. Singer. It was no longer difficult to confide intimate feelings. He told her about his relationship with Father Capehart.

"I want you to go to church, Bradley," his mother said.

"Why?"

"It will be good for you. You're a teenager now. Changes are coming."

"Changes have arrived."

"Talk to the priest about your problems."

"I don't have any problems, Mother."

"Everyone has problems, son."

"A priest is the last person I'd talk to about anything."

Not observant herself, Eleanor nevertheless wanted her son exposed to religion. He should regard the priest as a surrogate father. "Field trips to the city, Bradley. Church-related charity events, an occasional dance."

Bradley bunched his eyebrows in chagrin and frowned. A sophomore in high school at the time, he saw his mother's sudden religious advocacy, while sincere, as convenient retreat from parental responsibility. But no matter, she signed him up. Sodality classes on Thursdays with Father Capehart in the basement of the Church of the Incarnate Word in Wilberforce.

"This will be good for you," she said.

Bradley thus reluctantly delivered himself to the church basement, where, in a section partitioned off with room dividers, students sat on folding chairs. There was a portable green chalkboard at the front of the class. Wielding chalk and tap-tap-tapping on a green board, the priest drew circles, squares, and triangles representing cosmic enormities: Purgatory, Heaven and Hell; even Limbo (in days before its elimination by prayerful consensus). The priest rendered chalk-form Ten Commandments, the seven deadly sins, and without irony illustrated the nine orders of regimental angels, beginning with Seraphim. Bradley took passing interest, but he was not inspired. The priest was literal and earnest in his understanding of concepts that Bradley thought rather silly.

If religious instruction was tedious, there existed a true dynamism in Father Capehart. The priest had a special rapport with his students, a way of making each feel unique. His training as an actor made him adept at imitation and projecting character. A relaxed manner and youthful appearance brought him closer to his students, while his priestly office gave him unimpeachable authority. Often in class, the priest gave special attention to Bradley, a responsiveness that added a positive dimension to religious instruction which, no matter how Bradley approached it, was otherwise a dreary bore.

The first fall semester culminated at Christmastime in a trip to a soup kitchen in New York. The experience of the soup kitchen was a lesson in what to guard against becoming. A bus took them to homeless shelters on the Lower East Side. There he saw the war-wounded in life's battle, ghostly men and women shuffling under a burden of crushed hope. For the first time, Bradley saw what harm life can do, how some people had no luck, and how easy it was to make the poor seem wrong. Even in later years, he recalled the despair he had seen in the dejected faces he found there.

"Your minds are young and inexperienced. You are impressionable," Father Capehart told the class. "Some would say innocent—although I doubt that." The coy aside garnered self-conscious titters, to which the priest raised eyebrows of sham reproof until the class comported itself. He continued. "I will try to give you the experiences you need on the path Jesus found and shared with the world. Not an easy path, but, worthy to praise, a path that will serve you well throughout the rest of your lives." He pointed to his head. "This is your laboratory. You will learn to think for yourself, mindful all the while of God's guidance, mercy, and grace." Bradley's mother had a shrewd understanding of emotional want. Eleanor was aware that human history was a narrative of aggressive psychopathologies, and she wished to shield her son from deprivations. She felt Bradley needed male guidance, and she was correct in this. Bradley missed his father and unconsciously sought a mentor, an adult to respect and emulate. By the end of the term, Bradley was smitten by Father Capehart's attention to him. He admired the priest's wisdom, vitality, and knowledge of the world. Bradley wanted to be esteemed as a protégé and regarded as unique. As he described these feelings, Dr. Singer listened with an attentive ear. She well understood this desire, common to talented innocence and frequently exploited by craven experience. In the spring term, Father Capehart made a special trip to Bradley's house to see Eleanor. "A day in the city, just Bradley and me," the priest explained. "We'll rent bicycles at the Boat Basin, ride along the Hudson to Battery Park, and say hello to the Statue of Liberty. I should have him home by sunset."

Eleanor was delighted, and gave her blessing to the expedition. When the longed-for day arrived, Father Capehart came in his blue sedan, and it felt like Christmas. Bradley was so excited he could barely speak. His mother sent him off with a happy smile and twenty dollars to spend on anything he wanted, while sensing with a mother's uneasy awareness that this day was the end of childhood for her son.

The day unfolded in exquisite fashion. On the drive in, Father Capehart played music, and if he knew the words to a song, he sang loudly in full voice. Bradley too joined in, and a good mood spread like sunshine in him, echoing the joy he'd felt as a child at night when his father came home from work. Father Capehart parked the car on West End Avenue, near the Boat Basin. Bicycles could be rented nearby. The bicycle path at

Riverside Park was wide and not crowded, and you could ride fast along the river on a bike. The priest was an experienced rider; he held back to accommodate Bradley's slower speed. Along the way, they watched boats and barges on the Hudson, helicopters and airplanes flying low overhead, and Bradley could feel the rhythm and animation of the city, its pulse of life. All of this had been given to him by Father Capehart's attention and affection.

In Bradley's second year of religious instruction, the priest made a remarkable offer to Bradley, something the boy deeply appreciated. "Do you want to learn to drive?" His mood was jaunty, and his offer came as though he could read Bradley's thoughts. "Can I?" Father Capehart laughed. "I don't know, can you?" "I can try."

"That's the spirit. We'll go to the beach in South Granville with the big parking lot. You can take the wheel and practice there."

Bradley was fifteen. His mother had said she didn't want him driving until after his eighteenth birthday. Father Capehart, on the other hand, was treating him to yet another adult experience to be enjoyed and savored. Bradley was beside himself with pleasure and anticipation.

Father Capehart parked on the corner of the large lot and switched seats with Bradley.

"All right, adjust your seat. Good. Does that feel comfortable?"

The steering wheel seemed large.

"Can you reach the pedals okay?"

Bradley nodded.

"Okay, good. Put your seat belt on."

Adjusted and strapped in, Bradley put the car in gear. He stepped on the gas with his right foot, and the car lurched forward. He stepped on the brake pedal with his left foot, and it stopped abruptly, ungracefully.

"Okay," said Father Capehart. "First off, use only your right foot for acceleration and braking. It feels odd at first, but that's the correct way to do it. All pedal inputs should be gentle pressures. There's a lot of horsepower under the hood, and the brakes are very effective. You don't want any of it all at once."

Bradley tried again, stepping on the pedal gently, and this time the car moved forward slowly. He drove to the corner of the parking lot and turned onto the perimeter road.

"Use your turn signal next time," Father Capehart said. "I want you to develop good habits right away."

"Freedom was the dominant feeling," Bradley told Dr. Singer. "Freedom and a feeling of special attention." He remembered that bright sunny day, warm for early springtime, and the salt smell of the Sound, early flowers along the foot of the trees where the woods began.

"Tell me more about how you felt."

"I don't know how else to say it. An adult I respected was offering me a path to what I wanted from life at the time. I wanted to drive cars. Every kid does. I spent the whole afternoon driving around the parking lot at the beach. Hours. I think I used a tank of gas. Father Jim took the place of my real father—that's how I saw it at the time. I could relate to him. He made me feel equal and important."

"Well," Dr. Singer said. "We'll take this up again next time. I want you to think about a few things, Bradley."

"Don't you always give me a few things to think about?"

"Did Father Jim truly make you feel special? And if he did, were his motives always sincere?"

"Why do you think they weren't?" Bradley said. "I'm curious."

Reflecting on the charismatic personality which is so often narcissistic and monomaniacal, Dr. Singer smiled her enigmatic smile, professional, private, ironic. "I'll see you in a week."

PART IV

35

Sailing in a race excited Mallory. He looked forward to the experience. When he arrived on the dock, Father Capehart hailed him, hoisted him aboard, and introduced him to the four others in the crew. Mallory put names to the colors of clothes. Jack in the yellow sweater seemed to know more than the others and acted as a second-in-command. Bob in the blue and white jacket seemed a diffident but knowledgeable novice determined to efficiently set the spinnaker or reef the main on command. Carl in the green sweater moved forward to prepare to hoist the jib. Les Turner, the owner/captain, stood at the helm. He observed the preparations with almost formal executive attention, directing this or that action to crewmembers at their various stations.

"Jim will be forward," Les said to Mallory. "You stay here with me and just move from one side to the other when we change tacks."

That was easy enough. When *Second Wind* was ready to race, Les gave the signal to start the motor and cast off.

They motored out of the channel, and the sail covers were removed and stowed. The crew at stations on deck, Les steered into the wind and ordered the mainsail raised. Father Capehart, manning the main halyard, watched the luff clear to the top of the mast. Carl in the green sweater raised the jib and tightened the sheet. They left the last red nun to port on their way to open Sound under full sail, and Les ordered the engine shut down.

There was pronounced grace in the profile of sailing boats, beauty in the billow of a trimmed sail, in the steady cut of the bow through waves. Once established, Mallory enjoyed the irregular splash of the bow in unprotected waters, greater waves enhancing the pleasures that made sailing distinctive.

The crew listened attentively while Les gave them his briefing.

"We're going to win this one," he said. "Gary Adams in *Gwendolyn* is someone to watch. He's good at the start. If he takes the lead, we'll follow him until we find a wind shift. The others, Dirk Van Valkenburg in *Sea Beast* and Bernie Curry in *Varooom*, are tough competitors. If we have the lead, we might want to tack to pick up a thermal advantage near shore. Otherwise, let's be sure to get the spinnaker up without a tangle on downwind. I'm sure you're up to it, gentlemen. And so now let's kick some nautical ass and leave these dilettantes in our wake."

At the five-minute warning, the boats gingerly tacked or luffed in position, waiting for an opening at the starting gun. Their formations seemed chaotic, but there was a plan behind each maneuver. The gun fired and the race was on.

The first leg was a reach. *Gwendolyn* crossed the start in second place behind *Varooom*, but *Sea Beast* converged on a starboard tack and called right of way, forcing *Gwendolyn* to yield. Les maneuvered *Second Wind* to edge out *Sea Beast* as she came about and ran second behind *Varooom*, the lead boat. On deck, preparations were in progress for the downwind run after the first mark. Preparing the spinnaker, Father Capehart located the head and the two leeches. Holding them free, he stuffed the middle of the sail into its bag and secured it to the leeward shrouds. Jack in the yellow sweater attached the spinnaker pole to the mast and adjusted the topping lift and foreguy to hold it in place. *Second Wind* was on the inside as they approached the mark.

"Ready, about!" called the captain, and he pushed the tiller toward the mainsail as they rounded the mark to port.

The boat turned rapidly, and the boom swept across the cockpit to a starboard tack. Mallory ducked. *Gwendolyn* took the lead, but not by much.

Les, standing at the helm, called, "Hoist the spinnaker!"

As the bow came around, Carl, in green, raised the spinnaker swiftly. Jack manned the guy, and Father Capehart watched the sail spill out of the bag and dropped the jib to the deck. The spinnaker billowed magnificently with a tart snap.

"Hoisted!" Carl called when the halyard was two-blocked and cleated.

"On course!" called Les, waving to the skipper of *Gwendolyn*, now to port and slightly behind him on the run. The two boats were racing as though in formation, *Second Wind* slightly ahead to starboard. Bob played the sheet for maximum efficiency. "Trim the guy!" cried Les. He told Mallory to move forward and sit against the mast. Mallory jumped up and ran along the port gunwale, holding on to stays as he went to keep balance, and off they sailed with a following wind on the second leg of the race.

The boat rose on the waves and surfed down the rolling back side. The exhilarated crew were happy and relaxed in the moment. Ahead, vigilant and standing fast, *Second Wind* was good on the run, as her captain knew, and it remained his task to hold the lead and advance it when he could. Mallory watched intently and listened. The drama of wind and waves, of commands and scampering response, was exciting to watch, the raising and lowering of sails beautiful to behold—the endless motion—he loved it.

During these tasks and executions, Mallory observed Father Capehart. The priest was leaner and handsomer than the rest. His blue cotton boat-neck and canvas sneakers carried a sartorial panache greater than the brighter colors others wore. The priest worked swiftly and efficiently, directing or taking direction from the others, an equal among equals in a crew of one for all and all for one. When egos flared, as they did from time to time, his edges were less sharp, and he was able to dissipate tension with a joke, sometimes at his own expense.

Yet there seemed to the detective some essential thing absent in the priest, or perhaps it was the presence of some subtle quality others did not share. The detective noted how the priest lost himself in sensations of sailing. His eyes grew distant when he paused at the spectacle of sails and wind that gave the experience a special magic. He recalled the priest's pride in his audio system at the rectory. Perhaps his own prejudice was at work, but Mallory saw the priest living in the grip of one reality with his nose pressed to the enchantments of another. It crossed the detective's mind that what he saw in the priest was not a poet longing for a vision but a prisoner acting out a life.

Well established on the downwind tack, Father Capehart, free for the moment, came aft and sat down beside the detective for a few minutes while they rolled before the waves. "How do you like this sailing business?"

"I like it a lot," Mallory said.

"I thought you would."

"How long have you been a sailor?"

"I learned when I was a kid on Lake Michigan. My family summered there. Sailing was a rite of passage. Like learning to swim, it came naturally." The spinnaker rippled. "By the way, any progress on the Wheeler case?"

"I'm not sure, but I have some ideas."

"I'd be happy to hear them. Let's have drinks after the race. We usually get together at Cap'n Henry's for congratulations and condolences."

"I'm sure I'll be ready for a beverage by then."

Les called for a jibe of the spinnaker. "Whoops, got to go," Father Capehart said, jumping up. "I expect to be celebrating. See you afterwards."

Second Wind held the lead on the downwind course but lost it upwind on the third leg. The competitive boats were clustered together: *Second Wind, Varroom, Gwendolyn,* and *Sea Beast.* Eight or so other boats were far enough behind not to be threatening. The leaders held a close covering formation, each inside boat drafting tightly.

Les studied the shoreline. He sensed more wind close in. Mallory watched resolve gather in his expression. Finally, he called out: "All right, crew, we're going to tack to port and try to catch better wind closer to shore. The crew acknowledged. "Ready?" he called. "About!"

The boat turned swiftly from a starboard to a port tack, losing little speed. None of the other boats followed. The maneuver took *Second Wind* on a lone course away from the others. Mallory stood beside Les at the helm. It seemed impossible to gauge if this lone-wolf strategy would bring success at the finish. The cluster of other boats got smaller and smaller as they tacked to mid-Sound.

Second Wind held the inbound port tack almost to the shore, where a breeze generated by rising thermals was slightly stronger. "I think we can fetch the finish line from here," Les said, eyeing the committee boat in the distance. He waited ten seconds and then commanded a tack to starboard. The crew jumped into action. The boom swept from right to left across the deck, and the main and jib were close-hauled for a beat to the finish line. All hands sat on the starboard rail against the heel. Mallory was engulfed in the moment, as excited and involved as anyone. They could see their adversaries clearly in the distance, and as they closed, tension built.

Les offered insight. "If the other boats don't seem to be pulling ahead or falling back, that means we're dead even."

Mallory observed that boats converging held steady on the sight line; it was impossible to know who was ahead as they approached the finish.

Father Capehart, observing the unfolding of a strategy with a knowing eye, leaned into his ear. "Watch what happens next."

Mallory turned to him with a questioning expression. *Varooom* and *Gwendolyn* were neck and neck on a port tack coming up rapidly on what looked like a collision course. *Second Wind* held firm. The wind was steady from the southeast. The finish line ran an oblique favoring the others, but all at once Les yelled out: "Starboard!"

Curses were heard on the other decks, all on a port tack. In accordance with rules of racing, the boat on a starboard tack—wind across the starboard beam—has right of way. The tactic forced the others into changing course while *Second Wind* fetched the finish. The horn sounded and the race was won. The captain's canny strategy had paid off. The sailors of *Second Wind*, including Mallory, waved in happy triumph and shouted "Hooray!" to gracious waves, salutes, and antic insults from the other crews.

36

Mallory sat with Father Capehart at a small table across from a longer one in the middle of the room. The surge of sailors arriving piecemeal from post-race duties was beginning. Like the detective, the priest was in a state of excitement and pleasure. The race had been exhilarating for the strategies executed, risks taken, and tactics that scattered the challengers at the finish line.

Flush with the fine feeling of fellowship and victory, Mallory raised his mug of ale. "To winning," he said.

"To winning. Cheers."

They touched mugs and drank. The first sip of ale was cold and tasty and welcome.

"What a finish! Thanks for inviting me to come." The race had impressed the detective mightily. He felt a full share of pride in winning.

"It was a bit of a long shot," the priest said. "I knew what Les was thinking. A few knots of breeze near the shore might give us a boost." Father Capehart put down his mug and smiled in reflection. "The wind shifted slightly in our favor. That one long starboard tack gave us right of way at the finish. Sometimes everything goes right. Sailing, summertime. I love all of this, Gerry. It's all so civilized. It's all good."

"You grew up in Michigan?" Mallory asked.

"I did. Catholic. Middle class. Parochial schools. My mother was an idealist and my father sold life insurance." He shrugged and laughed. "Caught between optimism and pessimism, I learned to see the good in bad and the bad in good."

"A relativist priest?"

"Alive with contradictions." Father Capehart was exuberant and humorous. But Mallory sensed something else leaking like a blade of light through a broken door.

"I want to ask you a personal question. Feel free not to answer."

"You can ask anything you like."

"Do you believe in your religion, Jim?"

A shade of irony appearing in his smile, Father Capehart said, "I have to believe, Gerry, wouldn't you say? I'm a priest, after all."

Mallory shrugged. "Nietzsche said there are two types of individual. Those who want to know and those who want to believe."

"Which am I?"

"I think you are both. The actor and the monk are at war inside you. Neither is satisfied with the impulses of the other."

Father Capehart smiled wryly. "I am a man of faith in heart and mind."

Mallory cocked his head sideways in skeptical scrutiny. "Then you believe everything the Catholic Church teaches about God and man and heaven and hell?"

"God lives in the faith of those who seek him. He can have many manifestations."

"Yes, Virginia, there is a Santa Claus. But I'm talking about something else. I'm talking about a God that can be petitioned with prayers and persuaded by praise, a God that offers rewards for obeisance and condemnation for disobedience. An authoritarian God who knows your thoughts and holds you responsible for them. Is that what you believe, Jim, in your heart of hearts?"

"I do." The priest seemed not to mind this line of questioning as impertinent. He was open to intellectual engagement. "What do you believe, Gerry?"

"I believe that reason gives us meaning and purpose in life, and that reason is skewed by creed, which is in essence magical thinking. Let me ask you this," Mallory continued. "Do you advocate religion because you think it's true or because you believe that people would be better off *if it were true?*"

"Let me turn the question around on you," Father Capehart said, moving in his chair to face the detective squarely, to take up the debate directly. "If you knew something which, if disclosed, would cause unnecessary misery to millions, would you tell them anyway and allow them to suffer?"

"You mean acknowledge that God is a fairy tale?"

Hand raised to protect his faith, the priest shook his head. "People want to know what is right and what is wrong, Gerry. They want to know that there is a difference between good and evil. Faith asserts that good will be rewarded and evil punished, if not in this world, then in the next. This is God's assertion, not mine. Divine incentive, if you wish."

"You can't make that claim, Jim, nobody can. Evil is often rewarded in this world, and there is no indication of a life to follow this one."

"Faith allows what man can't prove."

"Faith denies what science knows is true."

"There are many mysteries unanswerable by either faith or science. But religion is affirmative. It adds a special desirable dimension to life."

"Science gave us airplanes and washing machines. These add desirable dimension to life. These are affirmative."

"Persons of faith enjoy greater certitude."

"Let me ask you this. Are you convinced that as a priest you have a special power that can change bread into the flesh of Christ after an incantation?"

"I do."

"Do you suppose that if we submit a consecrated host for DNA analysis it would come back with a code asserting the flesh of Christ?"

"God would prevent it as a blasphemy."

"That's magical thinking, Jim."

"Science says that nature has no purpose," countered the priest.

"Not exactly." The detective was adamant. "We human beings are a product of nature, and as a cognitive species create meaning and purpose for ourselves. What we make of it depends on what we think we need."

"Well, then, using your argument, I, as a cognitive human being, choose to understand that God has a purpose for each of us, and that God's hand in the affairs of man is at the heart of meaning."

"If God existed that might be true." Mallory threw out his hands. The priest chuckled and sat back in his seat. Meanwhile, the detective wondered: Do most people give these matters any but the slightest consideration? And yet they assert these things passionately. His sense was that most people let the priest or pastor carry the burden of faith. Father Capehart was comfortable with his assumptions, and his congregation mostly passively followed his words and affirmed him without criticism. His clients were his flock of sheep. Faith was their failure to think.

Father Capehart said, "Can you tell me why science can't approach a painting by, say, Rembrandt, and offer a competent treatise on beauty?"

"No, I can't," said Mallory. "Point taken."

Father Capehart slapped his hand on the table. "There then. Science has limitations."

Mallory smiled. "But art and literature exist to guide our sense of truth and beauty. Music moves us. The humanities, as it were"

"How about this," Father Capehart said. "Why is there something instead of nothing? Science can't answer that."

"It is perfectly reasonable to admit that we have insufficient knowledge," Mallory said. "There is a lot we don't know. But we can't embrace the false as a substitute for unknowing."

"Some entity had to be the creator of everything."

"Really?"

"We call that entity God."

"Jim, that's an absurd assumption."

"How so?"

"What if we reverse your premise and say this: *Everything we know could possibly be wrong.* If we proceed from that understanding and re-construct the world only from facts we know to be true, in this instance we don't reason down from a First Cause, but up from confirmed real-ities. We don't reason backwards to validate a wish but rather forward to report what we've discovered. You won't find God anywhere, I can assure you."

The priest pressed his point in response. "Some entity created the universe; can we agree about that?"

"Why? On what basis?"

"Surely it's self-evident."

Mallory, enjoying himself, laughed. "Then who or what created that entity? You can't have it both ways, Jim. Any system of contingent cause is itself contingent, into infinity."

The priest looked at the detective with interested curiosity. "Contin-gent cause? I haven't heard that phrase since college."

Mallory put his mug down and pointed at the priest, amused. "Evi-dently you missed that class, is that what you're telling me?"

Father Capehart grinned and raised his ale. "You're not a bad sort for an infidel, Gerry. At least you've given it thought."

"Reason is our only way of knowing what is, and facts are powerful tools, Your Priestliness. Faith and hope have no place in rational dia-logue. Anyway, you deflect."

They drank on that assertion. Then the priest put his glass down and scratched his chin as accompaniment to another thought. "Alright. But consider this, Gerry. If God is all powerful, He might have caused Him-self to exist. What do you think about that?"

"The difference between you and me, Jim, is that I don't substitute faith for doubt. Some people need explanations for everything. I understand that. But I can live without answers. I don't fear not knowing. Living with lies when facts exist that refute them, or accepting the false because proof of the true eludes us, is something impossible for me. I believe—with Bertrand Russell, I think—that if facts support a truth, you should believe it. But we should not fill in what we can't know is true with what we wish were so. If facts do not support something, then you can't believe in it without destroying your intellectual integrity. If facts are inconclusive, you must suspend belief until you can learn what additional facts might support. I would rather live in a world with no answers than in one with false ones."

"I've underestimated you, Gerry. I don't agree with you, but I admire your pragmatic thinking. Is this how you reason to solve a crime?"

"I don't make up clues, yes. There is no magical thinking involved. I follow hard evidence."

"But you have faith in your methods. That is, you believe in ultimate success."

"Reasonable expectations based on facts, not conjecture. Building a case is like building a story. I used to write for newspapers. You identify your subject."

"Go where the facts lead. That sounds reasonable."

"That's what I believe in. You make your argument, and the story begins to tell itself. In law enforcement it's the same. You identify your subject and turn up the heat. Eventually, the ending becomes clear."

"Have you ever had a Perry Mason moment where the perpetrator comes clean when you 'turn up the heat,' as you say."

"Sometimes, but it's rare. Human beings can have complicated motives for what they do. In some cases, punishment is the actual goal of perpetrators. Like Raskolnikov in *Crime and Punishment*. It happens."

"Guilt? Is that what you're saying?"

"Guilt can be a factor. It can be a large factor. Motives can be murky. It is important to know the distinction between guilt and remorse. But sociopaths have no guilt or remorse."

"Which means what?"

"Guilt is self-reproof for having wicked wishes or done wicked things. Remorse is regret for something that's already happened. Impulsive crimes are often driven by unconscious motives that become clear eventually whether or not guilt or remorse are factors."

"Why is that?"

"Facts are storytellers. They can be reverse-engineered to discover intent."

Father Capehart was listening, but his mind went to the next question. "Have you made any headway in the Wheeler case?"

"As a matter of fact, I have."

The priest was surprised. "Anything you can share?"

"Not at the moment," the detective said. He took a sip of his ale, and as he put his mug down, he raised his finger as a thought occurred. "Well, one item came up that concerns you."

"Me?" The priest retreated, sitting back in his chair.

"You were stopped on a routine matter of a tail light being out, do you remember that?"

"I do remember, yes. It was in May, I think. A female officer. She was very nice and gave me a warning."

"Was there anything that night, on that road, something that you might have noticed out of the ordinary?"

"Not really. I was on my way home. The stop was the only unusual event."

Mallory smiled, shrugged, and drained his mug. "I have to go."

Father Capehart extended his hand across the table. "Hey, it was a perfect day on the water. I'm so glad you came."

"It was wonderful, really. Thanks so much for inviting me. And I enjoyed our conversation."

"Me too," the priest said and winked. "I'll pray for you, of course."

"I can only hope."

A fine feeling between the men had been established, and as Mallory was standing up to leave, Father Capehart said, "Why don't you come by the rectory for lunch sometime next week? We can continue our conversation."

"I could."

"Good. I'll give a call, and we'll set a time."

As he drove home, Mallory meditated on the priest, his life, his work, his mind, his pleasures, and his ideas about God and man. Mallory wondered what torsions of the sacred and profane were at odds in him. He was robust in all his enthusiasms, a man of faith who yet took his worldly entertainments seriously. What was his life like: his inner life, his private world? Catholicism was an ancient and exclusionary institution of men. Celibacy expressed Catholic anxiety and morbidity on sex. He recalled the fig leaf covering the offending penis on pillaged statuary showcased at the Vatican museum, and a postcard of St. Peter's he had sent to his mother, where he had written: "God or Mammon?"

37

"Mother?"

"In here, Bradley."

He went through the foyer door, slightly ajar, to the parlor where his mother spent the larger part of every day in the warm season. Eleanor puttered with odd panache, standing by the birdcage wearing a red brocade robe with gold piping, cigarette dangling between her lips, squinting through smoke, reaching up, in her strange way stylishly feeding the parrot. The room, too, had definite distinction in its cozy clutter. The birdcage, the ceramic cheetah, her Persian carpet, the bookcases, her couch, and the mahogany coffee table made a snug nook. Bradley noticed she had added a potted palm, which stood in the corner.

"Why do you leave everything unlocked?"

"Maybe a dark stranger will savagely attack me." She chuckled, walking back to her place on the divan. "Sit down, son, have a drink with me. Pour yourself a scotch."

Bradley glanced at his watch. It was nearly noon. "I'll have a glass of wine."

"There's an open bottle in the refrigerator."

"May I freshen yours?"

"Merci, mon cher." She pointed to her empty glass on the table.

"Merci, mon cher," repeated the parrot.

Bradley rolled his eyes at his mother's voice emanating from a bird speaking French. "Did I ever tell you that a friend of mine had a parrot in college? He got it from a professor and his wife. Soon the bird began to repeat intimacies and arguments in their voices."

"That's very funny," Eleanor said. "Has there ever been a mystery written along those lines? I wonder."

"Why don't you write it?"

The familiar room evoked memories from Bradley's childhood. It was its own universe, safe from outside harm and influences, her world. He picked up his mother's empty glass and went to the kitchen for more scotch, ice, and wine. When he returned, Eleanor was ensconced against the pillow, the parrot perched atop the cage, animated, strutting back and forth sideways. Bradley handed his mother the freshened drink.

"Cheers," he said.

"Cheers." She raised her glass, and Bradley touched it with his in a proper toast. Then Eleanor said: "They kept her head, you know." Answering a private meditation, she shrugged and had a sip of her drink. His mother had that habit solitaries have of talking out loud sometimes, continuing a train of thought, the equivalent of how others hum songs audibly without realizing it.

"What are you talking about?"

"The French."

"What head?"

"Her head disappeared after the French executed her."

"Who?"

"Mata Hari."

"The spy?"

"She was put on trial for handing over the names of six Belgian agents to the Germans in World War I. After execution, her corpse was taken for medical studies." Eleanor shrugged, speaking with the cigarette between her lips so that she seemed to be chewing it. "But for some reason her head was embalmed and kept at the Museum of Anatomy in Paris. It disappeared in the 1950s. Someone may have it yet."

"Good Lord, mother."

"I can't remember your question, but that's the answer," she said authoritatively. And with a slight rasp, she exhaled a jet of smoke, stabbed out her cigarette thoughtfully, and chuckled to herself.

Bradley sighed, reflecting that her thoughts were like oil globs in a lava lamp, glomming on to a memory or a stray fact, her erudition random and accurate but eccentric. "How are you, Eleanor?"

"I've been better," the parrot said on her behalf, but in the basso accents of a gentleman. Bradley raised his eyebrows and looked up at the bird without affection. "What do you feed that thing?" he said.

Eleanor didn't answer but laughed instead, raising phlegm. She cleared her throat volubly and lit another cigarette. "How are you getting along at the library?" she asked.

"DVDs, CDs and electronic video games are very popular." He was being half facetious.

Eleanor exhaled smoke, and then, holding her cigarette in one hand and her glass in the other, she brought her drink carefully to her lips so as not to spill it. "Do people read books anymore?"

"They do. But not the way they used to. Miss Byrd and I have been discussing that. There has been a shift in favor of electronic media and audio books."

Eleanor had a second sip from her drink, and her face became abstracted. She seemed lost in thought. She put her drink down. "People will do what people will do." She sighed. "I'm old enough not to care."

"But you do care, Mother." Bradley reflected that for all her flaws and shortcomings, his mother was a woman of culture, a well-read and thoughtful woman who had instilled in him a love of literature. And from his father he had inherited a gentle and tolerant nature. He embodied most of their virtues and few of their faults. "Do you hear me, Mother? You *do* care."

"Ugly automobiles!" Eleanor, expostulating, started to laugh and then cough. When she finished coughing, she continued her roster of grievances. "The feckless corruption of politicians." She shook her head in private disgust and picked up her glass of scotch. "The dismal squalor of senators, their cowardice, their mendacity, their travesty."

Eleanor wasn't wrong, Bradley admitted. In the past she had noted American cultural decline, where instead of theater you had sports, instead of heroes, you had celebrities, instead of facts, you had opinions—a culture that mirrored Newton Minow's timeless analysis of television: "a vast wasteland." Social media was mediocrity in metastasis. But today his mother wasn't up to that sort of conversation. Today she was mainly in conference with herself.

"I've never liked the term class," she said. "It's louche."

"Who was talking about that?" Bradley's uncomprehending head twitched.

"Mata Hari had class."

"I suppose so. Are you warm enough?" Bradley eyed the blanket at her feet. "But she was a spy."

"Spying is as old as jealousy," Eleanor declared, circling back to the previous subject, continuing to wave her cigarette authoritatively. "People spy on other people, nations on other nations, governments on citizens, husbands on wives, wives on boyfriends, et cetera. Security cameras are on every city block, in every store, on every elevator. We're a culture of Peeping Toms. This is what we've become. What do you make of that?" She leaned forward to have a last drag of her cigarette and another sip of scotch.

Though impressed by his mother's sometimes astute clarity, Bradley could never tell what she really knew or how she knew it.

Eleanor said: "I gave Karen Jacobs, my friend in New York, a telescope for a housewarming gift. Every night she would spy on the apartment building across the way." Eleanor's left brow rose over a gimlet eye, giving her smile infinitely sly aspects. She put her cigarette out and then, looking up askance at Bradley, a wry expression of guile wavering on her tremulous features, said, "Karen told me that often she would see others in darkened windows holding binoculars or looking through telescopes also."

"I'm sure she saw some memorable sights," Bradley said while shifting nervously in his seat.

His mother, with her inexorable way of instinctively and minutely analyzing her son's body language, was aware of his discomfort and started laughing again, and coughing. Eleanor pursed her lips in the somewhat exaggerated fashion of someone coming to a point and about to dispense wise counsel. "The truth is, Bradley, life seems exotic from a distance, mysteriously resolved and happy. It's like seeing New York at night from an airplane, or how we imagine adulthood when we're children." Eleanor sighed at the thought of happy illusions in her mind and memory. And she had an observation for her son: "You don't believe in the worth of your own life when you think others are having a better time. Tell me, precious, have you been peeping into neighbors' windows? You can tell Mama."

"I have, as a matter of fact. But it's not what you think. And I've been using grandfather's WWII binoculars as an experiment. I took them from the chest at the foot of your bed."

She interrupted a sip of her drink, and shouted: "I knew it was you! You thief! You thought I wouldn't notice." Eleanor expressed petulance but not true anger, annoyance but not recrimination. She had no idea the binoculars had been missing.

"Who else would it be? You don't need them," Bradley said, sipping his wine.

Eleanor laughed, contemplating her drink. There was an understanding between them as among siblings who borrow each other's possessions wantonly and without permission. Bradley's astonishment was only that she knew his secret. Or maybe she had merely guessed.

"Oh, never mind." Eleanor lit another cigarette and took a deep drag on it, exhaling a cloud of smoke. She glanced at her drink, contemplating its remaining volume. Her eyes grew distant again. She shrugged.

"Bradley, you're so extravagant. I know you are a good and moral person underneath."

"Underneath what?"

Eleanor gave him a skeptical look. "Well, you know," she said. And, somewhat beside the present point, she continued: "The pious are ruthless and unforgiving because they suffer so much from guilt."

Bradley saw his mother showing signs he was familiar with, a kind of free-associative ramble as a symptom of growing intoxication. And yet she maintained a loopy coherence throughout. "What are you saying?"

She held her cigarette up to contemplate it. "The pious blame themselves for their thoughts, Bradley. They blame everybody else for their own darkest intentions. Imagine that. Imagine if you blamed everybody else for having your own evil thoughts! Their private suffering makes them insufferable." Eleanor laughed and continued. "There is, you know, a sect of nuns that perform self-flagellation. *Memoirs of a Nun on Fire* describes how, before becoming a poet, Philomene Long spent five years in a convent located in the Santa Monica mountains. The nuns there routinely whipped themselves."

"Maybe they deserved it."

His mother's eyes narrowed, and she looked at her son in unbreathing silence. Then she continued. "The good Sisters of St. Joseph of Carondelet Convent practice what Philomene called *The Discipline* with what she described as 'a very narrow steel chain, about a foot and a half long with a knob at the bottom and many little chains, each with a small ball at the tip.' The nuns called it the Saturday Night Special. After prayers on Saturdays, a required part of convent life was self-flagellation. But you know, the pious are an unforgiving lot, rather stern in their template for salvation. With the nuns, humiliation is their penance, mortification their path to redemption." His mother had an uncanny way of being lucid while seeming incoherent, all the more disconcerting because he didn't know if she was blathering or attempting to make a cagey point.

Bradley rolled his eyes. "Why are you telling me this, Mother?"

Her tongue was thick and visible between her teeth, and she seemed to chew on it until she became motionless and silent, staring at him, all seriousness in her aspect: "I think you should become a nun," she said.

Bradley coughed a laugh. "I don't want to analyze that." He sipped his wine.

Eleanor took a last drag from her cigarette, put it out in the ash tray, and began to laugh throatily, close to a cackle. But laughing made her cough, which made her laugh all the more, until this seizure of hilarity turned her red and threatened to asphyxiate her.

"Are you all right?" Bradley said. He went forward to help her, but she waved him off. She caught her breath and recovered herself, then continued an opaque analysis of her son through tipsy circumlocutions.

"Well, you can't help having thoughts, good or bad, they just occur," Eleanor said, vaguely. Wishing now to change the subject, Bradley said, "Did you hear about the couple who were killed while jogging, down by the Granville Country Tavern Inn?"

"Yes," Eleanor exclaimed. "Adele Rogers called and told me about it. Apparently, it was a bizarre accident, and they were crushed underneath a cement truck." Her eyes turned inward by staring into space. She began addressing a procession of her own thoughts, to which she apostrophized: "How terrible. How really awful."

The parrot began to pace back and forth sideways again, nervously expressing dread while conjugating his next impertinence.

Bradley noticed this and watched with casual interest. "They were neighbors of mine."

"Were you spying on them?"

"The Addisons live below me. I can see their house from mine. John Addison perished with Maggie Hawkins. Evidently, they were having an affair. She's the wife of the writer Nelson Hawkins."

"You haven't answered me," said Eleanor, with suspicion again. She looked askance at her son with narrowing eyes and said, "My binoculars! Oh, Bradley, why can't you be like other people and mind your own business?"

He laughed out loud. "Is that what other people do?"

"Well." She looked away, and her lips formed into a smile.

"It wasn't what you think," he offered defensively.

"What exactly do I think?" Her eyes fell on the bird again, strutting on the top of his cage and blinking, his gray feathers smooth and then ruffled and then smooth again as if he had thoughts on the matter also.

"It's not strictly looking through a window," Bradley insisted, articulate in his rationalizations. "It's as though I become an audience almost inadvertently, an audience of one witnessing the unfolding of a story telling itself in real time. It's still telling itself."

"Yes Bradley, it's called life—other people's life. It belongs to them, just as you have your own and it belongs to you. It is *not* a play or a film. It's their story, and frankly, I don't think they would appreciate your participation in it, passively or otherwise."

"Do you think it's a bad thing to do? Jimmy Stewart did it in *Rear Window*," Bradley argued.

"And Norman Bates did it in *Psycho*," Eleanor countered. In her heart of hearts, Eleanor was agnostic about nearly everything, but with a mother's concern for her child, she wanted to believe in the best.

"At first it was titillating, I'll admit it. I'm normal in my response to certain things."

"Normal. That's my boy," she said, seizing on the word, twitching her lip as if her nose itched. She leaned forward to rest her latest cigarette on the lip of the ash tray.

"One night I watched the four of them having dinner together. Two couples. I could see the stolen glances, the flirting and kissing and touching of each other secretly, and it was like a play, and there didn't seem to be anything wrong with watching."

"Detectives get paid to watch other people. You're not a detective. But there's a thought!" She sat up slightly. "Men who admire feet become shoe salesmen! No one suspects their fetish. You could find a profession for your obsession." Amused at the rhyming wit of her remark, Eleanor had a celebratory sip of scotch.

"As a matter of fact, I was down at police headquarters recently, talking to a detective," Bradley told her.

Eleanor looked at him with sudden concern. "What are you going to tell me?"

"A woman was murdered."

"Yes, I know. But oh, dear God, Bradley, you don't know anything about a murder, do you?"

"No, no. Her name was Ann Wheeler. A cable man found her dead at her home, about a month ago. I went to her memorial service."

"You bring me such pleasant news from the world. Has anyone been hanged in the town square recently?"

"Not that I know of."

"Bradley, I — " She interrupted herself when she realized she was down to the ice in her drink. "Would you freshen my cocktail? There's a good boy."

"Certainly, Mother," Bradley replied. He picked up her drink and left the room.

Eleanor, now alone, sat back in her divan, closed her eyes and, forgetting that Bradley was out of the room, continued talking as though he were still in front of her: "Why do you do it? It's unseemly. It's not legal, either."

"Mother," the bird said in a striking simulacrum of Bradley's voice, beseeching.

"And you could be arrested. Really, Bradley, why not take up a hobby? Learn to play golf. Hit things with a stick and get whatever it is out of your system."

"Mother," said the bird again.

"Don't interrupt me, Bradley. Listen to your mother. Collect coins! Do you know a 1913 buffalo nickel sold recently for over two million dollars? There were three. Find the others."

"Mother."

"Join the YMCA."

"YMCA."

"No, disregard that. Christians and their dreary repressions. Religion is a swindle, son, I've always said that. And even if I haven't, it is how fools fear death. Most people are boring, Bradley. They have dreadful little lives. So why do you peer into their windows? What gilding do you give to their squalor? How are their dreams less broken than yours or mine? What gives them elegance in your mind? Well, my son, Mother will tell you. All of it is in you, comes from inside you, Bradley, from your own life's longing for itself. You're a romantic. Do you see how it is? I make no judgment, but like any mother I want you to be happy."

"Mother." The bird's voice had now a declarative inflection.

"I know, Bradley, you don't want to listen. But you must keep your head and choose your relationships wisely, not as some fantastic goal. Engage life as it is. There is nothing to immunize you from heartbreak or average disappointments. Somebody else's window is not the path. Paint a picture, Bradley, write a book, travel to Zanzibar. Discover what there is to learn in the real adventures of life. Carpe diem!"

She held her finger up like a proper schoolmarm as Bradley entered the room holding a glass brimming with scotch. He had heard only her last bit of advice and said, "Excuse me?"

Eleanor opened her eyes and looked at him reprovingly. "Haven't you heard a word I've said?"

"Mother, I've been getting your cocktail."

"What?"

"Mother," said the bird, strutting crabwise, its talons wrapped tightly on the top of the bamboo cage. They looked at it together.

"Mother," it said again.

38

"Well, it's very embarrassing."

"Therapy is the process of confronting uncomfortable thoughts by sharing them, Bradley."

Bradley was silent.

"Remember our agreement," Dr. Singer said. "Absolute honesty."

Bradley sighed. "I'm shy about telling you."

"No embarrassment, Bradley. Disclosure without judgment."

Following a period of silence, Bradley's animated thumbs indicated deliberation, and then he said, softly, "I think I'm in love with you, Dr. Singer."

Good for you, she thought.

Bradley's analysis had reached a flash point. His disengagement from obsession was beginning to take place, this peeling of the onion, so to speak, differentiating what was real and imaginary in his emotional objects. His unpacked feelings were authentic and good and capable of redirection. The truth he could not yet see: Bradley, at last, was falling in love—with himself.

"Let's talk about it," Dr. Singer said with perfect cool. "When did you begin to have these feelings?"

"About a month ago, when I started to think about your life."

"What about my life?"

"What you do. How you live."

"Bradley, you don't know about my life."

"I know." Bewilderment embarrassed him. He sounded to himself like a fool.

"Let's talk about love."

"What about it?"

"You say you are in love with me."

"It feels like love."

"Does it feel like what you felt looking at Grace Addison through her window?"

"I guess it does. But that was different."

"I understand. But do you think that looking through her window was a way to get to know her, a way to develop a real relationship?"

"No."

"Do you think that looking through my window would give any greater satisfaction to feelings you say you now have for me?"

"Probably not."

And yet Bradley was imagining Dr. Singer's soft features, her commanding height, her intelligent demeanor and sexual appeal, the gray cotton dress she was now wearing, her scent, faint as memory but charged with intention. His mind began to spin imagined possibilities (her breasts, the rounds of her ass. Shameful!).

"We are here to find the truth of things as they are, not as we might wish them to be." Dr. Singer spoke in a neutral way that expressed cold facts. "You must understand how a picture of food is not the same thing as food, and that watching someone else eat can't satisfy your hunger. You and I have a relationship, but it is a very special clinical relationship. You share with me your most intimate details, but it remains the relationship of a doctor to a patient. A doctor might ask a patient to disrobe for treatment, but you can appreciate how that is very different than disrobing for sex."

"I like the way you look." Bradley again felt like a fool.

"Thank you, Bradley." Dr. Singer laughed. "I like the way you look. And I think it is admirable that you've made a commitment to therapy. Many can't do it. These feelings you have, by the way, are predictable. I want you to know, and eventually to appreciate, that love is part of the process of psychoanalysis."

"How is that?"

"Where there is trust, affection, admiration, and communication, there is love. Each component can be broken down into parts. Admiration and communication can, when appropriate, include sex, et cetera, and affection can include respect, integrity, and empathy. People fall in love when they tell each other about their feelings, hopes, and aspirations, but it's a two-way street. Life, love, friendship, these are not solitary endeavors. We are made to share feelings. Maybe now you are becoming aware of how isolating your pleasures had become."

"But are you saying that I have these feelings for you because I tell you about myself?"

"The short answer is yes. Analysis is like a small but fertile garden with richly authentic aspects that remain confidential and strictly clinical. You might think of analysis as a simulator, a testing ground for emotions."

"So if I want someone to fall in love with me, I should just listen to them?"

"You might try it. It's a good starting point."

Bradley laughed but remained intrigued. "I will."

Dr. Singer decided to carefully use his disclosure as a teachable moment and summarize his progress. "Bradley, our job here is to make a little of what was unconscious conscious, to enable you to see how defectively you moved through adolescence, pursuing your mother by means of her clothing, standing back from normalized relations with girls and later with women, falling into reclusive habits with emotional exaggerations and substitute gratifications that gave you no real satisfaction."

A long silence ensued. Dr. Singer let it go on for nearly a minute, hoping what she'd said was not too much. "Try to tell me what you're thinking."

"I don't think I'm thinking about anything at all."

"We are always thinking, Bradley. Remember? Something in your mind is being held back right at this moment."

Bradley's eyes were closed, and he had the giddy sensation that children lying on their backs have of falling into the sky. He realized that his thoughts were centered around a specific dream. It was on the night he was arrested, and the dream content was an alarming mystery. "I'm thinking about a dream."

"Tell me about the dream," said Dr. Singer.

Bradley fell silent for several moments and then overcame his resistance. "I was witnessing an exhumation of body parts by policemen. The parts were wrapped in clear plastic. Then I was aware that I had committed the murder myself many years before and had got away with it. Nobody knew. But now I had remembered, and the memory would force me to live as a pariah."

"No one else in the dream learned what you had done?"

"No. It just occurred to me as I watched. Nobody else knew."

"Do you know the identity of the victim in the dream?"

"No, I don't think I do. Or rather, maybe I do, but I've forgotten." There was a long pause. As the silence continued, Bradley struggled with the answer until, like fog lifting, repression broke. The identity of the dismembered corpse emerged not as a mystery in the least, but as something he'd known all the while, a characteristic of analysis he'd observed time and again when something unconscious at last was revealed: "Actually, it was my mother."

"Let's talk about repression," Dr. Singer said. "Some repressions are inherited. For example, the incest taboo is communicated generation to generation. Sexual desire continues to exist, but, because the incest taboo is repressed in the unconscious, we don't know about it. Does that make sense to you?"

"Yes, I suppose so."

"Follow me on this, Bradley: repressed desire even slightly felt would naturally create acute anxiety. A person might wish to destroy the cause of such painful, confusing feelings. Furthermore, a person under the spell of such feelings might manifest his confusion in ways that would disguise to himself the true object, displacing it. This can happen in varying degrees."

"Was cross-dressing calculated to make me feel closer to my mother in a roundabout erotic way?"

"Yes. Gold Star! Do you see how conflicting desires, even when they're unconscious, continue to exist simultaneously as a compromise?"

"I think so."

"Peering through windows was a similar imperfect attempt to have an intimate relationship. You are going through a change in perception that will free you to experience more direct and appropriate satisfactions. What you should begin to appreciate is that your feeling of love for me, while impossible to circumstances, is nevertheless the projection of someone capable of loving. You have created *me* from the whole cloth of *you*. You will soon meet a woman waiting to receive the rich fund of love that has been waiting for a way out."

"How can you tell?"

"You now have love to share. You just told me about it. You will soon find a more suitable object for that love."

"How can you be sure?"

"Because I'm six hundred steps ahead of you."

39

Wind-driven fat raindrops made the windows opaque, and the world outside became an indistinct blur. Bradley enjoyed the spectacle from his deck. He was thinking about what Dr. Singer had said about love and human connection while noticing a squall approach rapidly from the southwest. The sky darkened, and Bradley moved inside as low clouds brought sudden heavy rain.

In the swift passing of the storm, Bradley found parallels to his analysis—relentless rain was like obsession, the world opaque through rain-smeared windows of unclear emotions. The trailing edge of the squall moved across the northeastern sky, and it got lighter and the wind dropped off. The sun returned quite suddenly, and the rain stopped. Everything glistened in wet, fresh brilliance and new clear light. Bradley finished his beer and thought about what he should do next. Restless for outside, he went out on the deck and looked down at the lake. Deciding to go to the beach, he set out to stroll. He strode down the steep traverse. Leaves and twigs lay in runnels along the road. The sweet smell of lake and blossom came to him. When he passed Grace Addison's house, it seemed unfamiliar. Farther down, Nelson Hawkins's now empty home had a For Sale sign in front of it. Change had come in the aftermath of tragedy. He walked down the road to East Beach below.

He sat on a bench at the beach where the garden club had planted an array of daisies near a sandy patch. As Bradley watched the boaters and bathers resume their outdoor activities, his mind was using the beauty of the scene as a distraction from meditations he was not aware of having. His brain was quite active while seeming empty of thoughts. He was daydreaming.

A voice startled him.

"I've seen you," someone said from behind.

He turned around, surprised by a young woman close at his back. He had not heard her approach and had not sensed her presence. She had high cheekbones and blue Germanic eyes, rather girlish breasts under a thin cotton shirt, a young woman with blond hair cut shorter than suited her broad face, and a pleasant smile. She was a neighbor.

"I live over there in the gray house." She pointed in the direction of her home. "I've seen you walking past before. I saw you walk by, and I thought I'd come out and say hello."

"Yes, I, ah, I-I live around here, too. I … that is … after the storm, I thought I'd take a walk."

Although surprised, Bradley was pleased. Her intrusion came at a propitious moment, breaking the stream of his unconscious thoughts. He came out of abstraction and discovered himself to be glad of her interest and not at all resistant to her company.

"I'm Brenda, Brenda Robbins."

"I'm Bradley. Davis. I live up the road."

"I know where you live. Sunrise Lane. In the red house with the porch that hangs over the side."

"How do you know?"

"We're neighbors. Everybody knows where everybody else lives, more or less. You look in my window sometimes."

Appalled, Bradley blanched. "You must be mistaking me …"

"I waved to you. But you probably didn't see me. You were walking."

"Wait, I do remember seeing you," he said, recalling the moment she alluded to, about two weeks earlier. "You were watching television." He had wanted to wave back but, self-consciously fearing to seem untoward, continued on without acknowledging her.

"Why didn't you wave?"

"I didn't want you to think I was looking in at you or anything." The conversation seemed stranded as Bradley tried to deflect prurient notions which mainly existed in his own mind. But Brenda didn't seem to care at all. Her eyes shone with friendly humor, smiling in the sun. She had bright white teeth, a quite attractive smile, and she was smart, street smart, Bradley thought, though he couldn't say why that seemed so. Also, she was not shy. Confidence is an admirable trait. He wanted to be unafraid like that. He said, "You've got nice eyes."

Brenda began blinking like a silent movie starlet in a humorous way for exaggerated effect. Then she said: "Hey, I'm bored. Do you know why I'm bored?"

"Why?"

"Because the storm was exciting."

"The storm was exciting and that's why you're bored?" Bradley found himself enjoying her somewhat oblique manner. "Why don't you go for a swim?"

"I like to look at the lake, Bradley, not swim in it. Germs. Do you swim in the lake?"

"Not really. I'm on top of the ridge, so I mainly look down at it."

"Maybe I'll come up sometime, and we can look at the lake together from your house."

"Well, I-I mean, sure. Sometime. Give me your email."

But Brenda was not shy. "Let's go now. Unless you're busy. You're bored too, I can tell."

As a matter of fact, he was bored, but he was used to his own company, and it wasn't at all clear that spending time with Brenda Robbins was a desirable alternative. But giving weight to Dr. Singer's entreaty to

open his life to living others, Bradley made a conscious effort to overcome resistance to Brenda's manner and said, "Well, you can walk with
me back up the hill if you like." The words were out before he had rather
not spoken them.

"Great," Brenda said. Her eyes got big with enthusiasm.

Bradley's resistance was softening. They left the beach and walked
together up the transverse of ascending roads. Spending a few minutes
with Brenda won't hurt, he thought as they started out.

A smell of earth was strong in the air, a musk of things dying or coming to life. Bradley was slightly over six feet tall and Brenda was a foot
shorter. They made an odd couple walking up the street, not only for
their difference in size but because each had a unique gait. Brenda had
a kind of step-and-a-half skipping canter that made her look energetic,
enthusiastic, even childish. Bradley loped. Oddly enough though, they
seemed suited as they went.

"I love storms," Brenda said, frisking beside Bradley. "It's like a dream
when it rains."

"A lot of rain came down," Bradley said, stunned at the banality of his
comment, how he sounded like a yokel.

They passed the For Sale sign on the Hawkins residence Bradley had
seen earlier.

"Did you know John Addison or Maggie Hawkins?" Brenda said.

"Yes, I did."

"You know what happened, right? I mean the accident."

Bradley nodded.

Brenda grew animated. "I'm a nurse at the hospital. I was on morgue
duty that day. Grace was there to make a positive ID. She started to faint
on the elevator. I took care of her. She's a very nice person."

It made sense to Bradley that Brenda was a nurse. She had those per-
sonable qualities and an instinctive strong-spirited courage about things.

They continued walking, around the switchback and up toward the
Addison house, turning left onto Bradley's ascending road. The ground
was already dry, and the sun was bright and strong. When they got to

the top of the hill, which was flat along the ridge, Bradley's small red cottage came into view.

Brenda pointed to it and shouted, "That's your house."

Bradley turned to look at her, wondering if he'd made a mistake to let Brenda walk with him. It seemed necessary to ask her in, which he knew answered a perfectly normal expectation. One part of him wanted solitude, while an opposite impulse was responsive to her engaged manner.

"May I come in?" she said.

"Well, I—"

"Aw, come on. I don't bite."

For reasons he vaguely assigned to his mother (but in fact had more to do with his analysis), Bradley seemed incapable of resisting Brenda's imperative nature. He invited her in and took her to his outside deck. The chairs were still slightly wet, so he got a towel from the pile of laundry on the floor in his linen closet. He dried the chairs and when she was seated asked her if she'd like something to drink.

"Do you have any Châteauneuf-du-Pape? Maybe a South American Malbec, a California Pinot, or perhaps a bottle of Cristal?"

"How about a beer?"

"Sure."

She made him laugh.

In a few minutes they were sitting together in the afternoon sun looking out at the broad expanse of the lake to the south and west, drinking lager. Bradley pointed out the Addison house below.

"I used to see Maggie jogging past my house," Brenda said, recalling the tragedy. "I knew her to say hi. She ran a lot. She ran marathons."

Some impulse of the moment seized him suddenly.

"Actually," he said, pointing down again so she could see the house directly below. "I watched them sometimes with my grandfather's brass binoculars on a tripod."

"You watched them?"

"The way people in the city watch each other," he said, recalling his mother's benign-sounding account of her friend. "It's like a silent movie of people in their lives." He didn't mention his more strategic perch on the ledge.

"No way."

"It's like standing next to them as an invisible man."

Brenda Robbins jumped in her seat like a little girl ready for a treat. "Can I see? Where are they?"

"What?"

"The binoculars. I want to look through them too."

"There's nothing to see."

"I can look across the lake."

Responding tentatively with a shrug, Bradley got up and went into his bedroom and got the binoculars and the tripod and set it up in the living room. He aimed at a house across the lake.

Brenda looked through them. "You are *so* right. Wow. This is *so* sick."

"Excuse me?"

"Fun!"

"Is that what 'sick' means?"

"Of course. Silly man."

Idiomatically challenged, Bradley felt suddenly staid. Brenda's eyes were pressed to the binoculars as Bradley noticed her derriere, robustly visible beneath thin white cotton shorts she was wearing.

"I can see them in the yard. It's like I'm there."

"I told you."

Even at that great distance, the magnifying lenses brought people standing around a barbecue into sharp focus. As Brenda leaned into the lenses for a better view, Bradley was staring at her bottom, his imagination ranging. And then, almost shockingly, Brenda turned around and said, "Have you seen people having sex?"

Bradley stepped backward, as though from his own thoughts. "What?"

"Naked people. People having sex. Have you seen them doing it? Isn't that what you really hope to see?"

Her question seemed guileless, but Bradley, with all the sanctimony of the reformed, felt offended at the inference. "They might not appreciate it," he cautioned, advocate of privacy, moral parameters, and erotic restraint.

"If they leave their shades open, they're inviting anyone to look in!" said Brenda, demon of wicked intention. He understood she was being facetious.

"How would you feel if someone were watching you?" said Bradley, smiling inwardly while maintaining a façade of probity, devil's advocate to his own rationalizations.

"Great, if that's what I was into. People are into different things."

Bradley shook his head. He knew that if on the one hand she was goading him, on the other she shrewdly comprehended him. He didn't know what to think, but he liked her attention.

Head glued to the binoculars once more, Brenda began to chuckle at the sight of new targets for scrutiny on a beach farther down the lake. All at once she turned around to address him directly. "I know you're passive, Bradley. What makes it good is I'm active. And I'm a nurse. I've seen everything, and I have no inhibitions. And you know what they say."

"Okay, what do they say?"

"I'll tell you later."

She started laughing at her own thin, taunting joke. Brenda sensed Bradley's wry humor and also that he was wounded somehow. She astutely disarmed his inhibitions and made him laugh. Bradley felt happy. Brenda knew already what Bradley was only dimly aware of: they were a match.

"So, what do you think," she said, stepping away from the telescope.

"About what?"

"About everything. May I have another beer?"

"How about a glass of Châteauneuf-du-Pape?"

"Do you really have some?"

Bradley pulled the bottle from a cupboard above the sink and held it up expansively, tilting his head, scrutinizing the label. "We're down to the merely exceptional."

Brenda laughed richly as he got two wine glasses from a cabinet in the corner of the kitchen. They happened to be beautiful glasses, and she noticed. Brenda had deep appreciation for expressions of good taste. Bradley observed her approval.

40

Over the summer, the titular Mr. and Mrs. Fisher discovered the depth and breadth of their feelings for each other. They were emotionally wider and deeper than they had supposed. In confiding conversation, Grace described to Nelson the ebbing of tenderness in her marriage to John, her retreat into a private world of smaller expectations. A nonspecific sadness pervaded her married life. Nelson told Grace what was good and bad in his relationship with Maggie. They talked through what had happened. Both were honest. They talked about ambivalent feelings, about survivor's guilt. They shared the sense of betrayal and abandonment and discussed the place of chance in fate. They talked about the fragility of life, the importance of love, the dread of loneliness, and the inevitability of decline and death. They discussed whether or not their dreams had failed, deciding that together they had the will and resilience to keep dreaming. Most importantly, they at last found comfort in perhaps the only other person on earth who could understand the nuances of their particular experience. They found clarification, and they became devoted to each other. Slowly, skies cleared on their horizon, and it was no surprise that love came to them.

Nelson was meeting Grace for lunch. He sat at a table waiting for her to arrive from her attorney's office. As their relationship found its footing, Grace and Nelson had financial matters to resolve. Certain fiduciary concerns had to be explained to her by someone knowledgeable. As sole beneficiary of John's estate, all of her deceased husband's business contracts, property titles, stocks, and cash were catalogued to be explained to her in depth for disbursement or inclusion into trusts.

"Your portfolio is rather complicated," her attorney had told Grace. He asked her to come to his office. The attorney walked Grace through John's finances, the deeds and debt structures of numerous holdings, public notification requirements, pending zoning judgments, depreciation schedules, liabilities, and the whole drab process of law and taxes which had to be addressed with her authorization.

Nelson's worst fear for Grace was that John's businesses carried unanticipated debt or had some other costly entanglement. Further, John's reputation with women was widely known. What if a girlfriend or love child was revealed? As Nelson waited for Grace to join him for lunch, he wondered what she might have discovered. He felt relief then when Grace arrived in a buoyant mood.

Elegant in a tight blue sweater and flowing white slacks, broad-brimmed straw hat and sunglasses, she looked gorgeous and ebullient. When she sat down, she could hardly ¬contain herself. "I have news," she said, kissing him. Nelson ordered a bottle of champagne for brunch. "We may need two bottles," she said.

"What did you learn?"

Agitated with excitement, Grace said, "When I got to his office, Jack—Jack Epstein, my attorney—was sitting behind piles of paper, documents in folders mostly, stacks of them. He reviewed reports with me, one by one. It was a little overwhelming. I didn't know where he was leading me until he finally summarized the estate, and he said, 'Your husband was very creative with his business interests.'

"I'll read what he read to me." She took an envelope from her purse. It was a summary of assets her attorney had read to her about John's portfolio:

"'He financed the purchase of fifteen properties through an entity called the Mad River Trust. He did this by making interest-free loans to the trust, which offered tax advantages at the outset. Some of the money was his; the rest came from hedge-fund investors through a real-estate firm they owned. They were brought in as partners with an understanding that John's construction company would contract to refurbish or tear down the older structures and rebuild new units on desirable waterfront properties in eastern Connecticut and Rhode Island. It proved a successful strategy. Now as to what you have inherited: The worth of the commercial and private properties, with the assessment of future earnings as a bonus plus a two-million-dollar accidental-death insurance policy added to the assets from the business—'

"Then he stopped reading and looked up at me." Grace paused, as the attorney had. "I thought he was about to give me bad news. He started moving papers around, and I thought, Oh God, he doesn't know how to break it to me, and it can't be good. I didn't dare move. Finally, he said, 'Grace, I'm here to report that your financial inheritance, that is to say your net assets after taxes, are slightly under thirty million dollars and rising.'"

"How much?" Nelson said.

Grace held up a summary paper. "It says right here—29,859,323 dollars at the end of the last quarter." She leaned forward in her seat, shaking her head, and then laughed out loud and quickly put her hand to her mouth to suppress the laugh. "I don't mean to be light about any of this, impertinent or disrespectful toward John or Maggie, but Nelson, this is unbelievable. I had no idea. I don't know what to think. I'm in shock. And he drove that red Cadillac and fuck-awful rusted brown pickup truck!"

"It's unreal," Nelson said and puffed his cheeks in exhalation of surprise and mystification.

Grace continued. "The look on my face! And he told me, Epstein did, that current tax codes have put a moratorium on estate taxes, so there is no continuing liability. 'Congratulations, Grace,' he said. 'You are officially a very wealthy woman.'"

"And look at this." Grace opened her briefcase. She pulled out survey maps and photographs with titles to lands and homes that John had acquired.

Nelson looked them over, surprised at John's systematic development in targeted communities and the success of that strategy over time. He had quietly built an empire. But, unexpectedly, the news also unsettled Nelson. Money has no qualities, as he'd told Maggie, but it was a catalyst for many good and bad things in human nature. Decisions on new matters would be a litmus test of character, presenting a new challenge of choices.

"You won't change, will you?" Nelson said.

"I was going to ask you the same thing."

Grace put on dark glasses against the bright golden sunlight. She put on her hat too, the wide floppy straw hat so stylish on her. Nelson held up his glass, and they toasted a solemn acknowledgment with their eyes. Then Grace reached across the table and took his hand into hers in an effort to comprehend and assimilate the uncommon fate which had befallen them.

41

Alice Carpenter lived near the train tracks. Her home was about a mile down from where she worked at On the Beach. She sat in her living-room chair with a book in her lap, a glass of wine beside her, and the TV on with the sound off. A freight train passed by, the rhythmic click-clack of wheels on rails somehow consoling. As she gazed out at the train, she daydreamed about her army days, and how war changes human beings. Her thoughts were inspired by the silent television images in front of her: gunfire, men crouching behind cars shooting at each other. She changed the channel. An old Western movie featured more gunfire, cowboys shooting revolvers from saddles. Alice had seen soldiers killed in Iraq, and she had killed the enemy in firefights. Her thoughts drifted to speculation about Ann Wheeler and her assailant on the night she was murdered. She had invited the killer into her home. She must have known him. Were they lovers? When did she know she was in trouble?

Former Master Sergeant Alice Carpenter eyed her pistol in its holster hanging on a coat hook by the front door. The day her compound came under assault, a comrade standing next to her was felled by a sniper's bullet to the heart. Why him and not her was an unanswerable question. She remembered shock at the onset but none at the end. Adrenalin instantly turned fear into action. She fought furiously and survived. Her comrade killed that day was dead forever, and contemplating it brought no purpose to any of it, nor reason, and the passage of time made it worse. War never left you.

Thoughtful by nature and frugal by habit, Alice had a practical sense; after she left the army, in place of orders came choice, in place of certitude, questioning, and she grew in new ways. A military pension on top of the money she made managing and bartending at the Beach provided her more than enough to live comfortably. And she was comfortable. She could say with conviction that she was nearly happy! Her new independence was a state of mind that valued life. "I will fight no more forever," she said out loud, quoting Chief Joseph. Alice Carpenter, master sergeant and hardened veteran of foreign wars, honored and retired, was a pacifist. The train whistle sounded its fade into pathos and silence.

42

Nelson walked south down Central Park West, where uniformed doormen standing in lobbies looked like gatekeepers in Oz. His step was brisk. Cutting through the park at West 72nd Street in front of the Dakota, he strode at a good pace past Strawberry Fields, where the IMAGINE mosaic was decorated with flowers. Guitarists strummed for tourists who paused to honor the memory of John Lennon. Down a slight hill past the statue of Henry Clay and along the lake to the Bethesda Fountain, tall American elm trees lined the Literary Walk promenade where it began at the Naumberg Bandshell. Benches lined the walk. An origami artist was selling her paper animals. A trumpet man played cool jazz. In front of bronze Shakespeare, a violinist was playing the beautiful and dreamy "Romance" from the Shostakovich *Gadfly Suite*, somehow perfect in the moment. He was headed toward Fifth Avenue to pick up the wedding ring he'd ordered for Grace.

From where he now stood, Nelson could see the Plaza Hotel just beyond the southeast corner of the park. He went down past the Wollman

Rink and up to the horse-drawn hansom cabs along 59th Street. He walked across the street to the Oak Bar at the Plaza Hotel. Inside, the murals on the walls depicted people arriving in fierce snowstorms to that welcoming sense of sanctuary and sustenance before them. Waiters were dutiful in their attentions; customers felt prosperous, sheltered, and well served in a scene of New York to inspire a Gershwin rhapsody. Nelson ordered a brandy and surveyed the room with pleasure. New York gave him that good feeling you had about yourself for being there. No other city had that voltage. He could spend an afternoon happily reading and drinking here. On a ring mission today, however, he finished his brandy and continued down Fifth Avenue, past the windows at Bergdorf Goodman, Van Cleef & Arpels, to Harry Winston, a store famous for diamonds. Nelson pressed the door button and was buzzed inside. The high ceilings and bright light suggested a vault designed to look like a retail store.

A man approached him with a wide smile. "Good afternoon, Mr. Hawkins. Please be seated. We have your ring ready. I'll bring it to you."

He was led to a chair in a cubicle, and in a moment the manager returned and handed Nelson a dark blue box. When opened, a diamond ring sparkled on a mound of blue velour. He plucked it out and held it to the light—noble ice, clear as arctic air. The manager stood by ceremoniously as Nelson examined the diamond in its setting: four facets stood for Love, Duty, Faith, and Devotion, a rock upon which a life together can be built.

"It's beautiful," he said. He put the ring into its box again and slipped the box into his pocket. The manager escorted Nelson to the main floor. "Thank you," Nelson said, bowing slightly at the door. He continued his walk down Fifth Avenue.

At the Rockefeller Center Promenade, he looked down at golden Prometheus holding fire above ice at the skating rink. From there he walked north to 55th Street and crossed Fifth Avenue. At the St. Regis Hotel, uniformed doormen stood in front of the classical brass and glass taxi stand. They nodded to him as he went inside. Just beyond was the colorful King Cole Bar, with its eponymous Maxfield Parrish mural. The path to the bar took him past a harpist playing Puccini variations. From a quiet corner opposite the bar, Nelson sat and thought about Grace and their future together. He took the blue box out of his pocket and put it on the table. He studied it for a moment, and then then opened it to see the ring again. As he held it between his thumb and forefinger, the diamond drew in the ambient light and began to shine. The facets sparkled.

A young woman had been watching him from the bar. Curious, she stood and approached where he sat, and when Nelson looked up she was standing in front of him, smiling. In her style of dress, she was slightly too formal, and in her attractive ways of moving, too easy, too familiar; if she wasn't a lady of the evening, she was a woman of the afternoon.

"That's beautiful," she said of the sparkling diamond ring Nelson held in front of him. "For someone special?"

"Very special."

"Congratulations. How long have you been in love?" The question was impertinent, but Nelson knew the professional in her was not part of this conversation.

"From the moment she showed me who she was."

"Well, good luck," the young woman said, smiling broadly.

"Good luck to you too," Nelson said. She turned and, with a certain amount of theatrical poise, went back to the bar. For a brief instant, Nelson, the novelist, glimpsed her soul. She was a gorgeous creature of the jungle, not yet saved or damned, caught in a context of easy virtue and personal adventure, a young beauty in the Big City balancing the burdens of youth, feminine allure, money, ambition, independence, triumph, failure, and ruin. All of these qualities and possibilities stood before her against the press of time. Young if not innocent, she had no sense of the hurricane yet to bear down with furious and fatal indifference to her youthful expectations. But that storm had not yet formed. Her smile sang brightly and her eyes sparkled, canary in the coal mine of her own dark excursions. Nelson wondered if anyone would be there when her world began to give way.

43

Dr. Singer felt Bradley's analysis was moving in a positive direction. She saw the architecture of his troubled mind: Bradley needed love that his mother couldn't offer, and the images he had of his absent father were vague and confused. False enchantments of peeping and the artificial atonements of Mistress Angela had debased his essentially sound nature with erotic fixations and penitential humiliations. Dr. Singer suspected some trauma behind such acting out. As she was having that thought, she heard Bradley open the door to her waiting room. When he was on the couch, hands folded and eyes closed in his accustomed supine analytic posture, Dr. Singer began a deeper probe of his derailment.

"Today I'd like to talk a little more about Father Jim. At a crucial time in your life, he paid a great deal of attention to you. Have you given that period some thought?" Dr. Singer asked. Bradley lay mute and motionless for a long moment, silence connoting repression noted by the doctor.

"At first it was normal."

Bradley was struggling with something. The psychiatrist was silent. She waited. After perhaps thirty seconds of silence, Bradley began to tell a new story.

"There was an inner circle of boys, favorites of Father Jim."

"Tigers, you said."

"We were aware of those who were close to him and those who were not. I wanted to be in the group of favorites. In all the time I spent with him, even when he let me drive his car, I had not been invited to join that group. I thought it had something to do with my age. But anyway, one night I was invited to where he lived—"

"The rectory."

"Yes, the rectory. I stayed with him for dinner, and afterwards he proposed a ritual."

Dr. Singer leaned forward. "What sort of ritual?"

"He called it an initiation, an initiation to make me one of the chosen boys. He wanted us to believe that we were part of a secret society, like a fraternity, but there was an initiation everyone had to go through."

"Had others you knew gone through this initiation?"

"They had, but no one talked about it, because it was secret."

"How did he propose it to you?"

They had spent a day visiting museums in New York, touring the halls and galleries of the Metropolitan. The Edward Hopper paintings were Bradley's favorites, with their outlier loneliness and voyeurism. He was taken also by the Rodin figures in the sculpture garden, not only *The Thinker*, summarizing the evolution of man with its philosopher's skullcap hair above a Neanderthal brow, but also *The Burghers of Calais* with their tethered giant hands and feet. Balzac's enormous and mighty figure was also impressive. Father Capehart told Bradley that Balzac had been modeled from a naked figure holding his erection to symbolize creative passion. Rodin had thrown a coat over the model, deciding finally to cast the French realist as an image of implied creative energy. By the time they got back from New York, it was eight p.m. Bradley was tired and would rather have gone home, but Father Capehart invited him to stay for dinner. Because the boy thought the priest might be lonely for company, he agreed.

"Would you like a rum cocktail?" Father Capehart said.

"No thanks."

"Are you sure?" Father Capehart held up a bottle of Mount Gay. "You're almost fifteen. When I was your age, I had a false ID, a false driver's license, and I drove around an old jalopy I bought for fifty dollars from a dying man on my paper route."

Bradley noticed that Father Capehart's regular-guy references seemed rooted in small frauds but allowed that, because he was a priest, maybe minor moral misdemeanors seemed larger to a lay presumption of piety.

Father Capehart had taken off his jacket and shoes and was now relaxed, settled into his familiar rooms. "Do you mind if I have a cocktail?"

"No," Bradley said, wondering why Father Capehart should ask him at all.

"Make yourself comfortable. Would you like a coke or a glass of water?"

"Water, thank you."

Bradley sat on the couch. Father Capehart put music on, a quiet jazz of some sort, while Bradley absorbed the atmosphere. The rectory was dark and old-fashioned. The walls were paneled in wood. There was a large pewter crucifix above the fireplace. It was rather fancifully ornate. The Christ figure's outstretched arms nailed to the cross presented the spectacle of cruel death comprehensively. Bradley understood the crucifix as consistent with Catholic themes of punishment, repentance, and redemption. (While the cross as a symbol seemed right to Catholics, if a modern religion were to be founded on execution, he doubted whether an electric chair would work equally well as a pendant on a necklace.) There were other sanctifying artifacts and impliments of adoration related to the mass: the silver chalice, the gold paten, the radiant monstrance of transubstantiation, the fine crystal cruets of the lavabo, and those meticulous liturgical robes of lace and silk (and the bishop's hat, the cardinal's ring), all finely wrought material representations of Catholic religiosity.

Father Capehart returned with his cocktail and a glass of water for Bradley. Bradley leaned forward on the couch to take the water while Father Capehart stirred his rum drink with a swizzle stick from the Yale Club.

"Make yourself comfortable," he said again, sitting back in his chair, smiling. "Tell me about your girlfriends."

"I don't have any girlfriends."

Father Capehart laughed. "Well, you will. And then I'll see you in confession." He laughed again.

"I don't go to confession."

The priest leaned forward in his seat. "You should, Bradley. Confession is good for the soul. You'll feel less burdened, less guilty."

"I don't really feel any of that." This was true. Vigorously onanistic but technically chaste, Bradley was curious but rarely felt guilty. In any case, he was not inclined to share intimate personal information with any adult, especially a priest.

"If you don't feel burdened by sin, it's probably because you haven't had opportunities that would necessitate absolution."

"What is absolution, exactly?"

"Absolution is God's forgiveness, which allows you to get into heaven."

"Can't I get there just by praying?" Bradley was being facetious. Heaven was a foolish fairy tale to him. He didn't believe in any of it and was shocked that anyone did.

"You could. But confession is a sacrament, Bradley, created by God to assist us on our path to grace. It's worth receiving the benefits."

"Do you go to confession?"

"I do. And so does the pope."

Father Capehart began to tap his foot, as though deliberating some matter and weighing choices. He put his glass down and sat back in the chair. Then he leaned forward suddenly. "Bradley, I've decided to initiate you into a select group I call Tigers."

"Tigers?"

"Tigers are special. Tigers are strong and loyal. They are obedient."

It seemed that Father Capehart was asking him to be on a team. Bradley would instinctively resist any insinuation that he join the priesthood. Priests weren't allowed to have sex, which was something Bradley greatly wanted to experience but had yet been unable to manage, except by himself.

"Do you remember when we went to the soup kitchen to feel the homeless?"

"You mean feed them?"

"Yes. On the Bowery. There will be more field trips of that nature, sometimes to other cities. There is nothing that says doing good work shouldn't be interesting and fun. But to be a part of that, you have to become a Tiger."

"How do I do that?"

"First you are selected, and I have just selected you. Next you have to go through the initiation. After that, you are a Tiger."

"Initiation?"

"Like a fraternity. Well, in fact it is a fraternity. Every fraternity has an initiation. And every initiation has a theme related to the purpose of the group. Because those we serve have to put faith in us, this initiation has to be about trust. Trust and loyalty. That's what Tigers are about. Are you game?"

"I suppose so." Father Capehart was presenting an opportunity to enter an inner circle, exciting Bradley's desire to be thought of as special.

Father Capehart had been leaning forward in his seat as he explained the premise of initiation into the Society of Tigers. At Bradley's tentative agreement, the priest slapped his own knees with both hands as a way to seal Bradley's consent and began the initiation. "All right. Now stand up in front of me."

Bradley stood.

"Move over here."

Bradley moved to the spot the priest indicated, just to the left of his chair.

"Stand at attention, and I will explain the initiation."

Though he felt somewhat silly, Bradley stood at attention. He was aware that college fraternities famously humiliated their pledges until welcoming them as brothers and equals.

"Now I'm going to get the ropes."

"The ropes?"

"Trust, Bradley. That's the concept this initiation explores. I will take you outside your comfort zone. You will make yourself vulnerable to me in a way you have never been vulnerable to anyone before. Uneasiness and discomfort is what every initiation is designed to make you feel. Uneasiness is overcome only by trust. Nothing is achieved without it. That's the way of the world. I will put you in a position where you must trust me entirely. Are you ready?"

"I guess so."

"Stay standing at attention while I get the ropes."

Father Capehart appeared holding a neatly coiled line of quarter-inch braided Dacron halyard. "Are you ready, Bradley? Take off your clothes."

"Do what?"

"Take off your clothes."

Although Bradley wasn't aware of it, his mind began to spontaneously articulate the provocative lyrics of a Randy Newman song about a hat.

"You must be completely naked, Bradley. When you are naked, I will tie you up. We will then explore degrees of vulnerability. This is your trial of trust and obedience."

Bradley heard these words with deep misgiving, though he knew that military boot camp established parameters of power, that recruits must endure a shaming process connected to power that years later he would understand as in kind to Mistress Angela's transgressive dungeon. Bradley had none of the towel-snapping jock bravura of boys in gym and felt shame unclothed in the presence of others. Nevertheless, he did what was requested. He took off his shirt and unzipped his pants. He pulled them down and stepped out of them.

"And your underwear," commanded the priest, now standing before him with firelit eyes and, as it occurred to Bradley, the manic intensity of a drill sergeant. Bradley took down his underwear. He felt profoundly abashed. When he had disrobed entirely, he stood once again at attention. The priest's eyes combed over him.

"Becoming bound and naked in front of me makes you vulnerable. Do you feel vulnerable, Bradley?"

"Yes."

He certainly felt vulnerable, vulnerable and uncomfortable and uncertain. Though Bradley trusted Father Capehart implicitly, he was wise enough about his own sexuality to be wary. He looked for any sign of an erection in the priest but there was none.

"Put out your hands," the priest commanded.

For the next few minutes, Father Capehart bound Bradley's hands behind him and his feet together with multiple slip knots and square knots so that the rope was firmly but not painfully secure. He tottered but remained standing at attention.

"Now the blindfold."

Blindfold! *Blindfold?* Bradley's eyes conveyed nervous misgiving.

"Vulnerability," the priest reiterated. "Trust."

Bradley took a deep breath. After all, fraternities and secret organizations of all kinds had initiation rituals. He felt all of the emotions Father Capehart had predicted he would feel: unease, embarrassment, vulnerability, and, curiously, appreciation in favor of the initiation as inspired to a purpose, which was indoctrination into the mysteries of adulthood by someone he admired and believed. A litmus test of trust. He would tough through it and become that nebulous species of brave-heart, a Tiger. On the other hand, for the same reasons he thought military boot camp stupid, this was incredibly creepy, potentially proof of nothing so much as his own cupidity.

Father Capehart produced a blindfold and, to Bradley's surprise, displayed moistened cotton balls. Bradley continued to stand at attention as the priest slowly and methodically put the cotton balls on his eyes and attached the blindfold over them, tying it behind his head. Sightless, Bradley began to lose his balance.

"It's all right," Father Capehart said, helping him to the floor. "I've got you." Initiation or no, Bradley began to intensely dislike the whole experience. "You won't be able to stand," the priest said. "Now, for the next several minutes, I want you to try to get out of the ropes. Try to escape. Can you try that?"

Naked, bound, blinded, and lying helpless on the floor, Bradley felt awash in shame and confusion. Fundamentally, he did not like being naked and tied up and especially did not like being blindfolded. But truth admitted, disquiet had been foretold and did produce precisely the feeling of intense discomfort Father Capehart had said it would. Bradley wanted it to be over, but Father Capehart's voice came from the corner. "Try to struggle out of the ropes."

Bradley's hands were tied behind him. He tried to undo the knots. This caused him to writhe on the floor and move over to the edge of the carpet. His face went forward, and he was able to move his head and push the blindfold up using the carpet's corner to dislodge the cotton ball slightly from his left eye. This allowed him to see downward if he put his head backward enough. Reflexively, he positioned his line of sight in the direction of Father Capehart's voice.

And then he was able to see precisely what stood at the center of this initiation, the essence of this trial of trust, the point of it all. Father Capehart was standing in the corner masturbating furiously into a handkerchief. His face, grotesquely contorted, looked like a weight lifter struggling for a dead-lift record. He could not perceive that Bradley saw him. Meanwhile, corrupted Lennon/Little Richard lyrics were pyrotechnically exploding in Bradley's mind: *Lying with his eyes while his hands are busy working overtime*, interspersed with snatches from "Tutti Frutti" and other random lyrics washed through him. He lay naked, squirming in his degradation, while the priest, squinting where

he stood, made a whistling sound like pursed lips blowing across a bowl
of hot soup.

"Struggle a little more," the priest said, the timbre of his voice higher,
his tone tremulous. Bradley listened for the sound of a camera.

"And so how did it make you feel?"

"Betrayed. I had been taken in. I knew the initiation was a ruse. It
was ironic."

"How do you mean?"

"I didn't know much about homosexuality, I knew only that my own
sexuality had some extravagant aspects but that my nature was hetero-
sexual."

"And so what did you do?"

"I didn't have many options." Bradley laughed. "He didn't touch me,
and he didn't know I could see him. I lay there until his orgasm into
the handkerchief he was holding. Then his tone of voice changed. He
seemed a little embarrassed. Post-orgasmic remorse, I suppose. In a short
while, he untied me. I put my clothes on and went home and that was
that. I had achieved Tigerdom."

"And how did you feel?"

"Stupid. Humiliated. Credulous. Foolish. Mostly stupid."

"Violated?"

"Yes, I suppose that too. Taken advantage of at the very least. He
never touched me, and so I might have repressed a sense of violation."

"Do you think it was something you wanted also?"

"Me?"

"On some level."

"I was complicit in the initiation, yes, but it was under false pretenses,
a subterfuge. I don't think I wanted anything but to get out of there. He
was friendly to a fault afterwards, but I just wanted to go."

"What I mean is, you suspected a sexual motive in the initiation. You
were aware enough to check for an erection. And yet you let the process
continue."

"No, as I said, I went along with it because of how it was presented."

"Of course, I'm playing devil's advocate."

"I understand. The initiation idea took the weirdness out of it. That was pretty convincing. But I was wary about the whole thing from the beginning. I didn't like it. Even though at times I sensed a possible sexual intention, I felt no erotic response myself. He never touched me. He concealed his true motives. When I saw what he was doing, it freaked me out, and I just wanted to get the hell out of there."

"Any other thoughts?"

"I'm pretty sure that was the moment I stopped trusting people who say things like 'Trust me.'"

Dr. Singer chuckled audibly, softly. "I'm sorry that you had to learn that lesson in the way you did. This ritual, or initiation, was indeed about trust. About trusting your own inner voice."

"It was strange. I'll say that. And creepy. And probably sad."

"What became of your relationship with Father Capehart?"

"I left the church activities, but not right away. Shortly afterwards. My contact with him ended, but I do see him from time to time in town if I'm in Wilberforce. He sails. I've seen him at Cap'n Henry's."

"Does he know you saw him masturbating?"

"I don't think he does. But he knows what he did."

"Alright, Bradley. Let's talk about trust in a true sense. You trusted the relationship you have with yourself, because your instincts were correct on that night. You also discovered a person not worthy of your trust, someone who up until then was held in special high esteem. So you learned, albeit strenuously, that trust, like loyalty, is a two-way street."

"I guess that's true."

"You emerged from this 'initiation' with perhaps a clarified under-standing of life, but at a cost. What about some of the other boys? Some of the ones he called Tigers?"

"I spoke to only one other boy about it. He had gone through some-thing similar. He said he had got naked in the same way, blindfolded of course, but he never got his blindfold loose. He didn't know what was happening. When I told him what I had seen, it completely freaked him out. Come to think of it, that boy was Bobby Wheeler, Ann Wheeler's brother."

"The woman recently murdered in her home?"

"Back in May."

"What happened to Bobby?"

"Bobby left the religious class at the same time I did. But he died when he was twenty. He was poisoned by tainted cocaine on the Fourth of July about fifteen years ago."

The next day, Dr. Singer called Bradley at home, something she rarely did. "I can't force you to disclose these things, Bradley. It has to be your choice. But I do think that you should make Detective Mallory aware of the priest and what happened to you, and tell him about Bobby Wheeler. This sort of behavior is probably still going on, and you wouldn't want some other boy to face what you faced or worse. With your permission, I'll call Detective Mallory and tell him you'll be in touch. You can be candid with him, Bradley, as candid as you are here with me. Do I have your permission?"

The episode was ancient but still embarrassing to his pride. In addition, he did not want to get involved in any criminal charges. But he felt the detective was a decent man who had dealt fairly with him, and the argument Dr. Singer made was hard to refute.

"Sure," Bradley said to Dr. Singer. "You can talk to him. I'll visit him tomorrow."

44

Detective Mallory invited Bradley to sit. "I understand therapy continues to go well."

"Dr. Singer is different from what I expected. She's a very good listener. I like her a lot."

"And you feel she's helping you with a few things?"

"I do. Yes. Absolutely. She's very insightful."

While this exchange took place, Bradley noticed framed photographs he had not seen before and thought them beautiful. Classic racing sloops in a calamity of dynamic angles under full sail are elegant in their grace, he thought, and gorgeous in their precision.

"Dr. Singer called me, with your permission, as you know."

"She wanted me to tell you about Father Capehart."

"I appreciate the difficulty in talking about these matters, but if I can learn something, it might be helpful."

"What would you like to know?"

"You mentioned to me once that you knew Ann Wheeler's brother, Bobby." Detective Mallory leaned forward in his chair.

"We took classes together."

"What kind of classes?"

"Religious instruction. It was only for the year, on Thursdays, in the basement of the church in Wilberforce."

"The Catholic church?"

"Yes."

"When was this?"

"In the eighth and ninth grades? I was fourteen, fifteen I guess. Twenty years ago or so."

"Who instructed you?"

"Father Capehart. He was a young priest, just assigned there. There was also a monsignor. I forget his name, but he was old."

Detective Mallory leaned back slightly and folded his hands as he spoke. "I've interviewed Father Capehart. He mentioned Tigers and charitable works he proctored. He told me Tigers were his students with special promise. Tell me, what did it mean to be a Tiger?"

Bradley told Mallory what he had told Dr. Singer. It was news that saddened and angered the detective. Behavior had no stereotype; its range was as infinite as motives. As Bradley detailed the episode of the blindfold, Mallory issued a world-weary sigh, and when Bradley explained that Bobby Wheeler had been his close friend in sodality class, the detective grew attentive.

"How well did you know him?"

"We were good friends at that time."

"So you knew Ann Wheeler more than just a little."

"I knew her through Bobby the way you know a friend's little sister. Bobby and I didn't hang out. He was older and went to Wilberforce High, and I was at Granville, but we were friends at religious instruction, and sometimes I'd see him around town. I saw Ann once in a while."

"Do you think Bobby had a sexual relationship with Father Capehart?"

"Bobby wasn't the type. He was street smart, tough, and he certainly wasn't gay. He had the initiation, so probably something similar to what I experienced happened to him. But he didn't see what I saw."

"Did you tell him about it?"

"Yes. When I told him what the priest was up to, it made him angry. He quit religious instruction and never went back."

The detective leaned forward, and his expression got serious. "I'm wondering about something. Did Bobby's sister know anything about Tigers or her brother's relationship with Father Jim, whatever it was?"

"I'm not sure. Ann didn't like the priest. She was sarcastic. She used to call him Daddy Jim."

The detective moved in his seat. "Did the priest know that? That she called him Daddy Jim?"

"I don't know. Probably not."

Detective Mallory sensed that Bradley was tiring. He had been honest and forthcoming, but it was becoming uncomfortable for him. He stood up to end the meeting. "I appreciate the courage it took to talk about these things, Bradley, even if they happened long ago. It's important." Bradley stood up, and they shook hands. "And I'm glad the therapy is working for you," the detective added.

For his part, Bradley left the municipal building with a good feeling. The air was softer and warmer, the grass a brighter green on the square, with morning shadow and sudden sunlight alternating as clouds went by. Flowers were carefully tended along the fence in a pretty arrangement. He had to admit to a lightness of spirit that comes with unburdening. He had begun to feel an unfolding sense of new enfranchisement with the village he had been born into, energetic and wholesome, less isolated, freer in spirit, happier as a participant. He wanted to read a good book. He wanted to call Brenda. He wanted a day off to do whatever he felt like doing.

45

L inda Mallory was breading a filet of sole for their evening meal while Mallory was having a glass of wine. His expression was thoughtful, focused. She knew the look. His mind was engaged, processing data, mentally sifting through reports and accounts, analyzing facts and interviews. The husk of him was with her in the kitchen; the rest of him was elsewhere.

"Something happening in the murder case?"

"Maybe. I'm not sure. I can't quite put it together."

"Want to share what you've got?"

He looked up. "Remember Bradley Davis, the Peeping Tom I told you about?"

"The one you didn't prosecute?"

"Well, it turns out that years ago he was in a Catholic religious-instruction class with Ann Wheeler's brother, Bobby. They were friends"

"Do you think he had something to do with the murder?"

"No, I don't think Davis has anything to do with that. But I do think the priest is involved somehow."

"The Catholic priest?"

"Maybe. The priest preyed on young boys in his religious-instruction class."

"*What?*" Linda sat down.

"The priest liked to give them what he called an initiation."

"Are you serious?"

"He claimed it was a ritual initiation into a group of favored boys he called Tigers. That was the pretext. Bradley thought he was going through an initiation, so he let the priest tie him up and put a blindfold on him."

"Are you *serious*? He didn't think that was strange?"

"Yes and no. It was presented as a kind of fraternity ritual. A trial of trust, no less. He'd tie them up naked and blindfolded. But Bradley happened to loosen the blindfold and saw the priest masturbating in the corner."

"Wow, *that is creepy.*"

"He revealed this at long last to his analyst, and she urged him to tell me about it. In my office, Bradley also told me that Ann Wheeler's brother, Bobby, was a victim of the same sort of ruse. They were in this religious class together. Bobby didn't fully realize what the priest was up to until Bradley told him what he had seen."

"Are you going to follow up and contact Bobby?"

"He died years ago. Bad street drugs killed a bunch of students and college people. But I have a feeling."

"A feeling?"

"Maybe Ann Wheeler learned something about what happened with her brother and the priest. Bobby was her hero. He saved her from being raped in high school. His photograph was on her refrigerator door."

"Wouldn't she just bring the evidence straight to the police?"

"Maybe she wanted to be up close and personal with the padre to hear it from him. Maybe she didn't want her brother's reputation sullied. Her brother died at twenty. Maybe she discovered something that had to do with the priest and her brother and wanted to confront him with what she had. It's possible that she contacted him, and he went to see her to find out what she knew."

Mallory had a sip of his wine. It was beginning to rain. Linda could feel her husband's mind circling the idea. Raindrops on the rooftop made a consoling patter. He was once again the reporter in college, in pursuit, focused and relentless.

"Also, Ann Wheeler lived out in the country. The priest was stopped by one of our officers not far from her house. One of his taillights was out, but we have a record of the stop on a night that falls roughly within the time-frame of her death. All of this is circumstantial, but there is a connecting thread somewhere."

Mallory was thinking of various impressions he'd had of Father Capehart: a gregarious man dedicated to piety with a passion for jazz and young boys, a man of the cloth who had never come out of his own closet. Dr. Singer had suggested that the perpetrator, whoever it was, would try to get closer to him in a relationship that already existed between pursuer and pursued.

"I've got a definite feeling about this," he said.

"You do seem to," said Linda. Her belief in her husband's instincts was absolute. Falling rain lent an audible background to thoughts each were having.

In his office the following day, Mallory closed the door and fiddled with a rubber band while thinking, falling into abstraction. Every life has a story, he thought. Stories were the essence of the town. If news is the story of what happened, history is the story of consequences from what happened. Both define the identity of a place. In Granville, news of John Addison's wealth was a story. The engagement of Grace Addison and Nelson Hawkins was a story. Bradley's story (with its several chapters) might have had a different outcome but for the detective's intervention, which was part of that story. His thoughts were a train of associations. If the village was a social cell, its fabric was a web, and when people turned toward or against each other, their stories were its soul. Many things are invisible. God is invisible, life is invisible, time is invisible. Destiny? Merely the reverse-engineering of chance into story. Where were these thoughts tending? He had liked Jim Capehart, but contradictions in character had raised doubts and uncertainty; misgivings had swirled in his mind. Capehart seemed a man in conflict with himself and his God. Somewhere in such a man existed the possibility of personal crisis that could result in a catastrophic loss of boundaries. Mallory shot the green rubber band across the room. He watched in amazement as it ringed the only upright pencil standing in a can on a desk by the door. Stupefied as a lone golfer who makes an unwitnessed hole in one, he had an absurd impulse for validation, a token of recognition, public notification, and perhaps a small award. Coming out of abstraction, he laughed at his own absurdity, and then an unconscious thought below the surface boiled into consciousness: *It was time to pay another visit to Father Capehart at the rectory.* Almost following himself, he stood up, grabbed his jacket, and left the office.

46

Mrs. Reilly led Mallory into the living room. "The Father will be with you in a moment," she said. After Mallory was seated, she withdrew.

In the fine leather chair beside the couch, arms recumbent on the tufted rests, the detective reflected on the facts he knew. Clues were often in front of eyes that refused to see. The priest had been an actor. Mallory had observed him in his starring role: the Catholic Mass. And what was the Catholic Mass? A reenactment of death and resurrection, a narrative of sin and redemption through cannibal consummation, and (for Catholics) the literal eating of flesh and drinking of blood. Trading uncertainty for hope, they *choose* to equate worship with obedience, mainly so that sexual realities were papered over. Why the rule of celibacy? It closes its eyes to conflicts and contradictions of sex. The Virgin Birth as an immaculate conception! (You must ignore that God the Father Himself performs divine adultery and makes a cuckold of a mere man, St. Joseph!) Add to the mix priestly homosexual predation and—

But before Mallory could wholly integrate these thoughts, Father Capehart appeared, jaunty as always, familiar, hearty, and informal, this time wearing a short-sleeved Hawaiian shirt as though returning from a luau.

"Gerry, welcome once again," he said.

The detective stood, and they shook hands.

Father Capehart called loudly into the kitchen, not texting this time, sounding rather like an adolescent calling out to his mother. "Mrs. Reilly! Would you bring us the bottle of Bordeaux?" He waved his hand. "Please, sit," he said, and took the couch adjacent as the detective resumed the leather chair. The mullioned window looked out over the yard awash in late sunlight with deep shadows beneath the trees. Mrs. Reilly brought the wine, the priest poured it, and the men touched glasses.

"I'm still reliving our victory," the priest said, and though it had been a while, he repeated in detail some of the finer points of strategy they had discussed over ale after the race. "I also enjoyed our talks about faith and God," he said. "You're far more philosophical than one would suspect."

Mallory nodded but said nothing. Silence ensued between the men.

Detecting a neutral response, the priest began to feel uneasy. More time passed without words. An almost palpable awkwardness made Father Capehart feel a defensive impulse welling in him.

"Tell me, Gerry, what, if anything, have you learned in the Ann Wheeler murder case?"

From that hall of mirrors—the pious mind—this was precisely what the detective had been waiting to be asked.

"As a matter of fact, it is solved."

The priest nearly jumped to his feet. Mallory was himself surprised by his own assertion.

Father Capehart's face took on a queer expression of bewilderment, surprise, and relief. "Well, congratulations. Was it the Peeping Tom? I thought you were on to it when you said he was a person of interest."

"Bradley Davis was a student of yours about twenty years ago, I think. We talked about him." Mallory sat forward.

"Yes. Yes, he was. Bradley Davis."

"You mentored him. You had a close relationship with him at that time."

"He had family difficulties, but I remember him, yes."

"Something put him off though." Mallory scratched his temple and furrowed his brow. "He withdrew from class."

A gust of irritation blew across the priest's face then melted into false earnestness and a frown: the actor, thought Mallory.

"And I was sorry to see him go," Father Capehart said. "He was a quiet boy with some, well, eccentricities, but I would never have thought him capable of—"

"Bradley's not a suspect."

"But ... *Really?*"

"He left your classes for a reason. I think you know what that reason was." The detective's manner was not genial. "Or maybe you don't," he added.

The priest's expression changed again, settling into an aspect of chagrined curiosity. "I don't think I follow you, Gerry," he said.

"Bradley Davis quit your class after a ritual initiation in which he was disrobed, bound, and blindfolded, during which he was able to dislodge the blindfold enough to observe you masturbating."

The priest's expression froze this time, and the moment turned stone silent. Mallory paused, and then said, "Do you recall that?" The detective kept his eyes on the eyes of the priest, eyes that flashed the cornered gloom of a guilty man.

For a moment the priest looked confused, but for a moment only. He then assumed a simulacrum of geniality, but with an edge. "Gerry, I find it hard to understand your making such an accusation in my home after enjoying my hospitality."

"Is there ever a good time for these discussions, Jim?"

"I don't know anything about what you are accusing me of. There was an initiation. He might have been remembering that. Or misremembering."

"He saw you masturbating. Especially in that situation, not something a fifteen-year-old boy would easily misremember. Moments like that are hard to forget. And we know about other boys."

Father Capehart turned his head as though away from something profoundly distasteful, and for a moment he seemed to study the view outside. Then, turning back again, he said, "It is a very serious accusation. But I can tell you there is not a shred of truth to it."

"Well, it's old news in any case." Mallory's cold, uncompromising eyes pierced the priest's glare, "although Bradley Davis could, of course, press charges to the full extent of the law." He kept his eyes on the priest, waiting like a fighter for the exact instant to land a roundhouse. And it came.

"I'm here for this reason: you murdered Ann Wheeler."

"I *what?*" The stunned priest stood up and reflexively began to pace back and forth. He turned his head sharply, confronting the accusation. "What are you saying?"

"I've said it."

The detective kept his eyes on the priest. After a moment timed for impact, Mallory said, "You went to see Ann Wheeler, to have a talk with her about her brother, Bobby. You might not have intended to murder her, I can't know that, but she's dead, that is certain. And you killed her, that is also certain."

"Why would I do something like that? What could possibly be my motive?"

"She had learned something you did not want known."

The priest's face tightened as it passed through a rapid sequence of expressions. The veins rose at his temples. His defenses were melting away. His pacing slowed to a stop. He stood and then turned his head to the ceiling and spoke as though in petition to himself. "I am not capable of killing."

"And yet you did murder Ann Wheeler. And that's the tragedy." Figuratively building his case, Mallory put his hands down flat on the table and then raised them up, making a tent of his fingers. "Ann Wheeler intended to come forward with information about the nature of your abuse of her brother, Bobby. Abuse is in the wind these days, Jim, a movement for acknowledgment and accountability. Ann might have been emboldened by that movement. Bobby was a Tiger; ergo, he had gone through your initiation. She learned about it, what it was, and what it might have meant to her brother. Her brother was her hero. Let me remind you that there is no statute of limitations on sexual abuse with a child. My guess is that she made it clear that whatever took place between you and Bobby would come out. You went to her house to have it out with her."

Mallory paused to study the effects of his words on the priest. The detective continued: "Many victims of abuse have come forward in recent years. The Vatican has established a zero-tolerance policy. Ann Wheeler was about to speak out for her brother, Bobby, isn't that right? You thought you could reason with her. You tried to persuade her that old news in a new light was a bad idea. But she had more damning evidence than you expected. And you knew she'd act relentlessly as her brother's advocate. When you couldn't convince her, you silenced her in the only way that guaranteed she would never talk."

Oddly, and all at once, Father Capehart recovered his composure. Still standing, he reached for the bottle of wine and topped them both. Mallory watched the actor begin to work the moment, changing expressions like changing clothes, like swapping hats. When he put the bottle down, Father Capehart held up his glass as if conceding a lost competition. With almost a smile on his face, he said, "You are an interesting soul, Gerry, in ways I would not have guessed."

"I'm sorry, Jim."

"I have faults, like anyone," he said with head bowed, maundering, as hypocrisy collided head-on with truth. "But I have virtues too, like anyone."

Virtues but not contrition, Mallory thought. "You know your mind, Jim, but not your heart. Unhappily, you've lost your soul."

"Only God can make that judgment." The priest stood silently at the window, looking out at his garden. He sipped his wine and studied the movements of a squirrel there. The squirrel bounded and stopped, crouched on its hind legs to reconnoiter, then ran another few feet across the yard. The priest put down his glass. He continued to stand at the window. He spoke, measuring his words while watching the squirrel. "You know very little about me, Gerry," he said. "Like most nonbelievers, faith remains a mystery to you. The joyful sense of fulfillment that comes from putting trust in something larger, wiser, and more powerful than yourself is peace you will never know."

"Bradley and Bobby put trust in you. You failed the test of that trust."

Those words were landing like fearsome punches. Strong emotions fell across the priest's features in the rectory's gloomy luxury. Straining against truth, the priest's uneven attempt at composure seemed to suggest that denial at last was failing.

Mallory said, "You'll have your day in court."

The priest turned from the window, and when their eyes met, his voice thundered: "God is my judge!"

"Confession is the path to redemption, as you have preached. It is the only path."

Mallory stood to leave, but a scene began to take place, a literal acting out. Like a player at the edge of crisis, the priest began to move through emotions. He was at war with himself. His eyes blazed. Somewhat theatrically, he bowed his head, and when he spoke, it was in the voice of the pulpit.

"I submit that there is a balance between good and evil." He spoke in God's name with eerie biblical inflection. "And if I be judged evil, better it come from Him than from an average man of bland virtue." Here he paused and looked heavenward for a moment, then bowed his head. Silence ensued. He turned slowly toward the detective and lifted his gaze until their eyes met. He was now a man quite literally beside himself, expressing not shame, precisely, but self-abnegation, a man in extremis, in conflict with his God and with himself, an unaccommodated man.

"I won't let this go," Mallory said.

"I've enjoyed our friendship, Gerry, such as it was. But God is my judge."

"In the next life, perhaps."

47

On the following day, a picture-perfect September morning, a steady wind was blowing at fifteen knots from the southwest. Waves were cresting at three and four feet. The visibility was unlimited and temperatures unseasonably warm. With whitecaps foaming in sunlight under clear skies, a lone sailor held course. His sloop cut the waves smartly on a broad reach, sea, sailor, and sails making motion all as one. This was as fine a day as seen all season. Slight movements only of the tiller were required, which allowed the skipper to enter a dream state as he went along.

Though he sustained the idea of faith and God, he was troubled by secret dread. Over the years, resentment had grown against his early teachers. An inner voice spoke against their certitude. Is faith a myth of unholy imposture? If this were true, then he had spent his life falsely inside narrow limits of fixed ideas.

He was getting too close to shore, and reflexively, unconsciously, he pushed the tiller to starboard and began to come about. The bow moved through the wind line and the mainsail luffed and then filled while he tightened the jib to the starboard tack and made fast the sheet. Heading now toward open ocean, he picked up speed under trimmed sails. Sailing was his metaphor for navigating between shores, the claims of mysticism on the one hand, the logic of science on the other. The mainsail began to luff in a slight change in wind direction. The wind was strong. He fell off, and the sail billowed. He continued on. Faith was failing fast. The Christian claim of no atheists in foxholes was recalled to him, but also, he thought, no pope wishes for death. There are no men of faith on deathbeds, only men who die in hope of perhaps. What was truth? He squinted into the light. A strong sun stood in opposition to such blasphemies. God was incarnate in Christ, with blood and salvation inextricably entwined. Crucifixion was the trial put by God the Father to his Son. The story of Christ was a sanguinary tale. Navigating now between spiritual and material shores—between sin and redemption—perhaps everything was rationalization. His sin was grievous. Some other invisible force had taken him over. This force might indeed be the devil. He had not meant to murder. He knew the meaning of possession—of being possessed—of being driven to sinful action by evil impulse. It was a real phenomenon. In this one sense then, it was not he. But the detective would pursue him relentlessly, of this he was certain. Whatever bid for salvation he had in the next world, there would be harsh consequences in this one. He was diminished. Shattered. Shame had taken the place of pride in him, and he felt separated from God and man equally, with no path home, no sanctuary on earth, or in heaven. The wind and sea belonged now to the Last Judgment he was performing on himself. The bow crashed down, spray anointing him.

He used to think that life was a dream God was having of man. But if the opposite were true, if God was a dream man was having in life, well, dreams disappear with waking just as life disappears with dying. The material world is a place where, for a time, life can be felt and truth can be touched, but then the flame is extinguished. One sails to a destination using calibrated skills; the wake of a boat tells its story of passage, but the wake also fades and vanishes, leaving a memory only, and that too will evanesce in time, leaving nothing. Life is ephemeral and can yield only a story of its own demise, leaving scant trace of its journey through uncertainty and despair, and no witnesses.

He crossed turbid tide waters of the Race where ahead the open ocean beckoned, and he turned outbound. Seen from above, the solitary boat sailed into rising seas and increasing winds. The halyard in the wind started ringing like a bell against the mast. It tolled inchoate images that flew out like rushing air: his childhood, his learning, his life, his mortal sins. Holding a determined course to nowhere, forward and farther out, he sailed toward the open horizon.

THE END

The author wishes to acknowledge the following individuals for their critical reading, expert advice, technical input, and loyal support of this long-standing project: Ingrid Steblea gave insightful early comments on the manuscript; Dr. Jayne Bloch provided excellent feedback on psychological nuances of therapy; John Rousmaniere contributed his refined knowledge of the vocabulary of sailing and racing tactics; Marisa Bisi Erskine blessed me with her patient ear, keen wit, and a lifetime of insights; and last but not least, Silvia Fioretta Erskine gave me space, understanding, ongoing thoughtful comment, unflagging support, love, and purpose to complete this adventure. With every atom in me, I thank you."

Founder's Statement

Heresy Press promotes freedom, honesty, openness, dissent, and real diversity in all of its manifestations. We discourage authors from descending into self-censorship, we don't blink at alleged acts of cultural appropriation, and we won't pander to the presumed sensitivities of hypothetical readers. We also don't judge works based on the author's age, gender identity, racial affiliation, political orientation, culture, religion, non-religion, or cancellation status. Heresy Press's ultimate commitment is to enduring quality standards, i.e. literary merit, originality, relevance, courage, humor, and aesthetic appeal.

Other Heresy Press Titles

- *Nothing Sacred: Outspoken Voices in Contemporary Fiction.* "Twelve vibrant short stories by diverse authors who push boundaries and flirt with heresy."
  On sale: $19.95
- *Deadpan* by Richard Walter. "A mordantly funny novel that skewers prejudice and scoffs at ignorance, opposing hate with humor."
  On sale: $16.95
- *The Hermit* by Katerina Grishakova. "A successful Wall Street bond trader considers career suicide to save his soul."
  On sale: $17.95
- *Animal: Notes from a Labyrinth* by Alan Fishbone. "A radically uninhibited book, whose stories delve deeply into the muck and glory of life, tackling the enduring perplexities of love, art, identity, and our bondage to pleasure."
  On sale: $12.95

➜ Buy all four books as a bundle for 30% off the cover price: $47 (plus shipping & handling): https://heresy-press.com/books/

Newsletter

Don't miss the Heresy Press Newsletter SPEAKEASY: https://heresy-press.com/newsletter/